FATAL HATE

FATAL HATE

BRIAN PRICE

This edition produced in Great Britain in 2022

by Hobeck Books Limited, Unit 14, Sugnall Business Centre, Sugnall, Stafford, Staffordshire, ST21 6NF

www.hobeck.net

A CIP catalogue for this book is available from the British Library.

ISBN 978-1-913-793-62-3 (pbk)

ISBN 978-1-913-793-61-6 (ebook)

Cover design by Jayne Mapp Design

Printed and bound in Great Britain

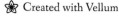 Created with Vellum

Are you a thriller seeker?

Hobeck Books is an independent publisher of crime, thrillers and suspense fiction and we have one aim – to bring you the books you want to read.

For more details about our books, our authors and our plans, plus the chance to download free novellas, sign up for our newsletter at **www.hobeck.net**.

You can also find us on Twitter **@hobeckbooks** or on Facebook **www.facebook.com/hobeckbooks10**.

To Simon, Rohan, Cait and Corin

Note from the Author

This novel is set in the imaginary town of Mexton in the early part of 2020. Covid is beginning to spread but nobody is doing much about it despite the fact that, by the end of the book, deaths are occurring.

I have attempted to portray police procedures credibly without becoming too boring. Of necessity I have telescoped some of the timescales required for post-mortems and forensic procedures. Please bear with me on this.

Also, I have deliberately omitted details from the 'bomb' on the front cover as I believe the food in Belmarsh is dreadful.

Brian Price
Weston-super-Mare
2022

Fatal Hate Easter Competition

Brian Price and Hobeck Books are offering readers in the UK the chance to win a very special box of chocolates from Maybrick and Cream, featuring such favourites as *Strychnine Surprise, Cyanide Swirl, Toffana's Toffee, Arsenic Delight* and *Belladonna Cream* (may also contain nuts)!

Hidden in this book are over thirty 'Easter Eggs' – quotes, famous sayings and cultural references from the 1960s onwards. Some may be slightly paraphrased, or split around other words, but they are there for you to find.

Send your entry, listing the Easter Eggs and where they come from, to hobeckbooks@gmail.com by midnight BST on 30 June 2022. The reader who finds the most will receive two prizes. Firstly, some delicious chocolates, hand made by Christopher, chocolatier of Weston-super-Mare, plus a signed copy of Brian's next book, provisionally entitled *Fatal Dose*.

For full details, and the answers after the closing date, go to www.hobeck.net.

Please note, the competition is open to UK readers only.

Good luck!

Prologue

Cambridge, Summer 2010

ONCE SHE STOPPED SOBBING, Iona knew what she had to do. The bastard had won, and she had no alternative. She had to protect her sister.

Her sister had supported her ever since their parents died in a car crash. The two girls had been inseparable, laughing, crying and mourning together, in sickness and in health. She had insisted Iona stayed on at school, helped her apply to university and cheered when she got a place at Cambridge, although the prospect of the two of them being so far apart appealed to neither. Then Iona told her about the tall, sophisticated, mature student reading law, who seemed interested in her. Oddly, her sister hadn't been as pleased as she had expected. At first Iona was annoyed at her reaction, but she trusted her sister's judgement and kept him at arm's length. But after the May Ball, Iona succumbed to his charms, ending up in bed with him at five in the morning, full of champagne and lust.

They carried on a relationship for a couple of weeks and at first she felt blissfully happy. Things seemed to be going well. Could he be 'the one'? But something niggled in Iona. Something wasn't quite right but she didn't know what it was. Her sister had sensed it. He seemed so out of her league; perhaps that was it. She knew she was attractive but what else did he see in her? She was just a scholarship girl from a nondescript town in Scotland and he was a posh boy from a rich family, clearly destined for power. She couldn't believe it would last. And, of course, it didn't, the moment she announced that she was late.

Two evenings later, she found them in her room. The child's father and his brother, all semblance of affection and gaiety replaced by cold stares and icy voices. They threatened her, they told her she had to get rid of the child and transfer to another university. They would help with her costs as long as she never made contact with them again.

Iona was shocked and horrified. She didn't know what to say. She wanted to keep the baby and knew she'd be able to cope, as she'd been without parents for three years. They ignored her protests and gave her one final warning; she had a week to do as they said or there would be fatal consequences for her and her sister.

Two days later, Iona found an envelope of photos pushed under her door. One was of her sister, chatting with her friends on the Lancaster University campus. The second was of a cemetery with a headstone, bearing her and her sister's names, photoshopped next to their parents' grave.

She lost all hope. Her life had been destroyed by those evil men and she knew that even if she complied with their demands, they would still be a threat to her and her sister. She couldn't allow that. She sat down and wrote a long letter, describing everything that had happened and urging her sister to be careful. *These men are dangerous* she wrote, *and I'm not telling you their names. Please don't try to contact them or tell anyone about it. But I owe it to you, my darling sister, to explain.*

Then she poured two teaspoons of powdered ketamine into a water bottle half full of whisky. She posted the letter as she left college, found a tree on Parker's Piece to sit under and emptied the bottle. She pulled her hat over her eyes so people would think she was sleeping and waited, in the warm summer sunshine, for her heart to stop.

Chapter One

Mexton, January 2020 | Day 1, Thursday

IF DYING of boredom was really possible, Duncan Bennett would have been a mass murderer. His reedy voice and prolonged diatribes, on matters devoid of interest to anyone but himself, were notorious in the workplace. Any meeting at which he spoke rapidly degenerated into little more than a slumber party, despite its participants pre-loading with espressos. In the canteen or at social functions, anyone seeing him approach almost wished their ears were filled with concrete. And it was concrete, applied with force to the back of his head, that finally shut Duncan up.

Duncan's body was discovered just before eight a.m. by the caretaker, who opened up the premises where Duncan had worked. He was slumped against a wall at the side of the building, away from any street lights, and a streak of blood on the bricks behind him pointed to a head wound. A fist-sized piece of concrete with a trace of blood on it was found some distance away. The caretaker called the police immediately. Within an hour, a tent had been erected over the scene. The forensic physician's preliminary opinion, after certifying death, was that Duncan had died from a blow to the head, sometime during the night, with more details expected from the pathologist after the post mortem.

DI Emma Thorpe shivered in the January chill as she suited up, signed the crime scene log and ducked under the tape forming the outer cordon around the scene. It was her first suspicious death since moving to Mexton and she was slightly apprehensive. She had handled plenty elsewhere but she was still getting to know the local people and procedures. Approaching the inner cordon, she nodded to the SOCOs methodically working the area where Duncan's body had been found.

'D'you want to take a look?' the Crime Scene Manager called.

'Please. I'll not get in your way.'

She lifted the second tape and, sticking carefully to the stepping plates, approached the body. She looked at the wound on the back of Duncan's head, taking care not to touch him.

'Found anything on him?' she asked.

A SOCO showed her a plastic evidence bag containing Duncan's wallet, his driving licence, a flash drive and a set of car keys, which corresponded to a Dacia parked in the company car park. She noted down the details on his licence, and realising that she would get nothing more from examining the body, authorised its removal to the mortuary. She then phoned DS Vaughan at the station to launch the murder inquiry.

'Jack – can you set up an incident room? Looks like we've got a murder. It's at the Maybrick and Cream premises on the industrial estate. Let DCI Gale know and call the team together for a briefing at two o'clock. Get a couple of DCs to find out all they can about Duncan Alan Bennett. His driving licence gives a date of birth as 12th May 1973. In the meantime, I'll talk to his employer and the guy who found him.'

'OK, Emma. See you later.'

Emma signed out and removed her protective clothing with relief. She was tall and slim, which meant that the suit fitted her height but flapped like a tent in the wind as she walked around. She approached the front of the building, a warehouse in slightly better condition than some of its neighbours. A plastic sign across the side door identified the occupants as 'Maybrick and Cream, wholesalers of confectionery to the nation'.

'Good morning. Police. Who's in charge?' she asked three men smoking, and shivering, in a rudimentary shelter.

'That's me. Malcolm Howard. Office manager,' the oldest of the three replied. 'You'd better come inside.'

He glanced at Emma's warrant card, dropped his half-smoked cigarette on the tarmac and led her in to the building.

'How was Duncan at work?' Emma asked, when they had found somewhere to sit in Howard's cluttered office.

'Well, he was conscientious, almost to the point of obsession. In the six months or so he'd been with us, he never arrived late or left early and hardly ever took a day off sick'.

'What exactly was his job here?'

'He was responsible for co-ordinating deliveries to our customers. We take in bulk loads of sweets and chocolates from the manufacturers and distribute them to retail outlets across the south of England. We have a computer program to help with this but he had to ensure that there were vehicles and drivers available to do the job. Thanks to him, we never missed a delivery.'

'So he was appreciated.'

Howard hesitated.

'I think his ability to do the job was respected but, in truth, he wasn't liked. But that doesn't mean we're not all shocked,' he added, hastily.

'Why was that?'

'He was a bit odd. He had his obsessions and he went on and on about them. Everyone thought he was really boring and tried to avoid him where possible.'

'Can you think of anyone who had a grudge against him?'

'No. There was no real animosity, just a general dislike.'

'How many people worked with him?'

'There are – were – six of us in the office. Me, Pavel Nowak, who handles orders; Jeannie McLeod, who is in charge of IT; Kerry Matthews, who deals with financial matters; Dave Bright, a general assistant, and, of course, Duncan. We also have drivers and warehouse staff but Duncan wouldn't have had very much to do with them.'

'Was there anything odd about him in the days before his death?'

Howard ran his hands through his thinning hair and thought for a moment.

'Not really. He was grumbling a bit about the mileage on some of the vans not adding up. Someone had probably borrowed one for a bit of house removal or shifting rubbish to a recycling centre. The drivers aren't really allowed to use the vans for private journeys, but they're a good crew so I tend to turn a blind eye.'

'I'd like to see his personnel file, please. We'll need to talk to his colleagues later but now I need to speak to the person who found him.'

'That's Kevin Cartwright. I think he's still in shock but you'll find him in the staff room. I'll have the file ready for you before you leave.'

'Thank you, sir. I noticed the staff room earlier. I'll find my own way.'

Emma walked slowly through the building, looking about her to get a picture of how the place worked. The building was around fifty years old, she guessed, and seemed to have been reasonably well maintained, although the carpets were worn. The paintwork was fairly new and the Health and Safety posters stuck to the wall looked fresh.

She noticed two large loading bays, where articulated lorries from the manufacturers were docked, and three smaller ones, where the firm's vans were being loaded. Half a dozen men scurried around, loading and unloading, while a couple of drivers stood smoking outside. Cardboard boxes were stacked neatly on pallets and a radio drowned out the sound of a fork-lift, which was unloading a container. The occasional profanity cut across the sound of the radio, while overheard conversations seemed to focus on football, cars and the physical attributes of the female office staff and TV celebrities.

Pushing through the staff room door, Emma spotted the caretaker sitting in the corner of the room, several empty tea mugs on the table in front of him and a faint, but unmistakeable, smell of brandy in the air. His crumpled brown coat and tobacco-stained fingers contrasted with his pale countenance.

'Are you OK to talk to me, Mr Cartwright? I'm Detective Inspector Thorpe.'

'I suppose so, but I've already told the uniformed lad what happened.'

'Yes, but it would be really useful if you could tell me as well. I realise it was a shock for you.'

'All right.' Cartwright's hands trembled as if he was in desperate need of a cigarette. 'I came into work about five to eight as usual. I noticed Mr Bennett's car was there, which I thought was odd. He normally comes in at eight fifteen on the dot. I was reaching for my keys when I saw someone's legs in the alley beside the building. It looked like a drunk had passed out there – the pub's just down the road – so I went to see if he was all right. When I got closer, I recognised Mr Bennett. I was surprised, as he doesn't really drink, but then I saw blood on the wall where he was sitting,' Cartwright flinched, 'so I went towards him. I didn't want to get close. I could see he was dead. Then I phoned you lot.'

'So, you didn't touch him or his clothes at all?'

'No, no. I kept well away. It bleedin' gave me the creeps.'

'Was there anything on the floor beside him?'

'Only the litter that the wind blows down the alley.'

'No phone?'

'No.' He looked aggrieved. 'Are you accusing me of pinching it?'

'Of course not, Mr Cartwright. It's just that his phone is missing.'

'Well, it's nothing to do with me.'

'OK. OK,' said Emma, moving back onto neutral ground. 'Did you know Mr Bennett well?'

'I knew him by sight but never had much to do with him. He's in the office mostly and I work all round the building.

Once or twice he's talked to me, going on about how people don't work as hard as they used to, how there were too many immigrants and how much better it was when Mrs Thatcher was in charge. I got away from him as fast as I could.'

'Thank you, Mr Cartwright. I'm sorry you had such an unpleasant start to your day,' said Emma, thinking that Duncan Bennett's day had turned out even worse.

Chapter Two

Driving back to the station, Emma could think of no obvious reason why anyone would wish to murder a middle-ranking employee in a confectionery wholesaler. Her team was already in the incident room when she arrived, wrapped up in coats and scarves, shivering despite the weak sunshine trying to make its presence felt. The heating system in the station was malfunctioning yet again and the portable gas heaters, provided by management, had been removed from the offices because the fumes were making everyone sleepy.

Emma perused the whiteboard, which displayed the results of the morning's enquiries, under the heading 'Operation Wombat'. Someone had thoughtfully stuck up a picture of a stout marsupial, presumably in case anyone didn't know what a wombat was. A Post-It note beneath the photo bore the message 'Wombats are the only animals to produce square shit'.

'OK,' she said, raising her voice to attract her colleagues' attention. 'Thanks to those of you who've done some digging already. Jack – what have we got?'

DS Vaughan got to his feet, unwound a Manchester

United scarf from his face and cleared his throat before speaking.

'So, we have Duncan Bennett, aged forty-six, without a partner and living alone. He'd been with Maybrick and Cream, distributors of chocolate and sweets to the trade, for the past six months. He started studying physics and chemistry at Leicester University but left after two years and did an HND in business. He had a variety of admin jobs and changed them every few years, before joining Maybrick and Cream. He had no enemies, as far as anyone knew, and he doesn't seem to have been involved in any torrid love triangles. Duncan has never come to our attention, not even a parking ticket, and wasn't a known associate of any local villains.'

'Thanks, Jack,' said Emma. 'Without the full PM results, we can't be sure of the cause of death. A blow on the head with a lump of concrete seems most likely so we must assume he was struck deliberately. We think he was killed during the night but we won't get a precise time of death. We'll know more later. Now, we need to look closely at his last movements and his workmates. DCI Gale has asked me to run things, reporting to her as and when necessary. I'll keep her fully briefed.'

'No surprises there,' whispered DC Martin Rowse to DC Mel Cotton. 'She doesn't think she's up to it.'

Mel grinned in response.

'Can you organise two teams, Jack?' Emma continued. 'One to question his colleagues and one to canvass the local area, including the pub, and check on CCTV. There's a camera covering the firm's car park. When did it pick up his car? Who saw him leave work? What was happening in the early hours of the morning? Get a notice put up by the roadside asking for help from anyone who might have seen an incident in the area last night.'

'What about his phone, guv?' asked Mel.

'Still missing, and we need to track it. I'll go to his flat with a DC and get the number from a bill, if he keeps them. If not, I'll ask the firm's office manager for it. We'll also see if we can find anything that could give us a motive. Thanks everyone. Get to it. Briefing tomorrow at eight sharp.'

Using the keys found in Duncan's pocket, Emma and DC Karen Groves entered his flat later that afternoon, pulling on nitrile gloves as they did so. The place was immaculate. The previous day's breakfast dishes had been washed up and left to drain, and Duncan had made the bed before leaving for work. The post that had arrived during the day was still on the door-mat, and there was no sign of him having returned in the evening to eat.

A small bedroom had been set up as an office-cum-study, and Emma searched that first. A couple of shelves held books on military history, particularly the French Resistance, as well as biographies of Enoch Powell, Margaret Thatcher, David Cameron and a number of eminent golfers, although there were no signs in the flat that Duncan played the game himself. Two T-shirts printed with the flag of St George hung on the back of the door, contrasting with the tweed jackets and twill trousers hanging in Duncan's wardrobe.

A modern, mid-range laptop sat on Duncan's desk. Emma put it in a plastic evidence bag for the forensic IT technicians to examine, along with a few recordable DVDs found in a drawer.

'Here's a phone bill,' called Karen, leafing through the recently delivered post.

'Good – anything else of interest?' replied Emma.

'Only junk mail. Nothing personal.'

'What about the lounge?' asked Emma, continuing to search the study.

'Very little in it. He's got a TV and DVD player. A couple of dozen DVDs – mainly British history and golf. A few thrillers on a bookshelf. And he likes fancy gins. Oh, and there's a pair of daggers above the fireplace. Look like Nazi weapons. They've got swastikas on the hilts.'

'OK. I'll take a look in a minute. Can you check the bedroom? I'll finish up here. We'll see what the techies can get from his phone number and laptop. On the face of it, he seems unexceptional, although a little odd, but you never know what his tech will reveal.'

Emma was just leaving Duncan's study when she heard Karen call out, a note of urgency in her voice.

'Boss. Come and look at this. I think we need a firearms officer.' Karen pointed to an open drawer in a bedside cabinet. Half-wrapped in a handkerchief was the unmistakeable bulk of a German army Luger pistol.

Chapter Three

Day 2, Friday

'OK, ma'am, OK. I know it was a replica. But for all we knew it could have been real, loaded and ready to fire. I'm not authorised to handle firearms and neither is DC Groves. So, we needed an AFO to make sure it was safe.'

Emma paused to listen to DCI Gale's grumbling.

'Yes, I know. I've seen the posters around the nick. But I'd rather have the piss taken out of me than a bullet in the leg. Now, if you'll excuse me, they're waiting for me in the incident room.'

'What is the matter with that bloody woman?' Emma fumed to herself, as she ended the call. 'I followed the correct procedure and she's moaning about embarrassment. It wasn't Gale who was photoshopped in a James Bond pose holding a pink water pistol.' Putting her irritation aside, she stepped briskly into the incident room and was hit by the smell of twenty officers and civilian staff cooped up in a cramped space with the radiators now going full blast. The vagaries of the station's heating system never failed to surprise her. She called the team to order.

'Right, Jack. What have we got?'

'Martin and Mel interviewed Duncan's colleagues. What did you find, guys?'

'They confirmed what we already thought,' replied Mel. 'He wasn't liked much and was generally considered to be a dreadful bore, with right-wing leanings. No-one knew if he had any friends outside work and he didn't talk about any hobbies. Surprisingly, he joined the rest of the office in the pub the night he was killed. He didn't normally socialise.'

'What's the timing for that?' Emma asked.

'They went after work, arriving about six, and ate there,' Martin spoke up. 'He was seen leaving around nine thirty, but others stayed until elevenish. A couple of people said he looked unsteady as he left but he'd only had a couple of halves. He didn't really join in with the party spirit, although it was celebrating a colleague's engagement.'

'And the other team?' Emma asked Jack.

'Trevor and Addy checked the neighbourhood. It's mainly light industrial around there so they looked in on a few places and knocked on the doors of the half-dozen houses nearby. No-one saw or heard anything suspicious. Addy made a note of parked vehicle registrations but nothing came up on the PNC. The pub staff confirmed that Duncan had been there with his workmates that night and that he didn't stay until the end.'

'CCTV?'

'Well, that's a bit more interesting,' replied DC Samuel Adeyemo. 'There's nothing in the street, but the pub's camera picked him up leaving at 21.35, wobbling a bit as he walked.

Twelve minutes later he was recorded getting into his car by the firm's car park camera. Nothing happened for ages, but three and a half hours later he got out again and walked towards the warehouse. That was the last time he was seen. The camera on the front of the building wasn't working.'

'That's convenient for someone,' said Emma. 'So, what do we think? He had too much to drink, slept it off in the car and went for a leak in the alley, where he was ambushed?'

'Possibly, but there was no sign of urine at the side of the building. Someone had thrown up and forensics are trying to find out if it was Duncan's vomit.'

'But it does seem likely that he met his killer there, or nearby, doesn't it? Anything on ANPR?'

'Nothing of any use, so far,' replied Martin. 'A few vehicles entering or leaving the industrial estate. We're still checking.'

Emma outlined the results of the search at Duncan's flat and was about to wind up the briefing when Amira Desai, the IT technician, stuck her head round the door.

'Something for me?'

'Yes, guv. I've managed to get into Mr Bennett's Facebook and Twitter accounts. It seems he was very busy on social media, posting some pretty unpleasant messages. I've printed the last month's off for you. We're still working on his laptop and USB stick. We're waiting for his mobile phone company to get back to us with his call records. I'll let you know as soon as we get something.'

'Thanks, Amira. Great stuff.'

Emma thought for a few moments and called DC Trevor Blake over, sending the others back to their desks.

'Trevor – you're a social media addict, aren't you?'

'Well, I wouldn't say that, boss. But I do use it a lot.' He looked slightly uncomfortable.

'I'd like you to help the IT guys analyse Duncan's use of Twitter, Facebook and whatever. Try and build up a picture of what Duncan was really like, since no-one at work had much of a clue.'

'Yes, guv. Glad to.'

He left the room smiling.

Emma asked Jack to send someone to the pub in the evening to talk to customers, in the hope that they'd been there on the night in question and had seen something of value. For the rest of the morning, she buried herself in paperwork.

'I see you've stopped wearing baby sick as a fashion accessory, Martin,' said Mel, who constantly teased him about his young daughter's proficiency at projectile vomiting.

'Yeah,' replied Martin. 'She's much better at keeping the milk down now and she's sleeping better through the night, as are we. I feel less like something from *The Walking Dead*.'

'How's Rosie coping?'

'Pretty good. We had some problems while I was first recovering from the stabbing, 'cos she was doing just about everything, but we're doing fine now. The rehabilitation's going better than expected and the doc says I can get out and about a bit, as long as I don't mix it with anyone. Believe it or not, Rosie's talking about having another one.'

'You'll have to sell your sports car, then. Get a nice family saloon.'

Martin looked gloomy.

'I hope it won't come to that. Her dad has a Clio he's getting rid of and he's offered it to us at a cheap price. I may be able to afford to keep the sportster.'

'Well good luck. I know how much you love that beast.'

'Thanks.'

Mel smiled and picked up her coffee.

Halfway through the afternoon, Trevor knocked on Emma's office door.

'Turns out Duncan Bennett was a very nasty piece of work, boss.'

'How so?'

'Some of these tweets are verging on the illegal. There's racist abuse, trolling of any politicians with remotely left-wing views and hundreds of 'likes' relating to tweets from far-right groups. His Facebook activity is similar. Also, he's viewed web pages advocating violence towards immigrants, vegetarians, gays, trans people and feminists, as well as supporting those wanting to 'Make England Great Again'. He seems to have approved of Donald Trump.'

'Is there any suggestion that he would have participated in violence?'

'Not so far. I think he was just an armchair thug. But I've only got one month's material printed out here.'

'Was he a member of a political party?'

'I came across an email in which he resigned from the Conservatives, claiming that they were too soft on benefits claimants, especially those with disabilities. There's no sign of him joining another party.'

'Thanks, Trev. Let me know if you find anything else.'

Emma switched off her computer at six o'clock and cycled home, brooding on the type of person Duncan had been. She knew that there had been few problems with extremism in

Mexton, although the Brexit issue had polarised people and some unpleasant graffiti had appeared on shops owned by Poles and Bulgarians. Could there be a group planning racial violence in the town she had adopted when she moved from Sheffield? She shuddered at the thought.

Chapter Four

Day 3, Saturday

BY THE FOLLOWING MORNING, technicians had printed out more evidence of Duncan's online activities, and some progress had been made with his phone.

'We're expecting a list of recent calls on Duncan's phone by midday,' Emma began, 'and triangulation data tracked it from Duncan's home to the warehouse and then to the pub. Around 9.45, it moved back to Maybrick and Cream, where it stayed until two a.m. After that there was no signal.'

'Failed battery or switched off?' asked Mel.

'One or the other,' replied Emma. 'This all correlates with the CCTV. What did you get from the pub, Martin?'

'Not much, apart from a wall of hostility from the customers, that is. They don't seem that keen on us. One of them saw Duncan talking to a man with a shaved head and a tattoo of St George's flag on his neck. He couldn't hear them but they shook hands as the other man left. One of the bar staff thought she saw a petite blonde woman add something to

Duncan's beer around nine o'clock, but she wasn't sure enough to warn him and make a fuss.'

'That would be Kerry Matthews,' called out Karen. 'I've been looking up the office staff on social media and she's the only blonde.'

'Thanks, Karen. Bring her in for a chat, would you?' asked Emma. 'Pick her up from her home. Discreetly.'

'OK, guv.'

'I've had a phone call from the pathologist,' Emma continued. 'He thinks Duncan died some hours before he was found, as his body was cold. He wouldn't be drawn on a precise time, obviously. Duncan could have been attacked some time before he died, as death wasn't necessarily instantaneous. He had a fracture to the base of his skull, and a haematoma – a large blood clot – had developed. This compressed vital centres in his brain and, together with other brain damage, eventually led to his death. There were traces of cement in and around the wound, which supports the theory that he was hit with the lump of concrete found in the alley.'

'How long between the attack and his death?' asked Martin.

'The pathologist couldn't say, but around the time his phone was switched off would be a good bet for the attack.'

'So, the killer hit him and took his phone, switching it off so we couldn't trace it,' continued Martin. 'Meanwhile Duncan staggered into the alley, or was dragged there, and died, maybe then or maybe a few hours later. Is that what we think?'

'Seems about right,' agreed Emma. 'We need more ANPR data, on any vehicles moving in the area of the industrial estate from, say, eleven p.m. to seven a.m. Can you get on to that, please, Jack? There shouldn't be too much at that time of night.'

'Yes, boss. We've got some but I'll get the guys to go wider.'

'Martin – talk to local uniform and see if they recognise the man who spoke to Duncan in the pub. Chances are, he's been involved in some kind of bother. Look at any photos and video footage the public order team have of far-right demos. Would the customer who saw him be able to help produce an e-fit?'

'I doubt it. He only saw him briefly. I'll ask him. If we can find a photo, he might be able to recognise him.'

Karen brought an apprehensive Kerry Matthews into the station in the late afternoon.

'Why am I here?' she asked, fiddling anxiously with an earring. 'I've done nothing wrong.'

'We'd like a bit more information about the night Duncan died, if you don't mind,' Emma replied.

'Oh, OK. What sort of information?'

'I'm a bit surprised that he joined the rest of you, given what we know about him. He certainly didn't seem popular.'

'Well, he didn't really want to go to the pub with us, although we felt we had to invite him. He declined at first but then had a call on his mobile and changed his mind.'

'Can you get the call traced, please, Karen?' Emma addressed her colleague before turning back to Kerry. 'That's helpful, Kerry, but I'm afraid that there is another, serious, matter we need to talk to you about. We have information that suggests you put something into Duncan's drink that made him unsteady and sleepy. Is that true?'

'Er...yes. I did, I suppose.' Kerry looked uncomfortable.

Emma nodded to Karen and spoke.

'Kerry Matthews, I am arresting you on suspicion of administering a noxious thing with intent to cause bodily harm.'

Kerry nearly fainted as Emma cautioned her and set up the recording equipment for the formal interview. She started to cry when Emma asked if she wanted a solicitor, which she declined.

'I can explain,' she sobbed. 'It was just a joke. He was so boring that we thought it would be a good idea to send him to sleep. I had some Valium in my bag so I crushed up a couple of tablets and put them in his beer. I didn't mean to harm him, I promise. I thought he would wake up at closing time and wander off home.'

'Did you know that combining Valium and alcohol can be dangerous?'

'No, I didn't.'

'Had you thought about him driving home and the risk he could pose to himself and other road users?'

'No, no,' Kerry whimpered. 'I'm so sorry. I was really stupid.'

'Did anyone else help you?'

'No. It was just me who did it. I can't remember who suggested it.'

'Where did you get the Valium?'

'My doctor prescribed it a few months ago. I had an anxiety problem and it helped me sleep. I'd left the tablets in the bottom of my bag.'

'That will do for now. You will be charged and bailed. I strongly advise you to consult a solicitor. Interview terminated at 18.27.'

Karen led a petrified Kerry out of the interview room and charged her before letting her go.

'That'll do for tonight,' said Emma, when Karen returned. 'I'll see you at the briefing tomorrow.'

'Night, guv.'

Chapter Five

Day 4, Sunday

MAINLY FOR THE benefit of DCI Gale, who had come into the office for the morning briefing, Emma summed up the results of the previous day's enquiries.

'Duncan went to the pub with his colleagues after work, although he didn't agree to go until after he received a call on his mobile. He was his normal self during the evening. His colleagues described him as 'boring as usual' and he didn't drink much. However, one of his colleagues slipped some Valium in his drink, which accounts for his unsteady gait as he left the pub. She has been charged.

'During the evening, he met a heavy looking bloke with a shaven head and tattoos and they had a few words, apparently quite amicably. He got back to his car at about 9.45 and stayed there until around 1.20, when he got out and wandered towards the building. It's most likely he was sleeping off the effects of the drug combined with the beer. At two a.m. his phone was switched off.

'From the PM, he was thumped with a piece of concrete between the time he approached the building and a few hours before the caretaker found him. It's reasonable to suppose the killer took his phone just before, or just after, hitting him and switched it off or smashed it, which gives us a probable time for the attack. There was no sign of his phone at the scene and it hasn't been used since. I've asked Amira to bring us up to speed on Duncan's electronics – Amira.'

'Thanks, boss. We've managed to crack the password on the flash drive and also a password-protected folder on his hard drive. They were very simple. Trevor's been looking at the hard drive and I'm still working on his cloud account.'

'What have you found so far?'

'Well, the flash drive had a series of maps and diagrams, mainly of shopping centres. Some of them we've identified, the London ones anyway. There's Bluewater, a market in Southall, Brixton Market and a number of places in Hackney and Tower Hamlets. And the Mexton halal supermarket. Each has a query scribbled at the bottom. The questions include 'Would this work?' 'CCTV?' 'How about this?' and 'Is there enough of them?'

'What's that supposed to mean?' queried Trevor. Emma looked at a sea of blank faces as a shiver crawled down her spine. DCI Gale spoke up.

'It's terrorism. These look like potential attack sites and most are noted for high populations of racial minorities.'

'You mean a boring little twerp like Duncan was a terrorist?' asked Mel.

'I don't think he was about to plant a bomb,' replied Emma, 'but he could have been advising others and plotting behind the scenes. How about his hard drive, Trev?'

'Lots of far-right literature, videos of speeches by people

like Enoch Powell, Nick Griffin, Tommy Robinson and so on. The protected folder was more sinister. That was full of material on terrorism and details of how to make bombs. *The Anarchist's Cookbook* was there as well as other, more recent material. There are several accounts of how to make TATP, mercury fulminate and other explosives. There's also a section on nerve agents. Possessing some of the necessary chemicals without a licence is an offence and it's illegal to download material likely to be useful to terrorists.'

'Could Duncan have been making explosives?'

'Not in his flat, that's for sure. He studied chemistry, so he would have had some skills in handling chemicals, but it's possible he was teaching others. He doesn't strike me as someone who would take personal risks.'

'Could he have upset one of his Nazi mates and got himself killed?' asked Addy. 'Perhaps they wanted him to get more involved than he was prepared to do.'

'That's certainly a possibility,' replied Emma. 'These are dangerous people. The shaven-headed man in the pub might have given him the flash drive when they shook hands. Has anyone recognised him?'

'Yes', said Jack 'His name's Derek Farren and he's got a dozen or so convictions for assault, affray and a couple of racially aggravated attacks. He's spent four months inside already and currently has a suspended sentence of six months hanging over him.'

'Nice chap,' commented Martin.

'Right, I'll get on to SO15 – Counter-Terrorism Command,' interjected DCI Gale. 'Send me the details please, Emma. This could be very sensitive and we don't want to get out of our depth. I'll ask if they've come across Derek Farren or picked up rumours of a planned far-right attack. They need to know what's on his hard drive as well. They may want to take over the inquiry, but please carry on in the meantime. I'll talk to the Super. Well done, everyone.'

When DCI Gale had left, Emma sat down at her desk and shivered. The prospect of a terrorist attack in Mexton chilled her. Working in a big city, she had been used to racial violence, bomb threats and the occasional genuine device that the army had to dismantle. But she thought she had left all that behind when she moved here. She looked again at the photos of Farren on far-right demonstrations, his face distorted with hatred. And Duncan Bennett seemed no better, with his vile tweets and links to appalling websites. Sometimes humanity sickened her, and she looked forward to getting home to her husband, having a shower and feeding her two cats, Gytha and Magrat. Messy they might be, but at least they didn't blow people up.

Chapter Six

Lancaster, 2010/12

JEANNIE MCLEOD DRAGGED herself out of bed around two in the afternoon and slumped on the sofa, too hung over to face breakfast. She looked around her flat, untidy and uncleaned, hardly noticing the mess. Her eyes lit, as they always did, on the Order of Service for her sister's funeral. A secular service that was supposed to provide closure but didn't. All it did was intensify her rage.

Wine for breakfast? she wondered. No, she had been warned by the bar manager about turning up for work pissed. She would drink some water and try to manage some food, then attempt to smarten herself up. She needed to collect a prescription for her immunosuppressants before work, and the pharmacist had warned her about mixing them with alcohol. Not that she cared. All the time, the old Rolling Stones number *Paint it Black* was going round and round her head, a malevolent earworm. She felt like the singer, who was complaining about a failed romance. But Jeannie's grief was much worse than Mick Jagger's.

———

The turning point came in spring 2011 when she stumbled out of the bar at closing time and a man stepped from the shadows.

'Bin waitin' for you, darlin',' he leered. 'Fancy it, then?'

'Not in a million years.' She was sufficiently sober to recognise the threat in his voice. 'Piss off. You're not my type.'

'Stuck up cow. I know you want it.' Angry now, he made a lunge for her, grabbing her hoodie and pulling her into an alley beside the bar.

'Let me go, you bastard.'

'When I've finished.' He fumbled for the buttons on her trousers, breathing fumes of tobacco and stale lager into her face, drops of spittle spattering her.

Jeannie struck out wildly. She'd never learned to fight but her elbow caught him in the eye. He swore and hit her in the stomach, knocking her to the ground. He straddled her, and as he started to unbuckle his belt, two figures stepped out of a car and the beam of a torch lit up the scene.

'What are you two up to, then?' a stern voice called out.

'Help! Help!' yelled Jeannie. 'He's raping me.'

Her attacker froze, leapt to his feet and dashed off, one of the figures racing in pursuit. Jeannie rolled over and threw up.

'Are you all right, love?' the second figure, a woman, asked. 'I'm PC Collard. Did he hurt you?'

'He hit me. Not too bad. You stopped him. Thank you. Thank you.'

'Did you know the man?'

'No. Never seen him before. He may have been in the bar but I didn't recognise him. Sorry. My head's in a mess.'

'We've been looking for a serial rapist who preys on women late at night. I think you were lucky we came along when we did.'

Jeannie's blood chilled and she felt like vomiting again.

'What's your name, love?'

'Jeannie. Jeannie McLeod. I work in the bar.'

'OK, Jeannie. What I'd like to do is get you to the police station so we can take some samples, in case he left any DNA on you. Is that OK? We can take you to the hospital first if you like?'

'No. I don't need the hospital. I'll come with you. I wouldn't be able to identify him, though. It was dark and he had a hat pulled down over his eyes.'

'Don't worry. That's fine. By the way, is there CCTV in the bar?'

'Yes. Some. The recordings are kept in the manager's office. He'll be in tomorrow at ten.'

'That's great. Thank you.'

At that point the other police officer returned, panting and cursing.

'Lost the bastard. Chased him down by the railway line. Climbed the fence and crossed the tracks. Nuclear waste train nearly hit him. Out of sight when it passed. Shit!'

'Never mind, Jeff,' his colleague replied. 'This is Jeannie. We stopped him in time. She's coming to the station to give us a statement. We'll get the forensic physician to look at her. Just in case. Come on, Jeannie, I'll help you up.'

The two police officers guided Jeannie to the unmarked police car and helped her in. She spent an uncomfortable hour and a half in the police station while she was checked over and swabs were taken of her face where her assailant's saliva had landed. Her own DNA was taken for elimination and she had to surrender her hoodie and joggers in case he had left fibres on them. PC Collard found her some clothes to go home in. After she had given a formal statement, they dropped her off at her flat at three o'clock in the morning, promising to keep in touch.

Jeannie couldn't sleep. The shock of the night's events had sobered her up and she realised just how narrow an escape she'd had. 'I've got to cut down on the booze,' she told herself. 'Turn my life around. Become the victor, not the victim. Just like Sarah Connor.'

———

Nervously, she pushed open the door to the gym and approached the reception desk.

'Hi,' she began. 'I'm Jeannie McLeod. I phoned earlier.'

'Oh, yes, Ms McLeod, welcome.' The receptionist smiled and led Jeannie to a seating area. 'Do sit down. Can I get you a coffee?' Jeannie declined the offer and the woman produced a clipboard with several sheets of paper attached. 'Would you mind completing this questionnaire? Then we can best see how to help you.'

Half an hour later, Jeannie returned the paperwork, which now included details of her health, her medical history and why she wanted to use the gym's facilities. The receptionist flicked through the sheets, picked up her desk phone and dialled a number.

'Hi Ade,' she said, 'I've got a Ms McLeod in reception. A potential new member. Can you come and have a chat with her? Great. Thanks.'

She turned back to Jeannie. 'Adrian, one of our supervisors, will be out in a couple of minutes. He can discuss with you what you need, and if it's acceptable, you can start as soon as you like.'

Jeannie smiled gratefully and settled back to wait. She'd hardly collected her thoughts when a wiry man of about thirty came up to her, studying her questionnaire.

'Ms McLeod. I'm Adrian Martin. How can we help? I see you want to improve your general fitness and muscle tone but aren't interested in bulking up. Is that right?'

'Yes. I was attacked a few weeks ago and want to be able to fight back, if it happens again.'

'Well, we don't do self-defence here but I can put you on to a martial arts club that does. What we can do is get your body fighting fit and stronger. Is that OK?'

Jeannie nodded.

'Right. What I'd recommend is a weights programme, based on dead lifts and squats. You can use some of the machinery as well, if you like, but weights should do the trick. We can provide you with a personal trainer for a modest fee or you can just roam free on the equipment once you've been instructed in its use. Which would you prefer?'

'I'd like a personal trainer, please. This is all so alien to me.'

Adrian's smile was reassuring. 'Don't worry. You're not the first woman to find herself in this position and I'm afraid you won't be the last. Come on. Let me show you around. If you like what we offer, Sally, on reception, will take your card details and you can make an appointment to start.'

Half an hour later, Jeannie had looked at all the equipment and had met her personal trainer, a dark-haired woman called Rachel, with a snake tattoo around her arm and a friendly grin. She decided she liked Rachel and arranged to start the following day. Once she had completed the paperwork and handed over her card details, she stepped out of the gym with a sense of optimism. Things were beginning to change. And the first thing she had to do was to buy some new trainers and suitable clothes for exercising in. All this was proving expensive for a part-time bar worker and she realised that she would need to get a proper job before her savings ran out.

She had never bothered to open the letter from the university, which confirmed her degree, and she didn't attend the graduation ceremony. It hadn't seemed worth it. But getting fit, eating properly and ruthlessly cleaning her flat had given her a more positive outlook, so now she opened the envelope. A first. She should have been overjoyed, but the fact that her sister would never graduate drained the pleasure from her achievement. Still, it would look good on her CV and she could begin to apply for real jobs.

She took a couple of temporary posts with local companies, which boosted her CV and provided her with useful experience, although she still didn't have a clear career plan. Doing basic data-entry work was all very well but provided few challenges and used only a tiny fraction of her abilities. Getting something better was now a priority. She still owned her parents' house in Scotland, her sister's share having reverted to Jeannie when she died. She hadn't been able to go back to live there as the memories were too painful. She would instruct an agency to sell it, furniture included, and would use the capital to get a smaller place somewhere else.

The anniversary of her being attacked was approaching, and her fear was resurfacing. She dreaded giving evidence in court but, to her relief, she wasn't called. The rapist had been caught through the DNA in his saliva on her face and an accumulation of other evidence. He confessed to a series of rapes and indecent assaults and was sent down for eighteen years. Jeannie declined the police's offer to return her clothing as it would only bring back memories.

Various locations, 2012–2016

Jeannie wanted to get out of Lancaster. Nothing was keeping her there and she could go anywhere in the country, as long as there was a job available. So she started scanning vacancies and moved from town to town, picking up short-term contracts with IT companies and businesses. None lasted more than six months but she built up a useful portfolio. She began to seek longer-term work, as constantly uprooting herself was beginning to get her down

Chapter Seven

Leicester, 2016-2019

JEANNIE MOVED to Leicester to take up a three-year contract with an IT firm. More confident now, she began to socialise. Her colleagues were a friendly bunch and usually went for drinks after work on Fridays. Their local pub was so packed with IT people that they called it 'The Programmers' Arms' or simply 'The PA'. Jeannie mentioned that she was interested in hacking, one evening, and told her colleagues about an assignment she'd done at university – *Data system vulnerabilities in the age of Tor*. The following Monday she found a note on her desk inviting her to call a mobile number if she wanted to learn more. She slipped into the women's toilets and dialled the number.

'Hi. This is Jeannie. I got your note. What's this all about?'

'Are you interested in a bit of mischief?' The voice at the other end was disguised.

'What sort of mischief?'

'The sort that could get you into trouble.'

'Depends.' Jeannie felt a stir of excitement. 'I'm not interested in stealing or trolling.'

'Nor are we. We're white hat hackers, finding holes in systems and telling people how to fix them. But we also like to have a bit of fun.'

'Then I'm in. But how do you know you can trust me?'

'We've checked you out, more thoroughly than you can imagine. And one of us remembers you from Lancaster.'

'Brilliant. So what happens now?'

'Get yourself a burner phone and text this number tomorrow evening.' The caller recited a string of digits. 'Don't give your name. Just send the word talpa.' He spelt it. 'It's Latin for mole, in case you're wondering. We'll get back to you with a time and location. This is just for you. Don't mention it to anyone else. OK?'

'Definitely. Looking forward to it.'

The call ended and Jeannie stood for a moment, clutching her phone. She was thrilled at the prospect of getting involved in something interesting and making new friends, but she also felt a little nervous. She had always been more-or-less law abiding, and doing something clearly illegal was a challenge. But it really looked like fun.

Jeannie got off the bus at the fourth stop from the town centre, as instructed. She was met by a gangling youth with floppy hair who she vaguely recognised. Craig? Clark? Clive? What was his name?

'Hi, Jeannie,' he said. 'It's me, Charlie. From Lancaster. Do you remember?'

'Yes, of course I do, Charlie. How are you?'

She did remember Charlie from the computing course. He sat behind her in practical sessions and always seemed to be staring at her backside when she stood up. If they're all like him, she thought, this could be a mistake.

Charlie led Jeannie along a roundabout route, doubling back on occasions and ducking through narrow alleyways.

'What's with the cloak and dagger stuff?' Jeannie asked.

'Just making sure you weren't followed. If it all goes OK, we'll give you the address and you can find your own way next time.'

Jeannie shrugged, thinking it was all a bit ridiculous. Finally, they arrived at a large Victorian house, divided into several flats and bedsits. Charlie ushered her to a back entrance and knocked on the curtained window of a basement. A shaven-headed man of about twenty-five, with a skull and crossbones tattooed on his neck, opened the door, glanced around furtively and let them in.

'I'm Miles,' he said, his pleasant Liverpudlian voice and welcoming smile contrasting with his fearsome appearance. 'Come in, Jeannie. Welcome to the Argus Collective.'

'Thank you.'

She looked around and recognised Davey Chen from work. He looked up from a screen and smiled briefly. A young woman, wearing leather trousers and a white T-shirt, with a tattoo of a dragon peeping out of her cleavage, ignored the arrivals, and a third person, of indeterminate gender, waved languidly while still typing furiously with the other hand. Tables supporting a range of computers were ranged around three sides of the room, and the hum of hard drives and cooling fans gave the impression of productive industry. An extractor unit failed to remove the heat generated by the equipment and the smell of takeaways. The main source of light in the room seemed to be from computer screens, although a flickering fluorescent tube in one corner illuminated a coffee machine and small fridge. Jeannie was glad she wasn't claustrophobic.

'OK, Jeannie. The collective. Charlie and Davey you know. That's Lucy and over there is Skip. We take on the bad guys in ways we'll explain, but we also like to have fun. We're in the middle of a project at the moment so they're not very chatty. Some rules. We have a load of equipment here, which is firewalled up to the eyeballs and virus-protected to a military standard. Please don't use your own gear for Argus business, and that includes your normal phone. Use the burner to communicate with us via WhatsApp. Don't do anything to harm anyone, apart from the bad corporations, or steal money. Anyone accessing child porn, or anything else evil, is likely to find themselves waking up outside a police station with enough material in their pocket to get them a long stretch. We don't drink on the premises but we do go to the pub when we've finished a job. And the first rule of Argus is...' he paused.

'You don't talk about Argus.' Jeannie completed the sentence and Miles smiled.

'Any questions?' he asked.

'A couple. Why Argus and why me?'

The first is easy. We named the group after Argus Panoptes, a character in Greek mythology. He had a hundred eyes and his name means Argus the all-seeing. And we can see almost anything, or at least that's the aim. We invited you because Davey mentioned you after a session in the PA. Charlie recognised your name and was very keen to recruit you. I think he fancies you,' Miles said, in a stage whisper. Charlie looked embarrassed. 'Are you cool with all this?'

'Yes, yes, it's great,' Jeannie replied, although she wasn't sure about Charlie. 'What are you involved in? I must warn you that I've never done any hacking, although I know some of the principles. You're using Tor, I take it?'

'Yep. Sometimes. And also a similar router that's even more difficult to track. Look, sit down next to Davey and he'll show you what's going on. We're engaging in a prank to infiltrate the *Daily Mail* website and substitute some of the shots of scantily clad celebrities on the sidebar of shame with pictures of fluffy bunnies. They won't be up there long but we reckon it will take them at least twenty minutes to notice what's going on and change them back.'

'Brilliant,' laughed Jeannie, dragging a folding chair over to Davey's desk and sitting down. Charlie looked slightly disappointed.

During the next three years, Jeannie became a proficient hacker and valuable member of the group, socialising with the others and sharing their excitement when they pulled off a particularly ingenious stunt. She quickly summed up their characteristics. Miles was an exuberant socialist, with a hatred of big corporations that despoiled the planet and exploited people. Davey was quieter, studious and extremely competent, while Lucy modelled herself on Lisbeth Salander, although she wasn't as good. Skip was intense but had a dry wit, while Charlie was competent and a little creepy. They often went for drinks together but never talked about Argus in public. Although Jeannie never forgot her sister, the memories of her suicide coming back to her in quiet, reflective times, she was generally coping well and enjoying life.

When her contract came to an end she looked around for a permanent job. Reluctantly, she looked outside Leicester and found a confectionery distributor in the southern English town of Mexton that was looking for someone to run their IT systems and help with general business operations. It didn't seem particularly challenging but it was permanent and she would be able to keep in touch with the Argus people remotely, honing her hacking skills all the time and still having fun. Her degree, a glowing reference from the Leicester firm and a confident performance at the interview got her the job.

Chapter Eight

Mexton, Summer 2019

WHILE JEANNIE WAS LOOKING through the local paper for a place to buy, a photo caught her attention. Her stomach lurched, her head spun and she could hardly believe her eyes. It couldn't be, could it? She fumbled in her bag and pulled out a crumpled photo showing two men in evening dress, obviously drunk, which she had found in her sister's things. Iona had written 'The brothers' on the back and drawn a heart. One of the faces was blurred and obscured but the other was reasonably clear. Mentally adding a few years to the clearer image, she confirmed it. The man in the paper was one of the people responsible for Iona's death. And the bastard was the local MP. She would send the picture to Miles, who had software that could age faces, just to be sure, but in her heart she knew she was right.

Fury boiled up within her and she reached for a bottle of wine. Two women's lives destroyed while that evil little shit had gone on to success and power. She waited for a few minutes while the alcohol calmed her down and started to think rationally. She would search for him in a moment and see if there was any way of tracing his brother. Then she would work out which one of them had impregnated her sister.

The MP's name was Maxwell Arden. Within seconds of Googling him she had identified Gavin Arden, the Home Secretary, as the man's older brother. Furthermore, he was tall and slim while Maxwell was clearly shorter and overweight. It must have been Gavin. Ironic, she thought. A murderer by proxy being responsible for law and order.

All the rage she had felt when her sister died came back to her, intensified by the success of those responsible. It was so unfair. Iona was an innocent, sweet girl seduced and discarded, like a used tissue, by the rich and privileged. For hours Jeannie paced around her bedsit, making plans for revenge and rejecting them almost as quickly. She wanted to strike back, but she didn't know how. She couldn't get them prosecuted. There wouldn't be any evidence of what they'd done. If she tried to name and shame them publicly, they would undoubtedly sue her and she didn't have the resources to fight them in court. Even the most scurrilous tabloid newspaper wouldn't risk accusing the Home Secretary without proof. What she needed was someone like the Denzil Washington character in the *Equalizer* films. Someone who rights wrongs with force, lethally if necessary. Of course, that was fiction. But why shouldn't she become her own Equalizer? She didn't have access to firearms but she was fit, skilled in martial arts and determined.

The diffuse anger that she felt about her sister's death became focused and sharp, a blade that she knew she would be able to use. And she would kill Gavin Fucking Arden and ruin his brother.

Obviously, she couldn't approach him directly. He was bound to have an armed bodyguard. But she would find a way to get close to the local MP and hence his brother. A new identity, some funds to live on and a safe house would all be needed and she wouldn't strike until everything was in place.

The more she found out about Maxwell Arden, the less she liked him. She built up a picture of a bigoted, perverted, misogynistic individual who had clearly entered politics to improve his own lot, rather than that of his constituents. She had no doubt that his demise would improve the human gene pool.

His brother, Gavin, was different in many respects. Although solidly right wing, he had striven to present his party with a more human face. He was charming, photogenic and rather smug. He looked after his cronies, obviously, but emphasised his commitment to improving the nation as a whole. These might have been empty words but Jeannie found no traces of skeletons in his closet. Apart from the death of her sister.

Her first task, then, was to ensnare Maxwell Arden. If she had to sleep with him, then so be it, although the thought turned her stomach. Her mission was too important to be derailed by her reluctance to share her bed with an obvious shit. Once he trusted her, she would ask to meet his brother and then she would strike. It would take nerve and careful planning but she had the skills, the time and the patience to do things properly. Sooner or later, Gavin Arden would die at her hand.

Jeannie made a point of attending every party meeting and social event at which Maxwell Arden was present, helping out at fundraising dinners and similar occasions. She called herself Shona and changed her surname slightly, in case he recognised her name, not that she thought that likely.

She always prepared for meetings with Arden carefully. She used make-up, which she didn't normally bother with, and dressed attractively, although not gaudily, with a shortish skirt and a hint of cleavage. She made a point of catching his eye and smiling whenever the opportunity arose, firmly planting herself in his consciousness. Her campaign bore fruit when she sat opposite him at a dinner-dance. Throughout the meal, she saw Arden staring repeatedly at her lingerie-enhanced breasts, and after dessert she made her play.

'I do admire your work, Mr Arden. We're so lucky to have you as our MP.'

'Thank you, my dear. And your name is?'

'Shona McKay. Shona's my middle name. I prefer it.'

'Such a pretty name. I've always liked Irish girls.'

God, this man was a fucking cliché, Jeannie thought. And he didn't realise she was Scottish. She smiled back at him.

'I think you're absolutely right about immigration. And benefits. We can't afford to support freeloaders. They're a drain on the economy.'

Arden looked surprised that an obviously attractive woman could also have political opinions. More to the point, they coincided with his own. He licked his lips.

'And what do you do, Shona?'

'I work in IT,' she said, deliberately vague. 'I was wondering, does the local party need any help in this area? I could overhaul the computers and update the software, if that would be useful?'

'I think that would be very helpful, my dear. Look, why don't you pop into the constituency office tomorrow evening? My PA will show you what's what and we can get to know each other better.'

'I'd love that,' she smiled, stirring her coffee and looking at him with demurely lowered eyes.

Chapter Nine

Day 5, Monday

THREE STRANGERS, and DCI Gale, were waiting for Emma when she entered her office.

'Good morning, DI Thorpe,' said a tall, middle-aged man in a smart suit. 'I'm DI Steve Morton, SO15, and this is my colleague, DS Angela Wilson.' He indicated a smart woman in her thirties, with a pleasant smile and auburn hair tied back in a ponytail. 'And this is David Cornwallis from the security services.'

Morton indicated the third man, whose rather unobtrusive appearance was belied by a piercing gaze and an impression of sharp intelligence.

'Thanks for coming so quickly,' said Emma, offers of tea and coffee having been made and declined. 'I take it you've seen the material DCI Gale sent over?'

'Yes, we have,' replied Morton, 'and that puts us in a rather delicate position. What have you found out and what are your conclusions?'

Emma summarised the investigation so far and offered the suggestion that Duncan had been killed because he had upset a fellow conspirator. She then asked the others what they knew.

Cornwallis nodded to Morton, who started to speak.

'Firstly, we have been keeping an eye on Derek Farren and his associates for some time. Most of these characters are just mouthy thugs, who preach hate on the internet and get involved in the occasional scuffle or racist demonstration. Farren is different – he's a bit more intelligent than most of the others and he harbours a bitter grudge against Muslims. He lost a sister in the 2005 London bus bombings. His social media postings have become more and more extreme, as if he's leading up to something. We fear he may be planning a revenge attack.'

'So what was he doing in Mexton? Why not London, Bradford or Birmingham?'

'We don't know. Perhaps he felt there was less of a security presence in a smaller town. Maybe he had contacts here or was recruited. We'd love to find out.'

'And why was he passing details of possible targets to Bennett?' Emma looked perplexed.

The MI5 officer sighed and checked that the office door was closed.

'This is for your ears only,' Cornwallis warned. 'Duncan was an informer for us. You could be right about one of the group killing him. Perhaps his cover was blown.'

'Duncan Bennett an undercover agent?' Emma's incredulity was palpable. 'I know you're not all James Bonds but Duncan was so boring and ordinary that it's hard to credit.'

'On the contrary, that's what made him effective. You don't infiltrate a terrorist group in a tuxedo with a Walther in your hand. Ordinariness is essential.'

'How did he get involved?'

'I'm not going to divulge operational details but he came to us. Yes, his views were right-wing, but he was very disturbed by what he found on some of the websites he visited. He offered to look into them for us. We're short-staffed so we were happy for him to help, once we'd vetted him. We suggested he created an ultra-racist web presence that might bring the more dangerous individuals out of the woodwork. He would then pass the details on to us. He quickly came across Farren and his brother, Steven, who also nurses a grievance but is thicker. We're keeping an eye on him, too, when resources permit.'

'That's outrageous,' snapped Emma. 'Duncan was an administrator, not a trained spy.'

Morton nodded his agreement and Cornwallis continued.

'The stuff on his hard drive was meant to boost his credibility with our targets, but he was told, emphatically, that he should not meet any of them in person. We would never put an untrained civilian in a position of danger. Unfortunately, Duncan exceeded his brief by miles. His grandfather had been in military intelligence during the war, so it's possible he told Duncan stories that made him want to follow in his grandfather's footsteps, albeit unofficially. Before we knew it, he was posing as an explosives expert, keen to blow up people of other races, and was going to secret meetings of far-right terrorists. We knew that some of that stuff on his laptop was illegal, but we allowed him to download it, as he was helping us.'

'And that's what cost him his life.'

'So it seems. And we do regret not keeping a closer eye on him. Do you have an alternative explanation?'

'It's the only one on the table at the moment. I suppose SO15 will be taking over the investigation.'

'That would be best,' said Morton. 'The fewer people who

know of Duncan's role, the better. I'll leave Angela with you, to pack up the evidence you've collected. Tell your colleagues that there are national security implications and thank them for all their hard work.'

Chapter Ten

Reluctantly, Emma called her team together and broke the news. 'The SO15 guys are taking the case away from us.'

A chorus of moans broke out in response.

'Yes, I know you've all worked very hard and SO15 are grateful for the material you've dug up. But they say there are national security implications relating to far-right terrorism and they will continue with the investigation. If we're lucky, they might tell us the result. Jack, can you put together everything we've got on paper and give it to DS Wilson? Keep copies, just in case. Trevor, can you copy any electronic files to a flash drive for her? She's waiting in the canteen.'

'OK, guv, but before I do, can we take a look at the stuff Amira extracted from Duncan's cloud account?'

'I don't see why not. Is it of any use?'

'It's rather odd. There were just a few photos of men loading vans. I couldn't make out any faces, or what they were handling in most of them, as it was too dark. The last shot was taken with a flash, though, and we can see the boxes that were being loaded.'

'Any distinguishing marks on them?'

'No – they seemed completely plain, with no labels.'

'What about times?'

'They were all taken between 1.45 and 1.55 a.m. and were uploaded to the cloud within a few seconds of the last shot.'

'And Duncan's phone was switched off, or smashed, five minutes later.'

'That's right.'

'So that's another possible scenario for murder. Duncan saw something he shouldn't have when he woke up, took some pictures with his phone and accidentally used the flash on the last shot. This alerted the loaders and Duncan tried to run, only managing to get outside the building before they caught him. They dragged him into the alley, hit him with a handy piece of concrete and smashed his phone. So what were they up to?'

'Theft?'

'Being caught nicking a few bars of chocolate is hardly a motive for murder.'

'So, what's in the boxes could be the key,' mused Jack. 'Any suggestions?'

'Cash?'

'Drugs?'

'Firearms?'

'Nicked goods?'

'Fake passports?'

'Illegal ivory?'

'Stolen organs?'

'Explosives?'

The team ran out of suggestions and Emma had to point out that some of them were highly unlikely.

'We'll take a closer look at Duncan's pictures,' she said, 'and try to estimate the size of the boxes. We should be able to rule out some possible contents on that basis.'

'I'll see if we can borrow PD Popeye and her handler from the drugs squad and get her to have a look around the depot,' said Jack. 'We'll do it discreetly, implying she's looking for blood.'

'Why Popeye?' asked Emma. 'Does she eat spinach?'

'Ha, ha,' replied Jack. 'PD Popeye is a highly trained drug sniffer dog. She's named after the detective in the film *The French Connection.*'

'Haven't seen it,' said Martin. 'One of your old time Hollywood greats, I suppose. Is it in colour?'

'Yes, Martin,' replied Jack wearily. 'I'm not that much older than you.'

'Can we get back to the case now please?' interjected Emma. 'We need to think about why someone would be clandestinely loading boxes full of sweeties, or whatever, into vans in the middle of the night. Where do they go? Who are the recipients?'

'I think they're distributing something,' said Mel. 'No-one would suspect that a van full of confectionery would contain illicit goods and they go all over the southeast. Ideal cover. If the drivers are dropping boxes off at other locations, as well as sweet shops, this would account for the discrepancies in the mileage that Duncan noticed.'

'Right,' said Emma, a hint of glee in her voice. 'This aspect clearly has nothing to do with national security, so I think we can follow up a few leads while SO15 take over the rest of the case. We won't mention it to them though, in case they get a bit precious about it. The DCI knows that they're looking into the terrorism angle and I'll only tell her about our continuing work when, and if, we find anything. Officially, we're just tying up a few loose ends for SO15. Be discreet.'

'You can count on it, boss,' said Jack. 'I hate it when the spooks stick their oar in.'

'They have their reasons,' said Emma, mildly reprovingly. 'But now we have to find out three things: what's in the boxes, where are they going and who are the drivers and loaders involved? Suggestions, please.'

'Could we follow the vans?' offered Addy.

'We would need to stake out the place every night until we saw one leaving at a suspicious time. The overtime costs rule that out, I'm afraid. Also, a tail would be easy to spot at night, when the roads are quiet.'

'How about fitting a tracker?' asked Martin.

'Firstly, we wouldn't have access to the premises without attracting suspicion; secondly, we wouldn't know which van to fit it to; and thirdly, we wouldn't get authorisation under RIPA.'

'Could we search the warehouse?' Addy asked.

'We wouldn't get a warrant and we have no grounds to search without one. And you know full well that evidence obtained from an illegal search is inadmissible.'

'How about CCTV?' suggested Martin. 'We've looked at the pub and the car park stuff, but there must be other cameras around.'

'That's a better idea. Addy, can you look at footage from cameras on roads around the estate between nine p.m. and seven a.m. on the night of the murder? Petrol stations, convenience stores, private houses, if their cameras cover the street outside. In the meantime, Trevor – run a financial check on all the employees. See if their lifestyles, houses, cars etc. match their earnings. Look on Facebook and Twitter and see if anyone has expensive holidays and so on.'

'We've got some idea of the size of the boxes,' interjected Jack. 'They're about twenty-five centimetres square and fifteen centimetres deep. It's difficult to be precise.'

'So, about the size of a wholesale box of chocolate bars.'

'Yes. They wouldn't stand out from the other boxes in the van, as far as we can see from Duncan's photos.'

'That rules out some of the suggestions, then. No kidneys in iceboxes or Kalashnikovs. Big enough to hold a serious quantity of drugs or a pistol, though. When is PD Popeye going in?'

'Later today, unless the drugs squad needs her for a raid.'

'OK. Let's get a package ready for DS Wilson while she "enjoys" a canteen lunch. We'll meet up tomorrow at nine, officially for a final debrief. Anyone without a task on this job can carry on with other cases until then. We've got plenty and I know some of you are still needed on the Maldobourne case from last year.'

Chapter Eleven

Day 6, Tuesday

'You're looking cheerful, Addy,' said Martin as the two detectives queued for coffee.

'So I should,' replied Addy. 'I've just got engaged.'

'Well done, mate. Who's the lucky woman?'

'Her name is Victoria,' smiled Addy. 'She's a nurse at Mexton General. I met her when we took in a drunk with a broken wrist and we just clicked.'

'When's the big day?'

'Not 'til the summer. There's a lot to arrange. We've both got big families, scattered all over the place. An organisational nightmare.'

'I'm sure it will be brilliant,' said Martin. 'Hang on, the guv'nor's starting the briefing. We'd better shift.'

The information presented at the nine o'clock briefing was detailed but not particularly helpful.

Emma kicked off. 'How did PD Popeye do, Jack?'

'Nothing very positive. She did seem slightly interested in the loading bay but she could have smelt something other than drugs. It wasn't strong enough for us to consider applying for a warrant.'

'So, if drugs are being distributed, they're very well wrapped up.'

'Exactly. How about CCTV and ANPR, Addy?'

'Well, there's definitely something dodgy going on. As you know, the cameras at the front of the building are out of action so it's possible to approach and leave without being recorded, as long as you don't use the staff car park. It's worth finding out how long they've been down, as you'd think they'd want to keep track of vehicle movements.'

'True enough. How about the roads nearby?'

'The industrial estate has a maze of small roads and paths, without cameras, so by the time a vehicle is picked up, there's no telling where it came from. However, around ten p.m. on the night of Duncan's murder a Maybrick and Cream van entered the estate, presumably returning from a delivery round. Later on, two motorbikes with conveniently dirty plates appeared, on two separate cameras, on roads serving the estate. They entered the complex, remained there for half an hour or so, then left, taking different routes from the ones they came in on.'

'The bike plates would have been cleaned up further along to avoid them getting pulled over, wouldn't they?' asked Mel. 'The traffic guys love stopping boy racers on bikes.'

'Indeed, said Emma. 'So we've no idea where they went.'

'Perhaps we've got it the wrong way round,' suggested Martin. 'Maybe Duncan saw unloading rather than loading.'

'You could be right.' Jack agreed. 'So, we have a possible scenario where small, high-value items are brought into Mexton by chocolate van and distributed by bike.'

'That would make more sense', agreed Emma. 'OK, I'm thinking aloud here. Suppose they are bringing in drugs or weapons from mainland Europe. An artic comes through the channel tunnel, or over on a ferry, stops at a derelict site and unloads the drugs or whatever into a Maybrick and Cream van, along with a load of Belgian chocolate.'

'It wouldn't have to be derelict. Loading chocolate into a confectionery wholesaler's van could be done at a distribution depot without attracting suspicion. It would look perfectly normal,' interrupted Trevor.

'Good point,' Emma acknowledged. 'The van then arrives at the warehouse, undetected by the firm's CCTV, which is switched off, and the drugs or guns are transferred to motorbikes for onward distribution. The Belgian chocolate would be put into stock as part of a normal delivery. The only detectable oddity would be more mileage on the van than expected – and Duncan was suspicious about this.'

'They would need someone bent in the office, as well as the loaders,' pointed out Jack. 'Do we think they're all at it then?'

'Not necessarily, but at least one other person is involved.'

'So what do we do now?' asked Mel.

'Well, it's nothing to do with national security, so we don't have to hand this over to Counter-Terrorism. I'll take it to DCI Gale and see what she says. She may want to run it past the Super. I'll also have a chat with the drugs squad. If they're not looking at Maybrick and Cream already, they'll certainly be interested. In the meantime, could someone check to see if any of the office staff, or the drivers and loaders, have previous, or are known associates of drug dealers?'

Martin volunteered and Emma nodded her thanks.

'Also, Addy, see if Malcolm Howard has a record of when the CCTV was switched off and whether it went down on other dates. We may see a pattern.'

'On it, guv.'

DCI Gale pursed her lips and tapped a pencil on the rim of her coffee mug. 'It's an interesting idea, Emma, but we need hard evidence. All we've got so far is a dead man and his photos of a couple of blokes doing something out of hours. What does the drugs squad have to say?'

'They've heard nothing. They've asked to be involved if it comes to a raid and arrests.'

'So how do you want to proceed?'

'Ideally, I'd like to put trackers on the vans, stake out the buildings and put hidden CCTV in the warehouse.' Emma knew she was asking for the moon.

'We haven't the resources for a lengthy stakeout and there's not enough evidence to authorise covert electronic surveillance. Do you have a plan B?'

'The only other option, as far as I can see, is to put someone undercover in the firm. There is a vacancy, after all.'

'Risky. Very risky.' DCI Gale looked sceptical. 'They've already killed once and anyone snooping around would put themselves in danger. Someone in the firm would have to agree and you don't know who's involved. If you did go down that route, do you have an officer in mind?'

'No-one on my team has undercover training, but perhaps I could borrow someone from the drugs squad.'

'I'm not happy about that. Undercover officers are highly specialised and they wouldn't want to waste one on a hunch. Look, I've got a management meeting now and I'll talk to the Super about resources afterwards. Explore the undercover angle discreetly and consider it a last resort. We'll talk again tomorrow.'

'Thank you, ma'am,' said Emma, a trifle disconsolately.

Wanting to clear her head and sort out her thoughts, Emma took a drive to the industrial estate and explored the area around Maybrick and Cream. It was obvious that the network of small roads provided plenty of opportunity for vehicles to get lost, change number plates and avoid CCTV. On her way out of the estate she noticed a For Sale sign in the window of a disused building a few dozen metres down from, and on the opposite side of the road to, Maybrick and Cream. That, she said to herself, would make a useful observation point.

'It's a bit of a long shot,' Emma explained to DCI Gale when she returned to the station, 'but I'd like to put a couple of people in the empty building overlooking the warehouse on Wednesday night – the same day of the week Duncan was killed.'

'You think it's a regular operation, do you?'

'Possibly. It's worth investing a few hours overtime to see if anything happens.'

'OK. I think we can afford that. Any progress with the undercover idea?'

'I haven't spoken to the drugs squad yet, but I've a meeting arranged with their DS Palmer on Thursday.'

'Well, be guided by him. He knows what he's doing. Good luck.'

'Thank you, ma'am,' said Emma, feeling rather more optimistic than she had after her previous meeting with the DCI.

Chapter Twelve

Day 7, Wednesday

'WHO FANCIES spending tonight in an empty warehouse?' asked Emma at the daily briefing. 'The Super's authorised directed surveillance. You'll get overtime pay but you'll have to bring your own coffee.'

'Do we get doughnuts?' Mel asked, cheekily.

'Don't be silly. Haven't you heard of austerity?' was Emma's riposte.

The team groaned. Mel and Trevor volunteered and followed Emma into her office.

'OK. Here's binoculars, a camera and a night-vision scope. Don't lose them. They're expensive.'

'We're not kids, guv,' said Mel, indignantly.

'Yes, I know. But DCI Gale is very particular about keeping costs down and the equipment budget is already overspent.'

'Right. I won't leave them at the back of the bus then.'

Emma smiled.

'Wrap up warm,' was her final advice. 'There's no heating in the building.'

Two hours after starting the surveillance, Mel was shivering and her fingers had started to go numb, despite her puffer jacket and woollen gloves. Their observation point was on the first floor and the windows didn't shut. The copious quantities of bird droppings on the floor and windowsills suggested that other species regularly took shelter there, not just watching police officers. They had seen no activity around the target building, although the sounds of motorbikes coming and going had punctuated the stillness a few times.

'Bored now,' said Mel.

'Oh.' Trevor perked up. 'What can we talk about? Did I tell you about the new computer game I've just got? The graphics are awesome. You really feel you're right in the middle of...'

'It's OK, Trev. I'll pass on that. I prefer the gym to computer games. I've never really got into them.'

'Well, they're supposed to improve your reflexes and working memory, according to something I read online. Anyway, Susie and I both like them. We play against each other sometimes and she often wins. We go out for walks as well. It's not like we're couch potatoes, stuffing ourselves with pizza and getting no exercise.'

'It's all right. I'm not getting at you,' smiled Mel.

'How are you getting on with Tom's Norwegian Blues?' Trevor teased.

'They're eclectus parrots. And they're noisy and crap everywhere. But they are beautiful. They cost a fortune to feed, as well. My tortoise is certainly easier.'

Trevor laughed and the two detectives turned their attention back to the warehouse.

Mel had made the mistake of nearly finishing her flask of coffee earlier on and desperately needed to pee.

'I'm going to look for a toilet,' she told her colleague,

'I just hope the water supply's switched on,' replied Trevor, 'or you'll have to go in the corner over there.'

'Not bloody likely,' Mel snapped back.

She had barely been gone ten seconds when she crashed back through the swing doors that gave access to their floor.

'Get out! The place is on fire.'

The opening doors had allowed the first tendrils of smoke to drift into the room, but by the time Mel and Trevor reached the stairs thick clouds were pouring upwards.

'Go up, not down,' yelled Mel, fumbling for her phone. 'We'll never get out through that lot. I'm calling the fire service.'

The two detectives started to choke as they leapt up the stairs to the next floor. Closing the doors behind them kept the smoke temporarily at bay while they cast around for an alternative exit or a fire escape. Following the Emergency Exit signs they came across a fire door, which someone had padlocked while the building was unoccupied.

'This wasn't in the bleedin' risk assessment,' spat Trevor. 'How the hell are we supposed to get out?'

'Maybe we're not,' said Mel. 'It's a bit of a coincidence, the building catching fire tonight of all nights, don't you think?'

'What, you reckon we were spotted?' said Trevor, incredulously. 'We didn't turn up with blues-and-twos and the car was unmarked.'

'Perhaps someone recognised it from when we questioned the staff.'

'Shit. You could be right.'

By now the smoke had reached the second level and they could feel heat from the burning building through the floor. The officers' eyes were watering and they had started to cough.

'Right now, I don't give a fuck how the fire started,' snapped Trevor. 'I just want to get out of here alive. I only wanted the overtime so we can get a new car. I thought it would be a doddle. My Susie'll be furious.'

Mel thought of Martin Rowse's near-fatal stabbing and forebore from mentioning that any day could be the day you got injured or killed in this job. Instead, she tried to block the smoke coming through the doors with some discarded plastic packaging she found on the floor, and went to the furthest corner of the room where she smashed a window with her baton. This gave them a source of fresh air, but the open window drew the fire closer and it was not long before her improvised barrier melted and then caught fire. Flames began to lick along the floorboards, their spread accelerated by the draught, while the room filled up with smoke from the ceiling downwards.

Despite sticking their heads out of the broken window, Mel and Trevor were becoming increasingly incapacitated by smoke. Below them they could hear parts of the building collapsing, and the heat behind was surging towards them like a dyspeptic dragon's breath. Only dimly did they recognise the blue lights and sirens of approaching fire engines.

Five minutes later, still choking, they were pulled out of the window onto the platform of a turntable ladder and lowered to the ground, while fire appliances poured water into the burning building. With oxygen masks on their faces and reflective blankets wrapped round them to keep them warm, the two police officers were stretchered into an ambulance and whisked off to A&E, too weak to talk.

Alerted by police control, Emma sped to the scene, her portable blue light clamped to the roof of her car. Her faced paled when she saw that her colleagues were gone, but she was reassured by the Senior Fire Officer on site.

'They've gone to the hospital for a checkup. They weren't burned but are suffering from smoke inhalation. They'll probably be kept in overnight.'

'How did it start?' asked Emma.

'There'll be a proper investigation and you'll get a report, but it's pretty clear to me that the fire was started deliberately. From the pattern of burning, it looks like an accelerant was poured over the bottom of the stairs. You can draw your own conclusions but I'd say that they weren't expected to get out. It doesn't seem like a random arson attack.'

Thanking the fire officer, Emma drove to the hospital. She wasn't allowed to see the two patients but was told that they were 'comfortable' and could be visited the following morning. She returned home, wondering how she would explain the surveillance disaster to her senior officers. It wasn't a particularly auspicious start to the job, she thought. Less than a couple of months in post and two colleagues nearly killed. She knew it wasn't her fault, but it didn't look good. Not at all.

Chapter Thirteen

Day 8, Thursday

AFTER VISITING HER HOSPITALISED COLLEAGUES, Emma pulled into the station car park a little after ten. DCI Gale stopped her as she entered the office.

'The Super wants to see you as soon as you get in – and he's not a happy bunny.'

Straightening her skirt, Emma knocked on Detective Superintendent Gorman's door and entered when summoned.

'A bloody shambles. A total bloody shambles,' thundered the DSup. 'Two officers nearly killed, six thousand pounds worth of equipment lost and the building's owners are trying to claim against us for the damage to their property. How the hell could that have happened? Didn't you do a risk assessment, for Christ's sake?'

An embarrassed Emma cleared her throat and attempted an explanation.

'Of course I did a risk assessment, sir. But the fire doors were padlocked by someone after the estate agent showed me round. The DCs did nothing wrong. They showed no lights in the observation building and sat far enough back from the windows to avoid light from the street lamps. The unmarked car was parked some way from the building, but it is possible that it was recognised by someone. It was used by officers interviewing the staff at Maybrick and Cream and also when canvassing local people.'

'Well, that was pretty stupid.'

'I know, sir, but I can hardly reprimand them, given what happened to them.'

'I suppose not. Has anything positive come out of this balls-up?'

'They didn't see anything, although they heard motorbikes buzzing about. But the fact that this was a deliberate attack gives credence to the idea that something dodgy is going on at the warehouse. Shall I contact Counter-Terrorism and let them know what's happened?'

'No. We don't want to look complete idiots and they may turn up something of interest through their channels. What are you planning next?'

'I'm now convinced that we need to plant someone undercover in the firm, taking Bennett's place.'

'You'll need to make a damn good case. The Assistant Chief Constable will have to authorise it and he won't be keen to put another officer at risk. Draw up a proposal with a risk assessment, fill in the form and include the names of any suitable officers. Clear it with DCI Gale then I'll put it to him. If he agrees, you'll have to square it with the office manager at Maybrick and Cream – unless you think he's in on it?'

'I don't think so. I've interviewed him myself. He seemed genuinely upset about Duncan's death. Still, it's a risk we'll have to take, and if our plant thinks they've been rumbled, we'll call it off immediately.'

'Keep me informed and let me have that paperwork as soon as possible.'

'Thank you, sir.'

Emma left the Superintendent's office, determined to catch those responsible for trying to burn her DCs to death. Someone had crossed a line here, she thought, and she wasn't having it.

Detective Sergeant Palmer, of Mexton drugs squad, pursed his lips and thought.

'So why do you think drugs are involved?'

'There's clearly something iffy going on, involving the distribution of smallish, portable articles. Drugs are the obvious conclusion,' Emma replied. 'Also, I'm sure someone at the firm was involved in killing Duncan Bennett.'

'A bit thin, isn't it? We don't send people under cover lightly. Apart from the risk, it takes a lot of planning. Finding a suitable officer and handler is far from easy. We don't have them hanging around, waiting for something to do.'

'I realise this, but I've no-one with the training and most of them have been seen by staff at Maybrick and Cream. I'd really appreciate it if you could help.'

'Well, I suppose we owe your team a favour for helping to crack the Maldobourne operation. I've got someone who's just come back from an assignment up north, so no-one should recognise her. I can spare her for a couple of weeks. Will that do?'

'That's brilliant. If she can't find out anything in that time there may be nothing to find. She'd better report directly to me.'

'Sorry. That's not how we do things. She'll have a dedicated handler within our squad, probably DS Alex Gordon, who'll pass on anything useful to you. I'll give you her alias but you mustn't disclose it to anyone. Fair enough?'

'Thanks, mate. I really appreciate it. I owe you a large drink for this.'

Palmer thought about Emma's pleasant face and lithe figure before replying.

'I might just take you up on that.'

Chapter Fourteen

Day 9, Friday

'IT SHOULDN'T BE DANGEROUS,' Alex assured Lorna Fraser. 'As far as the manager is concerned, you're looking into Duncan's death, trying to get a feel for his job and the people around him. He doesn't know about the photos Duncan took before he died and you mustn't mention them. He'll tell the rest of the staff you've come from a temp agency and may stay permanently, if things work out. We'll provide a convincing covering letter for their personnel files and cook up some references. Your alias will be Lauren Casey; preferred mode of address is 'Lor'. How are you with spreadsheets and accounting stuff?'

'Fine. I did an IT course before I joined the force and my partner runs a small business, so I can bone up on current practices.'

'Excellent. For the duration of the op you'll live at a safe house, not your flat. The address and keys are in this envelope. Here's your dedicated phone. Put a few personal contacts on it, with phone numbers and emails. We've put some stock photos from various dates and places on it so it looks convincing. Familiarise yourself with them. You know the ropes. In an emergency press star, zero and hash in quick succession. A call will go straight through to control and a unit will be dispatched to the GPS location immediately. We will monitor the phone at all times and if you are being coerced to make a call, include the word "cousin" in what you say. We'll send backup. Finally, in case someone gets hold of your phone and sends phoney texts, we will only accept a text as genuine if it ends with LoLLor.'

Alex spelt out the letters as they should appear and reiterated that there should be no spaces between them.

'I must emphasise that you should be in no danger, provided you follow your training. If you feel at all worried, get out at once. Any questions at this stage? You'll get a fuller briefing on the activities of Maybrick and Cream tomorrow and you'll start on Monday.'

'No, I'm fine sir,' replied Lorna, a note of excitement in her voice. 'I'll be careful. My partner would kill me if I got hurt!'

'An unfortunate turn of phrase, but I know what you mean,' said Alex, with a grin. Good luck!'

'Thanks, Alex,' said Lorna, leaving his office with a spring in her step and The Jam's *Going Underground* playing in her head.

'Some good news,' said Emma, as the team gathered in the incident room. 'We've got someone going undercover into Maybrick and Cream. Until we get some results, we can't do much more on Operation Wombat, so please get on with the dozen other active cases we're dealing with. Mel, keep working on the spate of burglaries, and Martin, carry on with the handbag snatches.'

'Perhaps he could dress up as an old lady and act as bait?' joked Mel.

'Nah,' Martin replied.' Handbags don't suit me.'

The other DCs laughed and Emma smiled as she continued.

'If there are any outstanding actions on Wombat, please finish them first. Be ready to switch back to it as soon as we get some intel. Jack, can you put together a file summarising where we are?'

'Yes, guv.'

'Thanks, everybody. You've worked really hard on this and we should get some results if we keep at it.'

As she walked back to her office, Emma hoped her optimism was justified. She had confidence in her team members, who, so far, had proved to be enthusiastic and diligent. But would that be enough?

Chapter Fifteen

Day 12, Monday

On Monday morning, Lorna knocked on Malcolm Howard's half-open door. She had exchanged her usual plain clothes outfit of trousers, a loose jumper and trainers for a skirt, blouse and kitten heels. She had also put on lipstick and eye make-up, items normally reserved for a posh night out.

'Come in er...Lauren,' called Howard. 'I'll show you the ropes here and introduce you to the others.'

After a crash course on Maybrick and Cream's business procedures, Howard ushered her into the main office.

'Everybody,' he called, 'this is Lauren. She's taking over Duncan's role for the next few weeks until we can find a permanent replacement. If you're nice to her she may even stay.'

There were a few chuckles and 'Hi, Laurens' as she was shown to the only empty desk, from which all traces of Duncan's former presence had been removed. Howard pointed to her new colleagues one by one, naming them and outlining their roles. She found herself sitting next to Jeannie McLeod, a neatly dressed, red-haired woman of about thirty with a friendly manner and a hint of a Scottish accent.

Jeannie smiled at her. 'If you need any help, just shout. I know the systems inside out and Duncan often asked me to troubleshoot.'

'Why did Duncan leave?' asked Lorna.

'Did you no' hear? He was murdered.'

'Oh,' replied Lorna, trying to look surprised. 'I didn't realise I was actually stepping into a dead man's shoes.'

'Was that meant to be funny?' someone called. Lorna didn't see who.

'N-no. not at all,' she replied, flushing and looking embarrassed. 'I'm so sorry. I didn't realise what I was saying.'

'Don't worry,' whispered Jeannie. 'No-one liked him much anyway. I'll give you the gory details at lunchtime.'

Aware that she appeared to have annoyed at least one of her new workmates, Lorna busied herself with getting to grips with Duncan's logistics system. It seemed fairly straightforward. Putting orders received into the spreadsheet generated vehicle routes that minimised the mileage driven between customers. Expected deliveries from manufacturers were also entered, so that the vans wouldn't leave until the required goods were available. Finally, odometer readings from the vans were entered at the end of each run, to check that the route planning worked. Within an hour Lorna had grasped the essentials, and within three she was already bored.

At midday, a van called with a range of sandwiches, cakes, fruit and yogurts. The staff room, with a coffee machine and water cooler, provided seating for people to eat their lunch. Some bought food from the van while others brought in their own, to eat cold or heat up in a grimy looking microwave oven adjacent to the sink. Lorna went for a wander around the loading bays during her lunch hour. Some of the men working there ignored her, a couple wolf whistled and a stocky, shaven-headed individual shouted at her to get out of the way.

'Office staff shouldn't be here, luv,' he shouted. 'You might get run over.'

'What's your problem?' she called back. 'I'm new here. I want to see how things work.'

'I'll show her how things work,' sniggered another man, just loud enough for Lorna to hear.

'Creep,' she muttered under her breath, avoiding a confrontation and speculating to herself about the effects of a pepper spray discharged into the commentator's priapic groin. Asking casually in the office, she identified the stocky man as Darren Lorde and the cat-caller as Mark Dickens.

Avoiding the mistake made by undercover cops on TV, Lorna didn't immediately start asking questions. She kept her eyes and ears open and confined conversations to routine matters, sticking to her cover story. Jeannie, however, was keen to share the details of Duncan's demise although she had a number of details wrong, points on which Lorna refrained from correcting her.

Back at her flat, she emailed her report to Alex and began to plan her actions for the rest of the week. None of the office staff had behaved suspiciously, although some had been a little reserved with the newcomer. They had little to do with the drivers and loaders and Lorna resolved to try to talk to them when the opportunity arose. She also considered staying late at night, to see whether anyone entered the premises illicitly. She didn't share her plans with Alex, thinking that she would give them further thought before doing anything.

Chapter Sixteen

Day 13, Tuesday

WITH MOST OF Operation Wombat on hold, awaiting information from the undercover officer, Mexton CID turned its attention to the stacks of other cases on its plate. High on Emma Thorpe's list of priorities was the series of handbag snatches carried out on pensioners as they left the post office with money in their purses. Many elderly folk, without conventional bank accounts, still used the post office card system and withdrew their pensions as cash. She stopped beside Martin's desk and asked him how he was getting on.

'Nothing much so far, guv. I've plotted where they've happened on a map and most of the small post offices in town have been targeted. They never hit the same one twice, and it's always on a Thursday morning. Two lads ride up on a small motorbike, with no plates. The passenger leaps off, grabs the bag and they ride away before anyone knows what's happening. CCTV, where there is any, is useless. The bags are dumped a few hundred metres away, minus the purses.'

'Hmm. Are there any post offices where they haven't struck? Could we predict where they might try next?'

'I've been looking at that. Of the three not yet touched, two are on pedestrian precincts where it would be difficult to take a bike. But this one, on Dalston Street, has a fairly narrow pavement and there are alleys nearby that would make a good escape route.'

'Right.' Emma thought for a moment. 'You know that crack Mel made about dressing up and acting as a decoy?'

'Yes, guv, and I don't fancy it.'

'I'm not suggesting you do. But if we could get a female volunteer, and have backup in one of those alleys, it could work. I'll ask around.'

'Fancy getting mugged in the line of duty, Karen?' Emma asked DC Groves.

'I suppose so. What do you mean, guv?'

'We think we've identified the post office where the handbag snatchers will strike next. We need someone to dress up as a pensioner and act as a decoy. There'll be backup around the corner and these wee shites aren't armed, so it shouldn't be too risky. Are you up for it?'

'Yes, guv, like a shot. My Mum left some old clothes of my Gran's that should fit me. With a grey wig and a stoop, I'm sure I could pass for eighty.'

'Good lass. You'll need your pepper spray, just in case. Can you be ready by Thursday?'

'No problem,' replied Karen, keen to do something a bit more exciting than desk work.

Chapter Seventeen

Day 14, Wednesday

On Wednesday night, Lorna decided to stay in the office after her workmates had left. She walked to the gate with them but then pretended she'd left something in the office and had to go back for it. Keeping the lights off, she used her phone torch to snoop around the offices, including Malcolm Howard's, but found nothing incriminating. She settled down in the dark building to wait, after texting Alex to let him know what she was doing. She set her phone to silent and prepared herself for a long vigil.

By eight o'clock she was seriously bored. Without a light to read by, she had nothing to entertain herself. She didn't have a Kindle and couldn't risk draining the battery on her phone any further by playing games on it. Just as her eyelids were beginning to droop, she was jolted into alertness by the sound of motorbikes approaching. Easing open the office door, she padded down the corridor on her shoeless feet to the staircase that led to the loading bay. She felt her way by referring to features she had committed to memory, such as windows, door-ways and fire extinguishers. She heard the sound of conversations below her and inched her way down the steps until she reached the ground floor.

'Stay calm,' she told herself, silently. 'Breathe quietly and remember your training.'

Convinced that she hadn't been heard or seen, she opened the door to the loading area, wincing as it scraped along the concrete floor. Lights from vehicles illuminated the area in patches, casting deep shadows that enabled her to remain hidden. She was just creeping her way closer to the action taking place around the vans when someone grabbed her by the hair, forcing her head back and catching it against a pillar. She couldn't see who it was but could feel the wool of a balaclava against the back of her neck and smelt a powerful after-shave over a stench of unwashed armpits.

'What the fuck are you doing here?' snarled a voice, which she recognised as Darren Lorde's. 'You should've gone home hours ago.'

'I did, I did,' Lorna whimpered, restraining herself from responding as a trained police officer and maintaining her role as an ordinary office worker.

'I left my contact lenses here, I thought, and I came back to look for them. I've been here ages and I can't find them.'

'How did you get in?'

'Jeannie gave me some keys. I was going to start early tomorrow, so I could leave in the middle of the afternoon to go to the dentist. She said I shouldn't tell anyone.'

Lorna hoped that her assailant wouldn't check with Jeannie.

'So why are you sneaking around here without any shoes?'

'I heard noises. I thought it might be burglars.'

'Have you phoned the police?'

'No. I wanted to be sure.'

'Gimme your phone.'

Lorde thumbed through her messages and relaxed slightly when he saw no calls, sent mails or texts to the police.

'Is anyone expecting you back?'

'Yes, my cousin Alex. We're supposed to be watching the new *Star Wars* DVD. Who are you and what are you doing here?'

'None of your fuckin' business. Now what you're gonna do is send your cousin a text sayin' you'll be back late. I'm gonna check it before you press send and if there's anything funny about it I'll snap your bleedin' neck.'

'All right, all right,' she said, playing up the panic in her voice. She figured that, with her training, she could probably get free of Lorde and maybe overpower him, but that would still leave the others to evade. It would also blow what was left of her cover. She would have to find another opportunity to escape.

With trembling fingers, she composed a text to Alex.

Hi Cousin. I still can't find my contacts in the desk so I'll collect my spare set from Gill's place. Back later. We'll still have time to watch the movie. LoLLor

'Who's Gill and what's this LoLLor bollocks?'

'Gill's my sister. And I'm Lauren, known as Lor. That's how I sign my texts.

Lorde studied the draft for a few seconds and looked at previous texts. Eventually, he pressed send and then switched off Lorna's phone.

'What now? Can I go please? I don't know what's happening.'

. . .

'You're going somewhere safe until we can take care of you. And if you make a noise, we'll hurt you. Got it?'

Lorna nodded meekly as she was bundled into a dark stock room, with a plastic cable tie binding her wrists behind her, worrying all the time about what 'taking care' meant. She didn't think it was tea and biscuits. Fighting back at that point would have been pointless. It would have wasted her energy and would have only led to her being injured.

As soon as the door was locked behind her, she cast her eyes around the room looking for a means of escape or a weapon. Fortunately for her, the lights were controlled from inside so she switched them on by butting the switch with her head, hoping her captors wouldn't notice. Piles of cardboard boxes were heaped against the walls, some empty and some full of confectionery. A dusty filing cabinet stood in one corner, next to a heap of derelict IT equipment. A sickly-sweet smell of chocolate pervaded the room, and the rough concrete floor scraped at her feet. There was no external window, just a series of small fanlights set into the top of the wall overlooking the loading area. She could hear muted conversations but couldn't pick out individual words.

She sat down on the floor and managed to manoeuvre her legs through her tied arms, mentally thanking her yoga teacher for her flexibility. With her hands now in front of her it was easier to explore. By standing on a chair, she could just see cardboard boxes being unloaded from a van, but there was no indication as to what they contained. As to a weapon, chocolate bars might be harmful if over-consumed but they would be useless in a fight.

Eventually her explorations yielded results. A small box cutter had dropped behind a pile of cartons, and three minutes, several small cuts and a series of silent curses later, her wrists were freed. While the box cutter was of little use as a weapon, the small carbon dioxide fire extinguisher she found in a corner was more so. She mulled over in her mind the principle of reasonable force and came to the conclusion that, if she was in fear of her life, she was justified in thumping someone with the item, preferably not fatally. To give herself an advantage, she clambered on a pile of boxes and removed the fluorescent tubes that illuminated the room. Once her eyes had adjusted to the darkness, she would have better vision than someone walking into the darkened room from the light. She settled down to wait, nerves on edge and sweat soaking the blouse beneath her jacket.

The men in the loading bay were arguing about what to do with her, although she couldn't make out what they were saying. After she'd been there for what seemed like hours, the door to the stockroom crashed open and Lorde stumbled in, still masked. He lunged at Lorna and managed to get his hands round her throat, a grip that only loosened when she slammed the fire extinguisher into his groin. Doubling over and yelling in pain, he threw a punch in Lorna's general direction, his fist glancing off her cheek. Before he could resume his attempt to strangle her, another man came in and hauled him away.

'We gotta go. The boss just phoned. The filth's on the way.'

Lorde hit Lorna in the face again and hissed.

'You say anything about this to anyone, you nosy bitch, and I'll find you and fucking kill you.'

Dazed and alone, Lorna slumped onto a pile of boxes, regretting her carelessness in getting caught. At least she knew who one of the criminals was, although it would be hard to prove in court as she hadn't actually seen him. It was a further five minutes before the cavalry arrived, blues and twos splitting the night. A crazy feeling of euphoria washed over her and obliterated the pain from Lorde's blows as her colleagues and a couple of paramedics burst in. They insisted on taking Lorna to hospital, despite her protestations that she was fine. In truth, she felt more wounded in her pride than in her body. An experienced undercover officer shouldn't have been caught like that. What on earth would she say to Alex?

Chapter Eighteen

Day 15, Thursday

LORNA SPENT the rest of the night under observation in hospital and was discharged the following day. Returning to the station, with a scarf covering the bruises round her neck and concealer disguising the marks on her face, she was anxious to discuss her next move. Should she pull out or carry on pretending that she was looking for her lenses when a burglar attacked her? Alex and DS Palmer were all for terminating the operation but Lorna was anxious to continue.

'I don't want to waste all this work, boss, and I could maintain the cover story of looking for my lenses.'

'You nearly got yourself killed. I appreciate courage but isn't this stubbornness?' Alex asked.

'Maybe. But it's my neck.' She fingered her scarf, almost unconsciously.

'But, if there's another villain in the office, they'll know you saw something you shouldn't have.' Palmer looked doubtful.

'I could look frightened and refuse to discuss it. Anyway,

I've not seen anyone acting oddly. I think the gang is being controlled from outside. Someone phoned and they let me go, just before the cavalry arrived. I reckon they were tipped off.'

'You mean a bent copper.'

'Possibly. Or someone else who knew a rescue was on its way.'

'I don't like it. I really don't.' Alex fiddled with a pen. 'But if you're sure you can handle it you can stay for one more week. Take a couple of days' sick leave from the firm. An office worker isn't supposed to be as resilient as a cop. And check your phone is set up so any speed dial comes straight to us. We'll treat the incident simply as a foiled burglary and assault, interview a few staff and give them a crime number. We don't have enough to arrest Lorde so for God's sake don't let him know you recognised him. Keep away from him as much as possible.'

'Will do. I won't go near the loading area and he rarely comes into the office.'

'All right, then. And if anything looks odd, clear out at once.'

Lorna smiled and stood up to leave, looking rather more confident than she felt. Yes, it was risky. But there was no way she was going to let Lorde get away with assaulting her.

Karen entered the Dalston Street post office just after nine, looking every inch as though she was there to collect her pension. She stooped, her clothes were old-fashioned and worn, and a grey wig plus some plain, heavy-framed glasses completed the disguise. The staff had been warned that she would wait there until called out by her colleagues, who were looking out for motorbikes ridden suspiciously up and down the street. She had spotted the white van, bearing the logo Tube Alloys plc, parked nearby and was comforted by the knowledge that there were three large PCs inside.

By midday, she had read every notice about posting times, prohibited goods and the benefits of Post Office broadband at least five times. She had leafed through the indifferent selection of greetings cards repeatedly and her feet were aching. She was beginning to consider the whole exercise a waste of time when her Airwave crackled.

'Potential suspects in sight, ten seconds away.'

Her heart racing, Karen opened the door, fiddling with her voluminous handbag as if she had just zipped her purse inside. She had barely stepped onto the pavement, slippery with rain, when a hand grabbed the bag's handle and yanked it. She held on and shouted 'Police!' while reaching for her pepper spray. Her attacker, a wiry youth with a face full of piercings, spat in her face, let go of the handbag and shoved her. Her feet skidded on the wet pavement and she fell on her backside, straight on top of a fresh pile of dog mess. A PC rushed to help her up, barely concealing his amusement, while the would-be mugger jumped on the pillion of a waiting motorbike, which roared off. The Tube Alloys van hurtled after the escaping youths, cutting in front of the bike and forcing it to stop. Karen watched them being arrested as she struggled to her feet, holding a bruised elbow.

'Are you all right, love?' asked the PC.

'I'm not really hurt. Just embarrassed. And look at this coat.'

'Look at it? I can smell it from here. I hope you're not planning to wear it in the van,' he chuckled.

Mortified, Karen cadged a large plastic bin bag from the

postmistress and put the fouled coat in it, tying the neck tightly to contain the stench. She trudged back to her car and headed for the station, not looking forward to the reception awaiting her.

———

Somebody whistled the song *Handbags and Gladrags* when Karen came into the office. Karen scowled and Emma glared at him. She called the team to order.

'Right, you lot. Please don't take the piss out of Karen. She was courageous in taking on this job and it's not her fault that she fell over. We've got the little bastards, so it's a result. Thanks, Karen. Well done. Write up your notes, then take the rest of the afternoon off. And change your clothes. You look a bit like one of Monty Python's Hell's Grannies.'

This time, all the team laughed, including Karen.

Chapter Nineteen

BACK IN HER NORMAL CLOTHES, Karen walked towards her car feeling low. Yes, they'd got a result but she'd let the little sod go instead of cuffing him, and had looked a right tit when she fell in the shit. She decided she would do some shopping on the way home and treat herself to a film and a takeaway this evening. Perhaps a bottle of wine, too. She really didn't feel like cooking and the stink from the bag in the back seat had put her off handling food. She would put it in the dustbin as soon as she got home. As she drove to the supermarket, she didn't notice the small silver hatchback that followed her and parked a few yards away from her own car. Nor did she take any notice of the person who watched her progress through the store.

Karen had almost finished packing her shopping into reusable bags when someone knocked against her arm, dislodging a box of eggs, which landed on the supermarket floor with a sticky crunch.

'Oh, I'm so terribly sorry,' said a smartly dressed, blonde woman. 'Do let me pay for those. Better still, have a box of mine.'

Karen's first reaction was to shout at her. Yet another addition to the catalogue of shit that had made up her day. But the woman's disarming smile and offer of reparation mollified her somewhat.

'Look,' continued the woman, 'let me buy you a coffee while I fish the eggs out of my bag. I think it'll be worth your while.'

Intrigued by the woman's last remark, and having nothing better to do, Karen agreed, and ten minutes later the two women were ensconced in the corner of the supermarket café with coffee and cakes in front of them.

'Now, Karen,' began the woman.

'How did you know my name?'

The hairs on the back of Karen's neck stood up and she began to realise that this was not a chance encounter.

'I know a lot about you. You're a detective constable based in Mexton. You're unmarried but your partner, who you lived with for several years, recently cleared off, leaving you with some major debts that you're having difficulty paying off. Your mother died recently but your father is in a care home and you need to contribute to the fees. Which you can't.'

Karen felt sick and the cake no longer had any attraction for her.

'Who the fuck are you and what do you want?'

'Never mind who I am. I want to help you. And, in return, you can help me.'

'I am not a bent copper. Do you hear?' She kept her voice low to prevent other shoppers hearing but it was charged with vitriol. 'I'll sort myself out and you can piss off. And I'll be reporting this conversation to my boss.'

'I wouldn't do that if I were you.'

'Why the fuck not?'

Her companion sighed. 'I had hoped it wouldn't come to this.'

She put a phone, in a clear plastic bag, on the table between them.

'It's best not to look at this in public. It's a sweet little film taken in a former senior policeman's office. It shows you leaning over his desk with your knickers round your ankles, while he takes you from behind. I hope you were enjoying yourself, by the way.'

It took all of Karen's self-control to stop herself from either vomiting or smashing the woman in the face.

'It's not illegal to have sex with a consenting adult. I know I could get into trouble for doing it at work but I was coerced.'

'True. But it wouldn't do your reputation as a police officer any good to have this all over the internet, would it? Also, that was my little mole, until he was found out. There's such a thing as guilt by association. I can arrange it so you seem to have been complicit in his corruption. Now he's dead I need another insider. And you've got the job.'

Karen felt her career crumbling around her and her self-respect heading straight down the toilet. She had vowed she would always do the job honestly and never do anything corrupt. But now she had no option. She sat quietly for a few moments then, with tears streaming down her face, replied, 'What do you want from me?'

'That's better. I knew you'd see sense. For the moment, all I want you to do is keep your eyes and ears open. I'll phone you now and then for a chat. I will have some business in Mexton soon and you may have to do a little more for me. Nothing that will put you at risk. I will give you something each month to help with your expenses, more if you have to do anything extra. So, what are you going to do?'

Karen wiped her eyes on a tissue and sniffed.

'I don't have much choice, do I? But I won't do anything to put fellow officers in danger. Is that clear?' She attempted a morsel of defiance, dreading the woman's response.

'It shouldn't come to that. I have no wish to harm individual police officers. But let me make one thing clear in return. If you attempt to discuss this with anyone, your career will be over, you will be ruined financially and you will go to prison.'

Karen nodded, unable to speak, as the woman eased the phone out of the plastic bag without touching it.

'You can keep the phone and enjoy the film at leisure. Oh, in case you are wondering, it's untraceable and I've left no fingerprints or DNA on it. I'll use it to contact you, so keep it charged and check your messages. One last thing. Here's a box of eggs. Your first payment is inside. Don't get anything scrambled.'

Karen watched the woman stride confidently out of the café, her elegant clothes out of place in a Mexton supermarket. She had no idea who the woman was, although she wondered whether the letter M on her expensive monogrammed scarf could be significant. She couldn't move for ten minutes, gazing at the box of eggs as if it was a bottle of Novichok. She wondered what was inside. Forty pieces of silver?

Gathering up her shopping and stuffing the eggs and the phone into her tote bag, she stumbled out to her car, threw her purchases in the boot and sat sobbing in the driver's seat until a young woman with streaked hair and a nose ring tapped on her window and asked if she was all right. She wound it down.

'Yes. Fine thanks. Just had some bad news. Boyfriend trouble.'

'Awww. I'm sorry. Bastards aren't they?'

Karen managed a weak smile.

'You can say that again. Thanks for asking.'

She wound up the window and drove off, fearing the future and dreading seeing herself in the mirror every morning. Perhaps it wouldn't be too bad, she tried to reassure herself. No-one would get hurt, she promised herself. But deep down she knew that, once a copper went over to the dark side, there would be no coming back.

Chapter Twenty

Mexton, Summer 2019

It wasn't long before Maxwell Arden's hand was on Jeannie's thigh. She had called into the party offices, as arranged, and spent a couple of hours updating software, optimising the performance of the computers and generally giving everything a digital spring clean. She had taken the opportunity to root about in Arden's emails and internet searches, and discovered that the right-wing views he espoused in public were diluted versions of his real beliefs. He seemed to be in touch with some seriously unpleasant people and these were just contacts on the party systems. She dreaded to think what might be on his personal laptop, so she sent him a 'test' email from the office containing a Trojan, supplied by the Argus collective, which she would use to gain access to his files in her own time.

Arden poured her a glass of whisky and sat next to her while she explained the work she had done. She took a swig of the drink to try to offset the smell of his sweat. She saw him leering at her legs, and the inevitable grope came a few seconds later. She felt him tremble as his pudgy fingers brushed the top of her stocking, and the bulge in his trousers was obvious. So bloody predictable, she thought. She had guessed that a short skirt and suspenders would arouse him and he went for her like a weasel on a field mouse. But she would keep him waiting.

'Mr Arden! Please!' she said, firmly removing his hand from her leg.

'Do call me Max, my dear,' he replied, looking like a baby whose rusk has been suddenly whipped away. 'You're a lovely girl and I'd like to get to know you better. You've been such a help here. At least let me buy you dinner.'

'Well, all right. I'm free tomorrow night if you like.'

'Excellent. I'll book a table. Can you meet me here at seven?'

Jeannie smiled sweetly, picked up her things and kissed him briefly on the cheek before leaving. 'I'll give it ten seconds before he's in the loo tossing off,' she chuckled to herself. 'Phase one complete, and now I need a shower.'

Over dinner, at an expensive restaurant that provided booths for discreet diners, Arden tried to get Jeannie drunk. She pretended to be more intoxicated than she actually was, although in other circumstances she would have been grateful for strong drink when in his presence. He turned on charm so oily that Shell could bottle it, and she responded as he had clearly hoped. It wasn't difficult to convince him that she found him attractive, despite his drooping jowls, thinning greasy hair and the prolific tufts of hair issuing from his nostrils. His high opinion of his sex appeal, which flew in the face of the evidence, needed little reinforcement.

'One of the things I like about you, Max,' she said, slurring slightly, 'is the strength of your beliefs. It's time something was done to take this country back from foreigners and immigrants. Another ten years and we'll all be forced to go to mosques. We must get free of the Eurocats...crats completely and be a great nation again.'

'I'm glad you think so, my dear. Very glad. I'm doing my best but much more could be done.'

'What do you mean?'

'There are many Englishmen out there who would fight for their country at home, to win it back. They just need resources and the right kind of prompting. Enoch talked about rivers of blood in 1968, but if we get our way it won't be English blood that flows.' He belched and looked worried. 'Oh dear. I think I've said too much. You won't mention this to anyone, will you?'

'Of course not, but I have an idea. Perhaps we could talk about it in the morning? Now if you'll 'scuse me I need the Ladies.'

Arden leered at Jeannie's behind as she swayed on her journey to the toilets. It looked like he was going to get lucky. Booking that hotel room had been a sensible move. His wife wouldn't miss him, as she was playing in a Scrabble tournament in Eastbourne and staying overnight. Of course, Shona was a little older than his preferred bedmates but she was certainly attractive and looked quite young. Anyway, he could always use his imagination.

After a night of clumsy fumblings, which Jeannie tuned out of with thoughts of revenge, she considered that Arden was ready to hear her plan. Encrypted conversations with Miles and other members of the Argus collective had given her the tools she needed. She had run over her pitch a dozen times in her head and figured he would be unable to resist. As they started on their room service breakfasts, coffee and croissants for her and full English for him, she began.

'Max, you know what we were talking about last night?'

'What in particular?' he leered.

'Your cause. To take England back.'

'Oh. Yes. You said you could help.'

'Well, I'm pretty good with computers. There are things I could do to, shall we say, divert money to places where it would be better used.'

Arden licked his lips and dragged his eyes away from her breasts.

'You know my brother's Home Secretary, don't you?'

'Yes, I do. I admire his stance on law and order. But this isn't really stealing and it's all in a good cause.'

'It's certainly tempting. But not as tempting as you, my dear.' He undid the belt of her bathrobe and pulled her towards the bed.

'Here we go again,' thought Jeannie, blanking out his attentions and focusing on memories of her sister. 'The things we do for love.'

Chapter Twenty-One

Day 19, Monday–Day 23, Friday

WHEN LORNA RETURNED to Maybrick and Cream the following Monday, she was embarrassed to find someone had taped a sheet of paper to her computer bearing the message 'Welcome back Jessica Jones'.

'I didn't do anything brave,' she protested to Jeannie. 'I just came back to look for my contact lenses and disturbed a burglar. If the police hadn't turned up, I'd probably have died.'

'Nevertheless, you've picked up a reputation as a crime fighter. I didn't know you wore contacts, though.'

'I don't need them all the time but I wear them at night when I'm going out.'

Anxious to change the subject, Lorna commented that the warehouse staff were thin on the ground and orders seemed to be backing up.

'Yes. One of them's off sick and we'll need to get a temp in if the lazy sod doesn't turn up soon. I think he's just having a duvet day, or was out on the piss last night and still recovering.'

The idea of Lorde snuggled under a duvet nursing a hangover, or sore bollocks, seemed strangely comical to Lorna. She wondered whether she had caused him significant damage when she fought back, and the thought made her secretly pleased.

Throughout the week, Lorna maintained a watch on the office staff, looking for any suspicious behaviour. None was apparent and she had no need to activate the emergency speed dial. She did manage to see a series of spreadsheets on Jeannie's computer when she was at lunch, but couldn't legally copy or photograph them. Otherwise, her undercover placement was unproductive.

On Friday afternoon, Lorna was invited to go for a drink with the office staff after work and they all drifted off to the pub down the road. A couple of the loaders joined them. She hoped that she could pick up something from gossip between the staff, their tongues loosened by alcohol, but most of the conversation revolved around sport and soaps. The others were downing pints or large glasses of wine but Lorna slowly sipped a couple of small glasses of red, explaining that she had a long drive ahead and didn't want to go over the drink-driving limit.

'We're all driving,' said Dave Bright, 'but the Old Bill never stops us.'

Mark Dickens, his manner now much more pleasant than when he had cat-called Lorna, nodded his agreement. Lorna made a mental note to have a word with the traffic division.

The group left the pub around seven and, as she stepped out the door, Lorna began to feel woozy. Her head started to spin and her legs felt like rubber. Surely, two small wines wouldn't have that effect, even on an empty stomach?

'Are you OK? You look weird.'

A concerned-sounding Mark took her arm and steered her into the back seat of a car.

'Sit down for a bit – that Shiraz must have been strong.'

Dimly it dawned on Lorna that this was not her car. As the door slammed, child locks set so she couldn't get out, she realised she'd been drugged.

———

Lorna's mind shuttled between delirium and unconsciousness. She couldn't tell how long the car was moving and had no idea where it went. When it stopped, she was hauled from the back seat and half-dragged into an unfamiliar building, where she was shoved roughly onto a wooden chair. Someone yanked her phone and wallet out of her pockets and secured her wrists in front of her with plastic cable ties. She fell asleep.

Sometime later – she had no idea how long – she woke up, still disorientated, with a thundering headache and a desert-dry mouth. Dickens and Lorde stood in front of her, the latter holding a pistol.

'Just what are you up to, bitch?' demanded Dickens. 'We asked Jeannie to look up your references and she said they're fakes. Well done, but fakes. So, who are you and what are you doing? You've been sneaking around and eavesdropping on conversations. And you pretended Jeannie gave you the keys the other night, which she didn't. Are you a cop? Are you wearing a wire?'

Dickens ripped open Lorna's blouse to check and searched her roughly, clearly enjoying rummaging beneath her clothes, but found nothing.

'You've got it wrong,' sobbed Lorna, playing dumb and hoping to bluff it out. 'I needed a job desperately and a friend with IT skills helped me with the references. I'm sorry. I'm not up to anything.'

The two captors moved to the back of the room and argued about what to do with Lorna.

'She's filth, or MI5,' said Lorde. 'We can't let her go. She's seen us and I warned her once.'

'Well, I'm not up for another murder. Your thick mate went too far killing Bennett and look at the attention that attracted.'

'I should have dealt with her at the warehouse. I would've if Anton hadn't phoned the boss from the nick to say they were on the way.'

Lorna couldn't hear all that was being said, and dropped in and out of sleep, but the mention of MI5 piqued her curiosity. Why would MI5 be interested in a bunch of drug dealers? And who was Anton? Clearly someone at the station, but she knew of no officers of that name. Of more concern was what was going to happen to her. And that was still under discussion.

'All right, Mark. We'll leave her here until we've talked to the boss. But if he says she goes, she goes, whether you like it or not. And we've got to find out what she knows.'

Dickens murmured his assent.

Lorde hauled Lorna from the chair and dragged her across a concrete floor to a large metal cupboard. Before he locked her in he hit her in the face, splitting her lip and drawing blood.

'We'll leave you here to have a little think,' he sneered. 'And when I get back in the morning, we're going to have a chat about who you are. You, me and my pit bull.'

Chapter Twenty-Two

MEL COTTON STEPPED out of the shower, wrapped herself in a towel and drifted into the lounge in search of her slippers. Her heart nearly stopped, and the towel almost fell to the floor, when she saw a thin, bespectacled young man in a hoodie and jeans, sitting on the sofa and nursing a laptop.

'Who the fuck are you and what are you doing in my flat?' she yelled.

The young man cringed. 'Don't hurt me, please. Tom said I could stay. I'm Robbie. Robbie Woods.'

At that point, the door opened and Tom Ferris stepped into the flat, carrying two bags from which the smell of curry emanated.

'Grub's up, love. Oh. This is Robbie. I've let him stay for a bit.'

'A word, please, Tom,' said Mel, stalking into the kitchen, leaving a confused Robbie sitting in the lounge.

'Just what the hell's going on? You've no business inviting a stranger in without asking me. We do share this place, you know.'

'Yes, I'm sorry Mel. It was an emergency. I tried to call you earlier but your phone was off. Then I forgot.'

'Forgot? How could you forget to tell me? I could have wandered in stark naked. And why didn't you leave a message?'

'Oh. I suppose I should have thought of that. Sorry.'

Mel usually found Tom's slight other-wordliness charming, but it also exasperated her on occasions.

'So, what's the story, then? Why do we have to put up an obvious geek?'

Tom closed the door to the kitchen and put the food in the oven to keep warm. He kept his voice low.

'Robbie's in trouble and needs somewhere to stay until we can find him safe accommodation. I thought here was the best place.'

'What's he done? Hacked into MI5? Nicked a couple of million from the Russian mafia?'

'Not exactly. He's a brilliant white hat hacker. He has a loathing of child abusers. He hasn't said why but I suspect it's something to do with his past. Anyway, he set up a phoney website to attract paedophiles and planted a virus in it. Any computer logging into it automatically sent an email to CEOP giving the user's name and IP address, with the subject heading 'I am a paedophile. Please come and arrest me'.

'CEOP? Remind me. There's too many acronyms.'

'Child Exploitation and Online Protection Centre.'

'Yes, of course. I knew that.'

'Anyway, two things happened. Firstly, the CEOP system nearly crashed and they were forced to divert these incoming emails to a separate account. It'll take months to process them and contact the appropriate local forces. Secondly, some of the users affected got wind of what was happening and Robbie's been getting death threats and had windows smashed. We suspect someone in the Job, who's involved in this sort of stuff, realised what he was doing and tipped them off. He's terrified and turned to us for help.'

'OK. These are nasty people. But wasn't what he did unlawful?'

'He was very careful. He didn't put anything illegal on his website. Just a few clips of Shirley Temple and a sequence from the film *Little Miss Sunshine*. He called himself Maurice and that dreadful song by Maurice Chevalier played whenever someone tried to enter the 'secret room' on the site. Users got a 'Temporarily Out Of Service' message while their details were sent to CEOP.'

'What song? And who's Maurice Chevalier?'

'Old French singer who sang *"Thank heaven for little girls"*, back in the 1950s.'

Mel cringed.

'Technically, the virus was illegal, but we realised it wouldn't be in the public interest to prosecute him,' Tom continued. 'But I'd like him to stay here for a couple of days, if that's OK. Sorry I didn't try harder to tell you.'

Mel smiled, pulled him towards her and kissed him.

'It's all right, you soft-hearted idiot. But is he house trained? He's not like Plague in Larsson's books, is he?'

'I'm sure he washes and won't leave pizza boxes all over the floor. Thank you. Now let's eat that food before it all dries up.'

Robbie ate his food quickly and nervously, glancing around as if someone was about to steal it from him. When the plates were cleared and the three of them sat back, their second beers in front of them, Mel tried to engage their guest in conversation.

'Do you have any family in these parts, Robbie?'

'No. No family.'

This was clearly a topic he wanted to avoid.

'How did you get into computing?'

At this he brightened up and his face became animated.

'I just loved the logic of it all. I could write code when I was seven and set up my own websites for fun.' He looked around cautiously. 'And hacking just followed naturally, I suppose. I've never stolen data or money. It was just the challenge of getting through barriers and going somewhere secret that I loved.'

At this point, Mel reminded him that his audience consisted of two police officers and that hacking was a criminal offence.

'Yes, I know. But I'll deny everything and I've taken steps to cover my tracks.' He smiled smugly. 'I've never done any harm and several organisations have tightened their security settings at my, anonymous, suggestions.'

'Do you have a job?'

'I used to work for a company distributing sweets. I set up their database and a system to increase the efficiency of their distribution routes. I kept the system running and ensured customers got their deliveries on time. But they made me redundant and gave the job to someone else. They said I was a lefty and I also think they didn't like me because I'm gay. I can't prove it, of course. I now work for a supermarket, co-ordinating their logistics.'

'Not exactly stretching, I would have thought,' said Tom. 'Surely you could do better than that?'

'Well, I've no formal qualifications. And I can't really tell an employer that I'm an expert hacker, can I?'

'I suppose not,' Mel replied. 'By the way, what was the name of the sweets company?' she asked, a note of excitement in her voice.

'Maybrick and Cream. They're on the Mexton industrial estate. Why do you ask?'

'Oh, nothing really. They've come to our attention in a different context, that's all.'

She glanced at Tom, who nodded in return.

'Right. Sleeping arrangements,' said Tom. 'You can sleep on the sofa and we'll find you a pillow and sleeping bag. We're both off to work early so help yourself to coffee and toast once we've gone. If you hear any strange rustlings in the night, it's only Ernie.'

Robbie looked confused.

'He's a tortoise. He lives in that pen in the corner. Mel rescued him. A long story. And you can't smoke as it upsets him, and the parrots, who you've met already, as well as us. Are you wanting to go online?'

'Yes. I need to. I've things to do.'

'OK. Please use 5G rather than our wi-fi. We don't want anything dodgy tracked back to our IP address. If you have to go out, take the spare key from beside the fridge. Do let us know if you're going to be out for any length of time, just for your own safety.'

'Will do. And thanks so much. Anything I can do, please let me know.'

'I wonder if he can help us with the Bennett murder,' mused Mel, as they were getting ready for bed. 'He might have noticed something at Maybrick and Cream.'

'Possibly,' replied Tom. 'But he's a bit vulnerable. No harm in asking, I suppose.'

'How did he come to you, anyway? I thought cybercrime didn't normally deal with child protection.'

'We don't. But he turned up at the station and asked for a computer expert. Jack Vaughan was in the lobby at the time and mentioned my name. The receptionist put Robbie through to me and I arranged to meet him. He sounded interesting.'

'He is that. But a bit weird, too. Just make sure he doesn't bring his shit down on us. Or surprise me getting out of the shower again.'

Tom smiled. 'Well as he's gay he probably wouldn't have been interested. I, on the other hand...'

He reached for Mel's dressing gown and pulled it open.

'Shhhhh. He's only next door,' she murmured, moving towards him.

Chapter Twenty-Three

'The little shit's around here somewhere,' Warren whispered. 'You'd think he'd have protected his phone better. He didn't realise he was downloading a tracker app when I sent him that text.'

'How did you get his number?' an admiring colleague asked.

'Naming no names, but I've a friendly copper who hates these vermin as much as I do. He did some digging and bingo!'

'Nice one,' said a third man. 'So, what do we do? Just wander around until we find him?'

'I'll park over here, behind this VW, and we'll see what happens. If we see anyone walking, and the app says the phone's on the move, we've got the bastard.'

The three conspirators parked in the empty space, oblivious to the police pass fixed to the VW's windscreen, and settled down to wait.

Robbie shut the lid of his laptop, stretched his legs and decided to go for a walk. At one o'clock in the morning, he felt sure no-one else would be about and he'd be safe. Closing the door to the building quietly behind him, he had barely walked a dozen paces when a light shone in his eyes and a voice charged with hatred screamed at him.

'Got you. You filthy bastard.'

Two muscular men stood in front of him, filming him on phones.

'Www...what do you mean?'

'You're a fucking paedo. And we've found you. And you're gonna get what's coming to you.'

He tried to step aside but the men blocked him. One dialled a number on his phone and spoke urgently into it, his voice barely audible.

'There's no escape, you bastard.'

Robbie turned to run, only to find a third man in the way.

'Please. I'm not. It was a scam. I never did anything to anyone.'

'Oh yeah? That's not what your website says, Maurice.' The name was uttered with loathing. 'You like little girls, don't you? And you know what happens to perverts who interfere with little girls,' the man sneered.

Robbie crumpled to the floor sobbing.

'Why won't you believe me? I was trying to catch them. I set up a fake website with a virus. They'll all be arrested.'

'Bollocks. You've got a secret room with the nasty stuff in it, when it works. I'm not stupid.'

'But that's how I caught them. That's where the virus is.'

'He's right. Leave him alone. He loathes paedophiles, just like you do.'

A woman's voice cut through the night, firm and author-itative.

'And who the fuck are you? Another pervert?'

'Detective Constable Melanie Cotton, Mexton CID. And you are?' She held out her warrant card. 'I can vouch for this man. Now leave him alone.'

The three men looked sheepish and stepped away from Robbie, who remained on the pavement, hugging his knees with his back to a low wall.

'We're paedophile hunters, officer,' Warren said. 'We track them down and report them to the police, with evidence of what they do. We've caught seven in Mexton already and five are now inside.

'You realise that what you do is on the borders of legality, don't you? And someone could get seriously hurt,' said Tom, who had joined Mel on the pavement. 'We appreciate your desire to get these people off the streets but we wish you'd leave it to us.'

'But you don't have the resources, do you? So you need help.'

'But vigilantes make mistakes. As you did tonight,' said Mel. 'So unless you want us to arrest you, you'll delete the films you've taken of this man, while I watch you do it, and you'd better not have uploaded or streamed them. Also, you'll refrain from mentioning his name to anyone, anywhere. Understand?'

At this point a patrol car, blue lights flashing, pulled up, prompting the three hunters to comply. A camera flashed and Mel and Tom realised that pictures of the two detectives, in coats over their pyjamas, would be all over the station by morning.

'Now clear off, you three. Up you come, Robbie. It's a good job I'm a light sleeper.'

Mel guided Robbie back into the flat and poured him a brandy, which he gulped desperately.

'Probably best if you don't go out on your own for a bit?'

Robbie nodded.

'Thanks, you saved me from a nightmare. I thought they were going to kill me.'

Chapter Twenty-Four

Day 23, Friday Night–Day 24, Saturday

THE DOOR to the building slammed as Dickens and Lorde left, leaving Lorna alone and scared. She had no idea where she was but guessed, from the way sounds had echoed, that she was in a large, empty building. She wondered if she was in a garage, as she had smelt diesel. Pushing horrific images of torture by pit bull out of her mind, she concentrated on trying to escape. There was no light in the cupboard and she could hardly move. Her neck was bent painfully over and her head was jammed against a shelf. There was space in front and to the sides of her, so she estimated the cupboard was about a metre and a half wide and a bit more than half a metre deep. She could smell cleaning products, and a metal bucket clanged when she moved her leg, so she assumed that she was in a caretaker's store cupboard of some sort.

She explored her prison by touch, discovering that the doors were locked by metal bars that moved into sockets at the top and bottom of the cupboard when the handle was turned.

She tried to pull them out of their sockets with her fingers but they were solid and immobile.

She was hungry, thirsty and desperate for a toilet. She didn't know how long she had been in captivity but knew she had to get out before Dickens and Lorde returned. They would kill her, for sure. But how could she escape? She contemplated rocking the cupboard until it fell over, in the hope that the doors would burst open, but realised it could easily fall on its front so that the doors would be held shut by the floor.

Then she had a thought. She couldn't move the bars with her hands but what about the bucket? She groped downwards and found the handle, the plastic ties biting into her wrists. As she pulled it, the end of a mop hit her on the side of the head but she managed to get the bucket level with the door lock. Her first thought was to try to use the handle to bend the bars inwards but she couldn't get it behind them. So she resorted to brute force, lifting the bucket through the narrow gap between the door and her body and smashing the base downwards on the locking mechanism. Nothing happened. She repeated the action, putting as much force behind it as she could, but the bucket bounced off the door and hit her in the stomach, winding her. Fear of a bullet in the head spurred her on, so she continued banging and bashing, her arms aching and her stomach throbbing from repeated impacts.

The combination of intense weariness and the after effects of the drug was taking its toll, and she was on the verge of giving up when, with a loud crash, the lock broke and the doors flew open. Disorientated and stiff, she clambered out and looked around her, barely able to stand up. So where was she?

A thin strip of light was visible low down on one side of the premises. Lorna guessed that it could be at the bottom of a door and slowly picked her way towards it. Her foot met air and she realised she was at the top of a ramp that led downwards towards the light. When she reached the bottom, she saw that the brightness was where a roller shutter met the ground. There was probably a light switch somewhere nearby, she reasoned, and searched for it on either side of the shutter. When she found it and switched it on, the brightness dazzled her for a few seconds, but she was soon able to identify the building as a warehouse with a loading bay.

Two vans, apparently undergoing repairs, were raised up on blocks towards the back of the building, while tyres, tools and motor parts were ranged against the walls. An electric fork lift truck was parked at the top of the ramp, next to a pile of old pallets. A handy tool box provided a utility knife, which Lorna used to cut the cable ties binding her hands. The outside door, next to the shutter, proved to be locked, and a quick survey of the building revealed no other way out. Although the shutter was padlocked to the floor, the strip of light she had seen beneath it gave her an idea.

Dragging herself back up the ramp, she climbed aboard the fork lift and tried to start it. No luck, no key. Resorting to the tool box again, she picked up a hammer, a handful of chisels and screwdrivers, and some jump leads. If the local kids could hot wire cars, she thought, surely she could do the same to a fork lift.

Ten minutes bashing, twisting and unscrewing panels enabled her to find a way of bypassing the key with the jump leads, and the fork lift came to life. She steered it down the ramp, after spending a few seconds working out which controls did what, and slid the tips of the forks under the edge of the shutter. Crossing her fingers, hoping that the machine was powerful enough and had sufficient charge in the battery, she raised the forks. At first nothing happened and the motor began to whine angrily. A burning smell filled the air. Eventually, with a crash and a tearing sound, the padlock holding the shutter closed ripped away from the floor and the shutter rose.

Dawn light flooded in and Lorna realised that she was on an industrial estate, somewhere on the outskirts of town. She was exhausted and aching, and the prospect of stumbling around looking for a friendly face or a phone did not appeal. So she used the fork lift to raise the shutter to its full extent and jammed her foot on the accelerator, hoping that the machine would clear the shutter before it came crashing down. The truck lurched forwards, caught against the falling shutter, then pulled clear. Lorna set off down the road, keeping the truck at a steady four miles per hour, searching for the way back into town. Looking back, she could just make out a faded signboard on the warehouse bearing the name Carter's Commercial Vehicle Hire.

Ten minutes later, with the battery beginning to fade and the jump leads smelling of burning plastic from the high current flowing through them, Lorna was approaching the exit to the industrial estate. A police traffic patrol car cut in front of her and whooped its siren, signalling her to stop.

'Good morning, madam,' said a perplexed PC, clearly unsure how to deal with a scruffy and bruised woman who had apparently taken and driven away a bright yellow fork lift truck.

'Are you insured to drive that vehicle and do you have the owner's permission? And you do realise it must be properly registered and taxed if used on public roads?'

The tensions and fear from the last few hours came to a head and Lorna started to smile at the constable. Then she giggled and was soon convulsed with laughter, interspersed with sobs.

'It's OK, officer,' she gulped. 'I'm CID. I've just escaped from a warehouse where suspected drug dealers were keeping me captive. I don't have my warrant card as I was working under cover.'

'Yes of course, madam. I presume you're working for Inspector Morse, or is it Superintendent Hastings? Why don't you come and sit in this nice warm car and we'll sort everything out.'

The PC looked as though he'd come across another of the mental health cases that, increasingly, the police have to deal with. Eventually, Lorna managed to convince him to contact Alex, who confirmed her identity and requested that she be given a lift to the police station.

'You look a bloody mess,' Alex said, his tone full of concern. 'What's happened to you? And what's this about you twocking a fork lift truck? You'll never live that down.'

After giving a brief account of recent events, Lorna refused to go to A&E for a check-up. She insisted on going home to change her clothes and sleep for a couple of hours, promising Alex a full debrief in the afternoon. She argued that she wasn't committing any driving offences, as the industrial estate was private land, and hot-wiring the truck was reasonable in the circumstances. Alex contacted Emma, who sent a couple of uniforms to secure the premises, and put in a request for SOCOs to gather evidence.

Chapter Twenty-Five

LORNA MADE her way to Emma's office at four o'clock, ignoring the cries of 'Hey, it's Lewis Hamilton' and 'Call that a getaway car?' that followed her as she passed through the incident room. Clearly her cover with the team had been blown and word had spread. She didn't mind the mickey-taking. The last thing she wanted was gushing sympathy or, worse, patronising comments from the more chauvinist males.

'Afternoon, ma'am,' she began. 'I gather you've heard about what happened.'

'Yes, I have – you're very resourceful, aren't you? Well done.'

'Thank you. But obviously I can't go back there. I thought it would be easiest if I reported to you directly. I've already spoken to my handler.'

'Much appreciated. Grab a drink from the coffee maker by the sink. It's quite good. Then tell me what you've found.'

Lorna provided Emma with as many details as she could, helped by notes she'd made before she went to bed. She identified Dickens and Lorde as her captors and recounted as much as she could remember from their overheard conversation.

'I don't understand why they should be worried about MI5,' she said, 'and they clearly have someone on the inside called Anton.'

'There are no officers at this nick called Anton,' Emma replied. 'We'll check out the civilian staff, discreetly, and find out if anyone could have known about the rescue party. Thanks for all your help. It has been useful and I'm really sorry it all went pear-shaped.'

'Don't worry, ma'am. It's not the worst situation I've been in.'

Emma stood up and shook Lorna's hand. 'Good luck for the future,' she said.

Lorna smiled and left Emma's office. The DI returned to the incident room where the rest of the team was gathered.

'Did the SOCOs find anything in the warehouse, guv?' Mel asked.

'No, Mel. They're still working there but, so far, everything seems legit. Apparently, it was going to be used as a temporary store for tinned goods in the run-up to Brexit but was changed into a depot for a vehicle hire business. It's a miracle there was any charge left in the forklift. The drug dogs are going in later today, when they've finished checking out a suspicious lorry.'

'Shall I ask one of the financial guys to look into ownership and see if there are any links with Maybrick and Cream? Perhaps Tom could help out if he's not too busy.' The idea of working with her partner again obviously appealed to Mel.

'Good idea. But I'm sure DC Ferris has enough on his plate in cybercrime,' Emma replied. 'Can you get vehicle ownership and leasing looked at, as well? Check out the fork lift, too. I presume Lorde and Dickens have gone to ground?'

'Yes, guv.' Mel looked slightly disappointed. 'No sign of them. Their registered vehicles are parked outside their home addresses, so they must be using others under false names. We've alerted ports and airports and circulated their photos. We executed search warrants at both their premises.'

'Did the search teams find anything?'

Jack looked up from his laptop and replied, 'Nothing much. Some unpleasant literature and a hungry dog at Lorde's place. A dog handler took it away and put it in our kennels before the team went in. Also, a couple of empty petrol cans, but forensics said that there's no way they can prove it was the same stuff that was used to torch the building Mel and Trevor were in. Apparently, petrol doesn't come in distinctive batches any more. Dickens' place was clean, so if there is anything incriminating around, it's somewhere else. One thing, guv. Before we pull them in, assuming we can find them, don't we need to know who the boss is?'

'Ideally. But we've certainly got them for kidnapping, false imprisonment and assaulting an emergency worker, and I'm buggered if they'll get away with that. Changing the subject slightly, Lorna said that Lorde mentioned someone called Anton, based at this station. He's not a police officer but perhaps he's a civilian. We need to identify him. Don't you have a friend in HR, Mel?'

'Yes, boss. Julie Hathaway. I'll give her a ring.'

'Thanks. Let me know what you find. When we get him, we could try feeding him some false info to flush out the others, but I don't see that working at the moment. Lorde and Dickens are likely to stay well under the radar for the time being.'

'There's something else, guv,' continued Mel. 'Tom's met up with a computer geek, on a different case, who used to work at Maybrick and Cream. He says he developed their routing system but was made redundant for being, I quote, "lefty and gay". Might be worth talking to him. He's currently staying with us.'

'Sounds a charming place to work,' commented Martin. 'Prejudiced workmates and the chance of getting drugged in the pub or killed. Makes this job look pretty safe, doesn't it?'

Martin's sarcasm prompted grins from his colleagues, who knew he'd been badly injured on a previous case.

'Yes, please talk to him Mel,' responded Emma. 'We've had one bit of good news. An off-duty PC spotted a known face acting suspiciously late last night. He stopped him and the lad did a runner, leaving a bag of stolen goods behind. He'd just burgled a flat and we think he's responsible for most of the other burglaries this month. Can you send someone round to pick him up, Jack? I'll arrange a Section 18 authority and give you the details. That's it for the moment, I think. Thanks, everyone. Carry on.'

'So, who's your lead, Mel?' Trevor asked as they stood by the coffee maker.

'A young lad called Robbie Woods. He's the computer geek who Tom's working with. I can't say what on.'

'Have you looked him up on the PNC?'

'Not yet – can you do that? Just to check?'

'Sure.'

Five minutes later Trevor dropped a printout on Mel's desk.

'Looks like he's been a busy boy.'

Mel looked at the sheet and burst out laughing. She called Jack over.

'Look at this. When Robbie was fifteen, he managed to hack the Number 10 press office and alter an electronic press release about how the government was trying its best to reduce the budget deficit, boosting the economy and working hard to alleviate poverty. He changed a few of the words and no-one noticed. "Trying" became "lying", "boosting" was changed to "wrecking" and "working" became "spanking". No-one noticed until it hit the inboxes of all the news outlets.'

Even Jack smiled at this.

'So, what happened?'

'Looks like Number 10 didn't want it to be known that a kid had hacked them, so they told us not to prosecute. He was given a stern warning, though, and he promised not to hack the government again.'

'Better be careful with him. Don't let him anywhere near our systems,' Jack warned.

'I won't. It's strictly Maybrick and Cream we want to talk to him about. I'll have a chat with him tonight.

'Hmm. Well keep me up to date.'

'Yes, Jack.'

Mel passed on Emma's request for a check on vehicles to Trevor and left the station to pick up a few odds and ends from the nearby convenience store. Still worrying about the mysterious Anton, she was brought up short when she saw the badge worn by the guard in the gatehouse. Under the logo 'Mexton Security Services' was the name Anton Kominski.

'Excuse me – Anton is it?' she addressed the man. 'Could you do me a great favour? My phone is completely out of charge and I need to make a quick call to the garage. They're mending my car but close in five minutes. Do you have one I could borrow? It will only be a short call, I promise.'

She put on her most winsome smile and hoped he would respond.

'Well OK. We're not supposed to have our own phones at work but I won't tell if you won't.' He winked.

'That's brilliant. Thank you so much.'

Mel made a call to her own mobile, so she could get Anton's phone number, and handed the device back to him with a grateful smile.

'I think I've identified Anton,' she told Emma, when she returned to the office. 'He works for the security contractor on the gatehouse. He would be aware of a raid leaving the station and could have overheard where it was going.'

'So how do we prove he alerted the gang?'

'I've got his phone number so, unless he used a different one, we can find out if he made a call around the time the rescue party was leaving. And we may find out who he phoned as well. Lorde mentioned "the boss" so we could get a lead on him.'

'Well done. I'll sort out the paperwork and you can chase up his phone company on Monday. If they come up with anything useful, we may have grounds for arrest. And I'm really looking forward to nicking the little sod.'

Chapter Twenty-Six

Day 25, Sunday

'So WHAT CAN you tell us about Maybrick and Cream, Robbie?' Mel poured tea for them both and took out her notebook, settling into the sofa at the flat, keen to put Robbie at his ease. 'This is purely informal, by the way. We might need an official statement later but this is just a chat.'

Robbie nodded, swept his floppy brown hair from in front of his eyes and relaxed.

'Well, they seemed a decent firm to work for, at least at first. I'd done part of an IT degree but couldn't afford to stay at Uni, so I dropped out and had to look for a job. They advertised for someone to overhaul their systems and I convinced them I was a whizz at databases. Which was more or less true. They took me on and I developed the logistics software to maximise the efficiency of their van routes. Then they made me redundant. I was only there for three months. For some reason the office manager took against me.'

'Any idea why?'

'There was nothing wrong with my work, I know. He once told me off for wearing a Jeremy Corbyn T-shirt to work but, apart from a few anti-gay remarks from the warehouse guys, there was no trouble. Jeannie, the IT woman, said I was no longer needed, but I know I could still have been useful. That's why I thought getting rid of me was because of who I am.'

Mel murmured sympathetically.

'Anyway, they brought this Bennett bloke in to run things. I heard later that he'd taken the credit for my work and there was no mention of me.'

'You must have been pretty angry. So, what did you do then?'

'I was. But I couldn't claim unfair dismissal. It was a short-term contract and I'd finished the project I was hired for. Maybrick and Cream gave me a decent reference, at least, and I ended up doing this logistics job, which is OK. It's permanent and pays the rent – when I have somewhere safe to live, that is.'

'You know Duncan Bennett's dead? Murdered.'

'Shit. Really? You don't think I had anything to do with it? I never met the guy.'

'No. No. Don't worry. We have a suspect.'

'Why was he killed?'

Mel thought for a moment.

'I can't really discuss it but it might have been something to do with his work. You didn't see anything unusual about vehicle mileages, or anything else, I suppose?'

'No. Not really. I just designed the system. There were a few teething problems but I sorted them out to Jeannie's satisfaction. If there were any discrepancies, such as people using the vans for private purposes, it was someone else's job to follow it up. How important is this?'

'It could be very important. Why?'

'Speaking hypothetically, of course. If an employee of a company had designed a system and felt they were being let go unfairly, it's possible that they might leave a backdoor into the system. Just in case.'

'I'm not sure I want to hear this.' Mel looked worried. 'That sounds illegal.'

'Well, it could happen. It would mean that the employee could get access to the system remotely and perhaps get up to mischief.'

'I am sure I shouldn't be hearing this. But go on.'

'All this is quite hypothetical, of course.'

'Of course. And speaking hypothetically, too, if a police officer had proof that information had been obtained from someone's system illegally, she would have to report it and the person responsible. And, of course, that information would not be admissible as evidence in court.'

'I understand that. But we are just talking hypothetically, aren't we?'

'Yes, we are,' confirmed Mel, gathering up the empty mugs.

'Well, if that's all you need to know, could you tell me whether there's an internet café anywhere nearby? I'm having a few problems with my 5G.'

'Yes, there is. Turn left outside the flat then right at the traffic lights. It's in a row of shops about five minutes' walk away.'

'OK. Thanks. I think I'll take a walk later on.'

'Well, be careful, won't you?'

'You can count on it.'

Robbie's demeanour had changed. His nervousness and diffidence seemed to have been replaced by confidence and purpose. Mel worried that he was about to do something illegal.

But if it helped catch Duncan's murderer, would that be such a bad thing?'

Chapter Twenty-Seven

Day 26, Monday

'I'VE GOT something for you, boss.' Amira knocked on Emma's office door while she was still taking her coat off.

'Something useful, I hope. I haven't had my coffee yet and I'm not ready for bad news.'

'Look at this!'

The IT technician waved a blown-up photograph at the DI, who peered at it hopefully.

'Where's this from?'

'We managed to enhance the photos Duncan took the night he was killed. This one, the one with the flash, shows a tattoo on this guy's neck. St George's flag. Is that helpful or what?'

'It is, lass, it is. That tattoo is Derek Farren's. This shows there's a link between the firm's employees and the far-right nutters. Well done, Amira. Well done.'

Emma reflected on the new evidence. Strictly speaking, they had edged into SO15's territory. She should pass the information on to DI Morton and leave it alone. But she had a murder to investigate and this could be useful. She decided to sit on it for the moment and made a note to discuss it with DCI Gale in a day or so. In the meantime, she would see what her team could do with it. After all, the counter-terrorist guys were probably watching Farren anyway, so he couldn't do a runner without being noticed. She made herself a coffee and joined her team in the incident room.

'Morning all,' she greeted them, raising her voice to be heard over the heating system, which was emitting a series of random rattles and clanks along with a trickle of heat.

'We've had a minor breakthrough. Amira blew up a photo of Duncan's and it identifies Derek Farren as one of the people either loading or unloading the vans. He's not on the firm's list of employees, so he's clearly there illicitly. From what Lorna heard while she was tied up, Lorde was also present, so there's just one more individual we need to identify.'

'But we can't touch Farren, can we?' Jack said.

'Not directly, no. We don't need to piss off SO15 and Five, at least not yet. I'm not sure how far this takes us though. Anyone got anything else?'

Trevor consulted his notepad.

'Carter's Commercial Vehicle Hire, boss. I've got the directors' names. The company secretary is an accountant based in Mexton, a George Meredith. Another is Maxwell Arden, the local MP, and the third is Gordon Lewis, a local councillor.'

'That's interesting. What do we know about this MP?'

'He's in the local paper a lot and I've Googled him. He seems very right-wing. He's spoken out against immigration, asylum seekers, gay marriage, trans rights and environmental laws. He was elected in 2017 and he's the Home Secretary's brother. Not exactly a favourite with the *Guardian*.'

A couple of detectives chuckled.

'Might be worth having a chat with him,' Emma said. 'See what he knows about the firm's activities. It'd better be me, given his status. Is he prejudiced against Yorkshirewomen, as well as everyone else, do you think?

A ripple of laughter flowed round the room.

'Addy, can you find out when Arden is next in Mexton, please? Does he run a regular surgery or show his face in the local party office?'

'Yes, guv.'

'Another thing,' Emma continued. 'The bugger who alerted Lorde is one Anton Kominski. He works for the private security company that staffs the gate. God knows how they screen their employees. Mel spotted him and got his phone number. According to his provider, he made a call just after the rescue party left. The receiving phone was a burner, now out of service, but Mel's requested triangulation data for the call in question. At least we'll know where the phone was when it received the call.'

'But didn't Anton's call give Lorna a chance to escape?' asked Jack.

'Mebbe it did. But he's still a bastard. We'll keep an eye on Anton and apply for a warrant to monitor his calls. We've enough evidence to justify one. How did you get on with the vehicle searches, Trevor?'

'Well, that's interesting. Maybrick and Cream's vehicles are all leased from Carter's, who rent, rather than own, the premises where Lorna was held. The place doesn't seem to be staffed. According to their website they only take bookings online. The collection and return of vehicles is by arrangement. Could be some kind of cover for criminality or a money laundering scheme. They don't seem to handle many hirings.'

'Great. That's good work. Look a bit further into the directors of Carter's. Do a financial check as well. See if there's anything suspicious there. Talk to a financial investigator if necessary. Also, we need to work out why Lorde and Dickens were concerned about attracting the attention of MI5. I don't want to ask Five directly, as they'll probably tell us to back off. So why would a gang of drug distributors be of concern to the Security Services?'

'Perhaps it's not the drugs themselves. Maybe it's the people involved or what they do with the money. Given the stuff we found on Duncan's electronics, could they be funding terrorism with it?'

'That's a thought. A bit of a leap, though. We need a forensic accountant to go over both firms' books, but we can hardly barge in there and demand to see them. Start with the accounts lodged at Companies House and see if that leads anywhere.'

Trevor perked up. 'OK, guv, I'll get on to it. I enjoy this sort of thing.'

'Nerd,' called someone at the back. Trevor ignored him.

'Package for you Mel.'

Trevor dropped a brown A4 envelope on her desk, nearly spilling her coffee.

'Careful, you idiot – oh, thanks. Where'd it come from?'

'Left at the station during the night, addressed to you. There's no return address on the back.'

Mel had her suspicions about the sender and these were reinforced when she removed the contents.

'Who's been sending you love letters, then?' joked Jack, who had been watching from beside the coffee machine.

'It's anonymous. But look at these.'

She spread half a dozen sheets of paper over her desk and the two detectives studied them.

'It's from Maybrick and Cream. It looks like records of one of their delivery routes.'

'So?' Jack frowned. 'What's it telling you?'

'I'm not sure. But look, here, in the mileage column. Every one or two weeks, on a Wednesday, the route is about thirty miles longer but the same customers are served. Perhaps this was what Duncan was concerned about.'

'Right. So, if we assume they are collecting drugs from somewhere under cover of chocolate deliveries, we can work out where.'

'We can. I'll get some maps and a ruler and do some drawing.'

'OK. Go ahead. Where did these come from, by the way? Surely the firm didn't send them?'

'Well, it was dropped off at the station overnight and there's nothing inside to show who sent it.'

'So, it was from your tame hacker, was it? Has he never heard of the Computer Misuse Act?'

'You might think that,' Mel grinned, 'I couldn't possibly comment.'

With that Mel gathered up the sheets and went in search of maps, a spring in her step, leaving Jack looking pensive.

Two hours later, Mel presented her findings to Jack and Emma, both of whom refrained from pressing her on the source of her information.

'I've assumed that the illicit journey was made after the last regular stop, otherwise the timings for the customers' chocolate deliveries would be out,' she began. 'It could have been between a couple of later ones but let's go with this for the moment. The last delivery is at a mini-mart in this village here.'

The others looked as she pointed to a map.

'I've drawn a circle around this point, representing a fifteen mile distance, but in practice, the rendezvous will be nearer to the village, as the roads aren't straight. That gives us a maximum area of about six hundred and eighty square miles to search in.'

Jack whistled.

'But you're going to tell us you've whittled that down, aren't you?'

Mel grinned.

'Yes, I am. Most of the land is agricultural, with a couple of small villages and a river. But within the circle is a service station on the M3. Using Google Maps, I found out that it's 14.2 miles from the last delivery point. And what could be better for a handover than the lorry park in a motorway services? It would all look perfectly legitimate, chocolate being unloaded from a container into a marked van from a confectionery wholesaler. So, all we need to do is watch the lorry park, with help from local officers, and we've got them.'

'Excellent work, Mel. Well done,' smiled Emma, with Jack also nodding his approval. 'But we can't do this on our own. First, we need to talk to our drugs squad and also the local force – Hampshire, is it? And we should probably inform the NCA as well. I'll sort all that out. And if a raid is planned, I'll make sure you're there to represent us.'

'Thank you, boss.'

As Mel collected her papers, Emma laid a hand on her arm.

'I don't know where your information came from and Jack tells me it was sent anonymously. But unless we have a source, and it was obtained legitimately, we can't use it in court.'

'I know, guv. I have no evidence as to who sent it. But surely we can stage a raid on the basis of information received?'

'Yes, but we're on thin ice. Everything will depend on our making a collar with evidence at the scene. We have some genuine suspicions about the firm so it would be worth monitoring a few of their vans via ANPR cameras, including the route we're interested in. Get Trevor to help you.'

'Yes, guv. Thank you.'

Mel was relieved that Emma hadn't pressed her over the source of the journey details. She hadn't lied. She didn't have any evidence that Robbie had sent them. But she was damn sure that he had and she worried about his safety. Could his infiltration of the Maybrick and Cream site be detected? She fervently hoped not.

Chapter Twenty-Eight

'PUT THAT OUT, YOU FUCKING TWAT,' Derek Farren yelled at his companion, a weedy looking youth with a shaven head and a T-shirt printed with the cross of St. George. 'Are you trying to kill us all?'

'Sorry, Del,' the youth said, stubbing out his cigarette on the concrete floor of the small basement. 'The smell's gettin' to me, 's all.'

'Well you can piss off and smoke outside when we've finished, can't you?'

'Yeah. All right.' The youth shuffled his feet sheepishly.

Farren looked around the room and grinned. Someone was in for a big surprise, he thought. The basement was lit by a couple of fluorescent tubes that threw sinister shadows in the corners. Damp stains covered the ceiling and there were streaks of mould, forming random patterns on the walls where the paint had flaked off. The mouldy smell was almost obscured by the pungent odour of chemicals. A long bench, made from a length of kitchen worktop fixed to a couple of old tables, stood against a wall. Bottles of nitric acid, some methylated spirit and an old barometer lay at one end, while a drum of hydrogen peroxide, bearing the name of a water treatment company, stood on the floor. Two large bottles of acetone and a couple of unlabelled bottles were visible in a plastic box, next to a range of laboratory glassware. A bag of nails, some tools, clocks, batteries and various lengths of wire completed the assemblage.

'When's 'e coming then?'

'When 'e finishes work,' Farren replied. 'We'll give 'im the first half of 'is money and leave 'im to it. I'm not fucking staying 'ere in case he blows 'imself up.'

The sound of feet on the stairs outside interrupted the pair and Farren reached into his pocket for his knife. They both relaxed when the door opened and a middle-aged man in a tweed jacket and grey trousers, carrying a briefcase, stepped into the room. He looked around suspiciously, as if checking that no-one had touched the items on the bench.

'Did you bring the money?'

'Half now, as agreed,' Farren replied. 'Are you sure this will work?'

'Of course. For me this was a full-time job. It'll take out dozens of the bastards if you place it right. Just behave yourself and don't drop it on the way.'

'I'm not stupid. I ain't gonna play football with it.'

'I'm sure you're not, Mr Farren, but these things are tricky. Now if you'll excuse me, I've got work to do.'

The man removed a lab coat from his briefcase and put an envelope of cash, which Darren had proffered, in its place. He put the coat on over his jacket and took out a complicated looking face mask.

'You're better off elsewhere. This could be dangerous,' he advised. 'I'll be in touch when it's all ready.'

'Quick as you can,' replied Farren, as the newcomer reached for the barometer and a plastic tub.

'It will be ready when it's ready. Now please leave.'

'Why's he doing this?' asked Farren's companion as they climbed the stairs and shut the door to the basement behind them.

'He's committed to the cause. His son was killed by ISIS in Afghanistan. He hates Muslims. He's not a street fighter but he joined us after seeing our stuff online.'

'Like Bennett you mean.'

'Yeah, but not so fucking nosy.'

'Does he know what he's doing?'

'Reckon so. He was in the army a while back. Ordnance unit or whatever it's called. Dealt with bombs all the time. And he teaches chemistry at the college. Useful for getting chemicals. Pub time?'

'Course. That stuff's got to my throat. And any time is pub time.'

Farren smiled thinly, wondering whether his mate was really up to the job. His enthusiasm wasn't matched by his intellect but he could still be useful, he supposed. He would have to be very careful about what he told him to do.

Chapter Twenty-Nine

Day 27, Tuesday

'So what do we know about Lorde and Dickens?' asked Emma, at the start of the morning briefing. For the first time in days the heating seemed to be working properly, without emitting any distracting noises. She didn't expect it to last.

'Darren John Lorde, 26, lives in a flat in town that hasn't been visited since he did a runner,' replied Trevor. 'He's from Mexton and has come to our attention a few times for affray, assault and drunkenness. He's been behaving himself for the past four years or so. Never been married. He has no social media presence under that name but Amira managed to find him through tags on other people's Facebook pages. He uses the alias PatriotDL to post nasty rants about immigration, gays, women – the usual targets. Drives a seven-year-old Porsche, which is a bit pricey for someone in his job as a warehouse operative. He's had a few jobs, but he's been with Maybrick and Cream for five years. That seems to have settled him down a bit. He was brought up in care from the age of 11, after his mum died of cancer in 2005. His dad was in the army and was killed by an IED in Iraq the year before.'

'Thanks, Trev. How about Dickens?'

Mel spoke up.

'Mark Paul Dickens. Age 27. Rents a bedsit on the edge of town. Also been in trouble for violence, frequently of a racial nature. He did nine months for supplying cannabis but has no known involvement with Class A. He's not been in trouble for a couple of years, apart from when he was stopped for driving his Corsa with faulty lights and without tax. His parents are deceased, killed in an RTC when they hit a minibus of Muslims returning from a pilgrimage to Mecca. There were a few injuries but none of the pilgrims was killed. The coroner blamed Dickens' father, who was drunk at the wheel.'

'Thanks, Mel,' said Emma. 'Neither has a particularly ostentatious lifestyle it seems, apart from Lorde's Porsche, although we don't know about savings or any offshore accounts they might have. No exotic holidays, as far as we can see. Dickens blames his father's victims for the crash so they both have a motive for racism.'

Someone snorted.

'By the way, guv,' said Jack, 'Lorde and Dickens are the only employees at Maybrick and Cream with anything serious on their records. A few of the other drivers and loaders have the odd conviction for traffic offences or disorder, but the office staff are all clean. None of them is a known associate of drug dealers. We'll keep looking, though.'

'Thanks, Jack. In the meantime, we do need to talk to this MP and see if he knows anything about the activities of Carter's Commercial Vehicle Hire. We've got the dates for when he's next in Mexton. Can you phone his office and make an appointment, please, Addy?'

'On it, guv.'

'Oh, something else. We've tracked down the phone, a burner, that Anton called to warn someone about the rescue party. As expected, it was in the area of Maybrick and Cream's warehouse. Also, he made a call to the same number about the time Mel and Trevor were leaving for the surveillance job that nearly got them killed. He must have found out about it somehow. So, it wasn't carelessness on the part of you two.' She smiled encouragingly at Mel and Trevor. 'I think we've got enough for an arrest, so I'd like Mel and Addy to pick him up as soon as.'

'Sure thing, boss,' Addy replied, grabbing his jacket and stab vest.

'How's the ANPR tracking of the firm's vans going, Trev?'

'We've been watching three of them, boss. Two of them just stick to logical routes between customers. But one visited the service station Mel identified last Wednesday. We're getting CCTV footage.'

'Good. I think that gives us grounds to set up a raid. I'll talk to DS Palmer and liaise with Hants Police. I'd better let DCI Gale know, as she, and the Super, will need to sign it off. I'll speak to her after lunch.'

Anton Kominski was leafing idly through the *Sun* and drinking tea, standing in the police station gatehouse, when his boss phoned.

'Anton. I've had the police on the phone, asking about you. What's this all about?'

'No idea, boss. They haven't been speaking to me. What did they want?'

He sat down abruptly, his legs no longer able to support him.

'They asked how long you've worked for me, what you did before, and who gave you your references. Is there something I should know? You're in a position of trust and I can't afford to have them doubt your honesty.'

'No, boss. Is all good. They're checking all civilian contractors.' He groped wildly for a reason, his mouth suddenly dry and his heart thumping. 'Something to do with data protection, I think. GDRP, is that it?'

'OK. Well, you tell me if there's anything for me to worry about. Mexton Security has a good reputation and I don't want to lose it.'

'Yes, boss. Sure. No problem.'

When his boss ended the call, Anton felt sick and his thoughts went straight into panic mode. Were they on to him? Surely not. He'd been so careful to hide his habit and his contacts with Derek Farren. Undecided as to whether he should run, or stay and brazen it out, his mind was made up when he saw two police officers approaching, grim expressions on their faces. 'That's the girl who borrowed my phone,' he thought, as he grabbed his jacket, rushed out of the gatehouse and ran to his parked motorbike. He shoved his helmet on his head, turned the ignition key and pressed the starter.

'Stop, Anton. We want a word with you,' yelled Mel Cotton.

Anton ignored her and kicked the bike into gear, almost doing a wheelie as he shot through the gate. By the time the officers had piled into a police car and got it started, he was half a mile away, confident that he hadn't been followed. He pulled into a side road and reached for his phone, dialling a number from memory.

'They're on to me,' he gasped, when the call was answered. 'What do I do?'

There was silence for a few seconds.

'Meet me at the depot. Soon as you can. And take the battery out your phone. They can trace it. Don't worry, mate. We'll sort it.'

Chapter Thirty

'I'm not sure, Emma. I'm really not sure.' DCI Gale straightened her pen on her immaculately organised desk and frowned. 'We screwed up last year when a drugs raid found nothing and it cost the life of an undercover officer. I think we need more than just some suspicious van movements. What does the drugs squad say? And how about Hants Police?'

Emma tried to conceal her frustration.

'Derek is fine with it. Hants are happy for us to run the op. They can spare us an ARV in case firearms are involved but that's it. They're overstretched, as are we all.'

'No. I don't think we can do this at the moment. We need a bit more evidence to justify the costs. I'm sorry. But do come back when it looks more solid.'

'Yes, ma'am. Thank you.'

Emma's formal farewell concealed an urge to shout at the woman. But she closed the DCI's office door gently and walked back to the incident room, resisting the urge to kick something on the way and muttering rude things about bureaucrats who don't understand real coppering. She wondered how Fiona

Gale had reached the rank of DCI. Perhaps she would have an unofficial word with Jack Vaughan. He obviously knew what was going on in the team and she'd heard him let slip a few remarks about DCI Gale that were less than complimentary.

Emma cornered Jack beside the coffee machine when no-one else was about.

'So what is it with DCI Gale, Jack? She seems a pretty good administrator but doesn't seem to be that much of a cop. Normally, I wouldn't have this kind of conversation, but you seem to know how things work around here.'

'I have to say you're right, Emma. She was given the SIO role, as a DI, in a major case last year. She was expected to fail but, thanks to her team, she didn't. That stood her in good stead when the DCI vacancy came up. She talks fluent management-speak and she is good at that side of the job. But the fire went out of her years ago. Some personal event, I believe. She'd rather stay in her office and not get involved, especially with the press.'

'That makes it bloody difficult to work with her, surely?'

'I think it's more a case of working around her. You'll get used to it. As long as the paperwork is up to date, and you don't screw up anything major, she'll leave you alone.'

'Thanks, Jack. Appreciated.'

Emma stirred her coffee thoughtfully. She would just have to get on with the job and disturb her senior officer as little as possible.

'Bad news, folks.' Emma addressed the detectives, who looked up from their desks, surprised at the tension in her voice. 'DCI Gale has vetoed an op at the service station. It seems that catching drug dealers is too bloody expensive, but please don't quote me on that. She wants more evidence before approving an operation. So, if anyone has a good idea about how to get it, please let me know.'

'How about CCTV from the lorry park?' asked Mel.

'It's come in but it's not very useful. The van was careful to park so it couldn't be seen, behind an articulated lorry,' replied Trevor. 'Any transfer of boxes was completely concealed and the lorry's number plate was out of range.'

'We really need someone on the spot,' said Emma. 'But Hants Police can't spare anyone and I'm damn sure the DCI wouldn't authorise us to follow the van. It would take several cars and cost a fortune. So, keep looking for grounds to pull them, people. Thank you.'

The disconsolate team turned back to their duties. Mel thought for a while at her desk and then approached Jack Vaughan.

'Can I take a day's leave tomorrow, Jack? I'd like to take a trip down to the New Forest.'

'What on earth for? I didn't think you were a nature girl.'

'Oh. You know. It would be nice to get out of town. Look at some trees and things.'

'You wouldn't be going anywhere near a certain service station, would you?'

'Me?' Mel looked as innocent as she could manage. 'Well, I'll probably need to fill up at some point.'

'For fuck's sake don't do anything to compromise the investigation or get yourself hurt. You know I've told you about this before. This lot have killed once and were prepared to murder an undercover officer.'

'Course not, Jack. Forests are supposed to be good for the soul. I'm bound to come back refreshed after a bit of tree therapy.'

'Well OK, then. Enjoy your nature walk and don't get into trouble. Fill in the leave request and I'll approve it.'

'Thanks, Jack.'

Mel grinned and wandered over to the coffee machine with a sparkle in her eyes. She'd been accused of being too impetuous in the past and it had put her in danger. Since the Maldobourne business last year, she felt she had gone some way to proving herself. Although she had gained the respect of colleagues, she knew that she would still have to work at it. But hanging around a lorry park for an hour or so was perfectly safe. Wasn't it?

Chapter Thirty-One

KITTY MICKLETON WAS a bit of a busybody. Long since retired from her job as a dispensing assistant in a local pharmacy, she had time on her hands. She spent some of this watching antiques programmes on daytime television, hoping that some of her father's war mementoes would be worth a fortune, and the rest of it setting the world to rights.

She was a regular contributor to the letters page of the local newspaper, bemoaning the lack of manners of young people, dog fouling on the pavements and the unreliability of the recycling collections. Should anyone hold a house party within a hundred yards that extended beyond midnight, the Council would hear about it. Courteous as their responses always were, the helpline operators had had enough of her. That was why they initially dismissed her complaints about the smell coming from the basement flat.

Kitty lived on the ground floor of a slightly run-down Victorian house, on the outskirts of Mexton. She kept her home spotless and did her best with the hall, which served the whole building. The behaviour of the other tenants, who generally didn't stay long, frequently annoyed her. Their uncollected post, muddy footprints, which could have been prevented by a more diligent use of the doormat, and the smells from their takeaways arriving at weekends often had her fuming in silence. She wouldn't tackle them about it, of course. She didn't want to cause an upset. She still had to live there. So, despite an arthritic hip, she would sweep and tidy the hallway, almost on a daily basis. No-one thanked her and sometimes she worked herself up to a silent rage at the sloppy behaviour of her fellow tenants.

The basement, which had a separate entrance, was supposed to be unoccupied, because of inadequate light and pernicious damp. The landlord used it for storing paint, ladders and other equipment. But she was sure she heard people moving around down there, at odd times of the day and night. There were peculiar noises, from machinery she thought, but worse was the smell that somehow drifted up through her floorboards. It reminded her of some of the chemicals she came across when she did her dispensing certificate, many years ago, at the Technical College, but she couldn't remember which ones. So she phoned the Council helpline and made a complaint. When nothing was done about it after a few days she phoned again, and again three days later.

Eventually an Environmental Health Officer knocked on her door, one Tuesday afternoon, and made notes while she described what she could smell.

'It's not all the time,' she explained. 'But sometimes it's overpowering. Sometimes it smells like acetone, sometimes it's like acid and sometimes like something else. I'm sure it's not healthy and I do have a touch of asthma.'

'OK, Ms Mickleton. Let's see if there's anyone in and I'll have a word with them.'

Kitty showed him the entrance to the basement, at the bottom of a flight of stone steps. The EHO led the way down, with Kitty following close behind and holding on tight to a rusty handrail.

'You're right. There is a chemical smell.'

He knocked on the door and it swung open, the last users clearly having forgotten to lock it properly.

'Well. What can you see?' Kitty asked excitedly.

'I don't really have the authority to go in, Ms Mickleton. But I suppose it won't do any harm to look from the doorway.'

He flicked on the light switch beside the door and gazed at the debris scattered over the floor.

'Looks like someone's been using the place and left in a hurry. Hang on. What's this?' He stepped into the room and crouched down to examine some empty containers. 'Acetone. That's what you mentioned, and oh sh...' He swallowed the imprecation before he could utter it. 'Hydrogen peroxide. That worries me.'

'Why? What's the matter?'

'I think, perhaps, we should leave and contact the police. Immediately. I went on a course last month that mentioned these chemicals and I think something bad has been happening here. Can you go back to your flat and I'll make the call?'

As Kitty scurried away, he looked once more at the contents of the basement. A small pile of beige powder lay on a workbench, and as he approached it, he tripped over a cardboard box. His phone flew out of his hand and landed on the powder. A sharp explosion echoed round the room and the phone was thrown a metre into the air, accompanied by a yellow flash and a cloud of grey smoke.

The EHO fled as his ruined phone tumbled to the floor.

Within half an hour, the street outside the house was cordoned off and the residents evacuated. Police cars and an unmarked bomb disposal van had blocked off the street. It took an hour for two explosives technicians, appropriately dressed in forensic suits, to declare the scene safe and deal with anything potentially dangerous. It was then the turn of the SOCOs to record the scene and gather evidence. Miscellaneous chemicals and various electrical items, together with DNA swabs and fibre lifts, went to the forensic science contractor, while items for fingerprinting were dealt with by Mexton CID's own lab. An interim report was promised for the following day.

Chapter Thirty-Two

Day 28, Wednesday

DI THORPE WAITED until she'd received a report from the labs before calling the team together after lunch. Unusually, DCI Gale sat in on the briefing, and before Emma started, she stood up and addressed the team, introducing a grey-suited man.

'Ladies and gentlemen, this is DI Steve Morton from Counter-Terrorism. Some of you have met him already. He'd like to say a few words to you but, before he does, I must emphasise that what you hear today is strictly confidential. No-one, and I mean no-one, is to discuss these matters outside the station or with anyone not connected to the investigation. That includes family. Am I clear?'

A murmur of assent went round the room and DI Morton stepped forward.

'Thank you, ma'am. Good afternoon. It seems that, quite by accident, you've found a bomb factory, or, rather, the remains of one. We found no completed devices on the scene but plenty of evidence indicating what had been going on.

Empty acetone and hydrogen peroxide containers were discovered, and as I expect some of you know, these chemicals are used to make TATP, the explosive used in the London bus and tube bombings in 2005. We also found various electrical items suggestive of a timing mechanism and detonating system. The Council chap, who first found the place, dropped his phone on a pile of powder, which exploded. That was mercury fulminate and is used in detonators. His phone, incidentally, was covered in mercury in the explosion and is now hazardous waste.'

One or two officers grinned at this but the expressions on most of the faces in the room ranged from puzzlement to alarm.

'I must tell you,' continued DI Morton, 'that I am extremely concerned. Judging by the evidence we've seen, and much of it has not been processed yet, a significant explosive device has probably been manufactured and could be deployed at any time. The potential loss of life, should it be used in a crowded place, does not bear thinking about. But it is our job to think about such things, which is why I'm speaking to you today.'

Mutterings of 'Oh fuck!', 'Dear God' and similar circulated and Morton let the hubbub die down before continuing.

'It is vital that we find this bomb before it's used and we need the efforts of every officer available. I will second some SO15 officers to the inquiry and will also alert the security services. I should also mention that there seems to have been enough chemicals on the premises to make several devices.'

At that point Emma's phone vibrated and she stepped away to take the call.

'The first thing we need to do is to identify the individuals who were present in the basement,' Morton continued.

'I think I can help there,' interrupted Emma. 'We've processed prints from the site. They belong to Derek Farren and Michael Harris. You know Farren, and Harris is another local scrote with convictions for racial violence. There were no other retrievable prints on equipment, but the SOCOs did find a trace of blood on a fragment of broken glass. It's been sent to the outside lab for fast-track DNA profiling.'

DI Morton looked surprised, thought for a few seconds, then spoke.

'Then it looks like the murder of Duncan Bennett and the bomb making are linked, if only tenuously. We will need to consult at a senior level to decide how to handle this. But, for the moment, could I ask you all to focus your attention on the bomb threat? I'll now hand you back to DI Thorpe. Thank you.'

Morton took a seat at the side of the room while Emma wound up the meeting.

'We'll meet again tomorrow at eight sharp, please. I know it's tempting, but please do not mention what's happening to your partners or spouses. DCI Gale has assured me that over-time will be available but you must make excuses if you are called out at unusual hours. Spend the rest of the day tidying up and leaving things where you can pick them up again. Then go home. Thank you.'

Chapter Thirty-Three

IT WAS dark by the time Mel arrived at the service station. The motorway had been crowded with homeward bound commuters and the services were busy. She cruised around the car parks and found no sign of a Maybrick and Cream van. Realising she was early, she bought a takeaway coffee and a Cornish pasty from a stall and settled down to wait. Ten minutes later she saw an artic with Belgian plates pull into the lorry park, busy with truckers heading to the transport side of the services, clearly eager for their evening cholesterol blast. She moved her own vehicle to a position where she could watch it, hoping that no one would challenge her car's presence amongst the goods vehicles. Glancing around, she could see that the lorry was parked in a CCTV blind spot. A few minutes later, a Maybrick and Cream van pulled up behind it.

Mel was tempted to film the scene on her phone but realised she didn't have the authority for surveillance, so she contented herself with making a note of the artic's number and the van's. She watched as the lorry driver climbed down from the cab and conferred with the two men in the van, then lost sight of him as he moved behind his vehicle.

She nearly spilled her coffee when there was a loud rap on her window. Her heart thudded and her mouth dried up despite her drink. The lorry driver had circled his truck and come up behind her, his expression full of menace. Deciding to play the innocent, she wound down her window.

'Yes? Can I help you?'

'What you doing in ze lorry park?'

Despite his Belgian accent, his English was clear.'

'I'm having a quiet coffee and something to eat. What's it to you?'

'Zis is for trucks only. You shouldn't be here. There might be an accident.'

The underlying threat was clear.

'There's no law against it. It's a free country.'

'Are you a cop? Are you spying on me?'

'No. Course not. I'm an estate agent.'

The driver didn't seem to understand the term. He produced a large spanner from his overalls and tapped it threateningly on Mel's windscreen.

'I sink you'd better go, missy. Drink your coffee back there where it's safer.'

Realising her cover was blown, Mel put her car into gear and let off the handbrake. As she pulled away she tipped the remains of her coffee over the lorry driver's crotch. Although it was nearly cold, he leapt backwards in fury, but before he could strike back, Mel was well out of his reach.

She cursed her luck as she hammered back up the motorway, just keeping to the speed limit. All that time wasted and she wouldn't even be able to claim for her petrol. At least she had the number of the lorry. She would pass it on to the Border Force. Perhaps they would stop and search it when it returned. If they had the resources. She wasn't looking forward to seeing Jack Vaughan, but at least she hadn't been hurt. This time.

Chapter Thirty-Four

Mexton, Autumn 2019

'This money you're going to provide for the cause,' began Arden. 'I'll need some of it in cash to pay for certain services connected with the campaign but we need to make the rest look legitimate. Just in case anyone starts asking questions.'

'Obviously we need to launder it somehow,' Jeannie replied. 'Massage it through the books of a company or a phoney charity or something. You've got plenty of business contacts. Do you know any bent accountants?'

'A few. But they wouldn't want to touch something like this. There is a company I'm involved with, though, which could work. I have another...project on the go that will generate some income I'll need to conceal. Perhaps you could help with that as well?'

'I could, if I knew what it was about.'

Arden thought for a moment. 'I recently met some charming Belgians who, like me, are concerned about the future of the white race. We got talking and they told me that they funded their activities by selling cocaine. I don't see any great harm in it. I take a little myself, when things get stressful. They did say that, if I wanted to do the same, they could supply me with the occasional modest shipment. The only problem is how to import and distribute the stuff without getting caught.'

'Belgians, you say. The company I work for, Maybrick and Cream, imports chocolate from Belgium. And they have a fleet of vans. I think we could work something out, here. You'll need someone reliable on the inside. I can't be directly involved but I can help cover a few things up.'

'Excellent. I'll chat to some of my colleagues in the movement. See if anyone sympathetic already works for the firm – Maybrick and Cream, did you say?'

'That's right. You'll need a means of distributing the product once it's in Mexton, but I'll leave that up to you. One thing, though. They know me by a different name at work. It's a personal thing from the past. You won't mention my name, will you?'

'No. Of course not. Now are you coming back to the hotel with me, my sweet? Helen's away again.'

'You know I'd love to but I've lots to attend to. Another time. Soon, I promise.'

She kissed him briefly and headed for home. Keep the prick dangling, she thought. Always leave them wanting more.

Over the previous few weeks, Jeannie had made plans to divert money into Arden's grasp from a selection of sources. Small scale computer scams, unlikely to be spotted, would raid the accounts of a number of prominent right-wing people and organisations, including Arden's own party. The prospect of using her hacking skills exhilarated her and she comforted herself with the knowledge that she wasn't generating new funds: she was just recycling them. The drug money could easily be laundered, if necessary, although much of it would probably remain as cash. She would keep detailed encrypted records of transactions as insurance. She would probably release them to the authorities at the end of her mission, clearly linking Arden to illegal activity.

Darren Lorde was extremely pleased with himself. When Derek Farren approached him after the meeting, with a scheme to help fund the cause and provide him with a useful amount of wedge as well, he didn't have to think before agreeing. He knew there was a gap in the market, since Campbell's operation had been broken up and no-one organised had moved in so far. He'd worked for Campbell occasionally, a bit of dealing here and there, and he knew many of his customers.

The idea of collecting the goods from a Belgian supplier in the firm's van was sweet and he knew of several young lads with motorbikes, ideal for delivering to customers, who would be keen to help. He also had a mate on the firm who shared his beliefs, so setting things up and running them would be easy. Derek had told him he would be put on the payroll of a vehicle hire firm so his 'wages' would look legitimate, not that he would have to do any work there, and he would get a bonus every time things went well.

Chapter Thirty-Five

Day 28, Wednesday

'OH GAWD. Twitty Kitty's at it again.'

The *Mexton Messenger*'s Letters Editor groaned as he scanned another missive in Kitty Mickleton's distinctive, precise handwriting.

'Banging on about terrorists this time. As if.'

'What did you say?' Jenny Pike pulled up short as she passed his desk, her hawkish face lighting up at the prospect of a story.

'It is our favourite correspondent. Not. She's always writing in to complain about something daft, and this time it's about her landlord letting people use the basement below her flat to make bombs.'

'That's odd,' Jenny mused. 'I've not heard anything from my police contacts about bombs, although there was that chemical leak the new boy, Ricky, covered. Maybe the police are hiding something.'

'Slipping, are you? Not enough tenners in the right pockets?'

'No, George, I am not slipping. And I don't actually bribe police officers, as you well know. That would be against the law. Of course, the odd social drink helps to lubricate tongues. It's not illegal if they find my company charming.' She fluttered her false eyelashes in an exaggerated manner and attempted to pout.

George ignored her.

'So, I can dismiss this as nonsense and spike the letter?'

'Hang on to it for a bit. I've got a spare half hour. I'll go and talk to your Ms Mickleton and see what she's on about.'

'Good luck with that. She'll bore you to tears with trivia if her letters are anything to go by.'

Jenny noted down Kitty's address and left the office with a thoughtful look. She had a hunch there could be something in the woman's claims. After all, every now and again the most preposterous idea proves to be true. Look at relativity.

'Ms Mickleton? Can you spare a moment? I'm from the *Mexton Messenger*. It's about your letter.'

Jenny Pike smiled warmly at the woman, who seemed quite unlike the daffy, sub-Marple old lady her colleague had implied. She looked around seventy but her eyes were bright and her clothing was sober and clean. She hadn't dyed her hair, but her tightly permed curls gave her an old-fashioned look. Her thin frame moved slightly awkwardly and Jenny could see she had a problem with her hip.

'You'd better come in. And it's Miss.'

Her handshake was firm and she ushered Jenny into a tidy

lounge, furnished with several well-stacked bookshelves and a three-piece suite that had seen better days. A framed certificate from Mexton Technical College, attesting to Kitty Mickleton's qualification as a dispensing technician, hung on the wall above the 1950s fireplace, alongside an ornate, beribboned china plate printed with a picture of an elderly terrier. The inscription read 'Gone but always in our thoughts'.

'Thank you, Miss Mickleton. Our editor showed me your letter and asked me to come and talk to you personally.'

'Look, sit down, will you? Do you want tea? A biscuit?'

'Yes, please. That would be lovely.'

Jenny pulled her short skirt down as she sank into the sofa. She didn't really want tea but realised that it helped to build a rapport. As she waited, she wondered whether this would be a waste of time. Another old woman with nothing better to do than make a fuss. But Kitty did have a technical qualification so she couldn't be completely daft.

'Let me help you with that,' she said, as Kitty returned bearing a tray loaded with china cups and saucers, a teapot, a milk jug, a sugar bowl and a plate of digestives. Jenny carried the tray to a small table.

'Is it OK to record our conversation on my phone?' she asked, as Kitty poured the tea.

'Yes. Of course.'

Jenny switched on her phone and placed it on the arm of the sofa.

'What exactly did you mean about bombs in the basement?'

Kitty put her cup down and arranged her hands in her lap before speaking.

'Well, I had to put up with the smells for more than two weeks. And odd noises. People coming and going although the basement is supposed to be unused. I kept on at the Council about it but they wouldn't listen, until Tuesday.'

'So did you think that there were terrorists there?'

'No. I just hated the nuisance. I could smell chemicals and thought there might be a fire risk. And I've got a bit of asthma. But a pleasant young man from Environmental Health came round, eventually, and had a look. He seemed really worried. I went back to my flat and there was a bang from the basement. He borrowed my phone and I heard him calling the police and asking for the bomb squad.'

'What happened then?'

'Lots of people turned up and we were evacuated for over an hour. Had to sit in a freezing church until they let us back in. When we were allowed back the policewoman in charge said there was nothing to worry about, there had been a chemical spillage of some sort but we weren't in danger. People would come and deal with it.'

'You sound as if you didn't believe her.'

'Well, if it was just that, why didn't they leave it to the fire brigade or the Council to clean it up? That's what they do. Why was there a Scientific Services van parked outside for most of the day with CSIs in space suits going to and fro? I've seen enough TV to know that something was going on. All the neighbours, those that talk to me, that is, believed them and lost interest. But what I want to know is why the landlord let people store chemicals in the basement in the first place. And what were they there for?'

'Why did you write to the paper?'

'I tried to speak to the Environmental Health man again, but he was always unavailable when I phoned. The police just fobbed me off. I thought the paper would publish my letter and someone might respond.'

'Well, I think we can do better than that. If the authorities are keeping quiet about a bomb threat in Mexton, it's a scandal. I've got plenty from you here. It's OK to quote you, isn't it? And can I send a photographer round?'

'Quote me by all means. But I don't want my picture in the paper. I'm not interested in celebrity.'

'That's fine. I'll just ask him to take a shot of the building from the outside. I may have some more questions, if that's all right. Can I have your phone number in case I need to check anything?'

Kitty gave Jenny a landline number and stood up to show her out.

'I'm glad someone's taking me seriously. It took ages for the Council to do anything. Useless blighters. Still, the man they sent was nice.'

'Well, I'm taking you very seriously, Miss Mickleton. Very seriously indeed. Thank you very much for talking to me.'

Jenny almost skipped back to her car. This was big. No-one else had it. And it could even be picked up by the nationals. Perhaps it was time to spread her wings and leave the *Messenger*? After all, it was just a provincial rag, permanently under threat from online media. She deserved better and this might be her chance. She would scan Twitter, Instagram and Facebook, to see if there were any photos of the scene, and talk to a few of Kitty's neighbours. She didn't expect anything from the police press officer but knew she could guess at some things and make up others if she needed to. It wouldn't be the first time.

Chapter Thirty-Six

Day 29, Thursday

SOMETHING WAS CLEARLY wrong when Mel turned up for work early the following morning. Officers and civilian staff wore frowns and expressions of fear. The usual morning banter was absent.

'What have I missed, Jack?' she asked.

'While you were communing with nature, we had a briefing from SO15. That basement we were called to on Tuesday was a bomb factory. Derek Farren's prints were all over it and there's a device in play. A big one.'

'Oh shit.'

'I don't suppose you happened to notice anything of interest while you were on leave? Apart from a few New Forest ponies, I mean.'

'Well, I was having a coffee in a motorway services when I noticed a Maybrick and Cream van pull up behind a Belgian artic. The lorry driver suggested I should move on as the place was dangerous so I gave him my coffee and went home. I got the number though.'

'Have you been taking stupid risks again?'

'No, of course not. I just happened to be in that particular place. I wasn't in danger.'

Jack looked sceptical.

'So what's this about a bomb?' she asked.

'There's briefing at eight so get a drink and find a seat. It's not good news.'

Jack sat back and thought about Mel, as he often did. He was still, officially, her mentor as well as her supervisor, but she rarely came to him for advice. Supervision sessions were sometimes fraught, as Mel was extremely keen to progress but sometimes cut corners. She wasn't exactly insubordinate but tended to strike out on her own. Jokingly, he had likened her to a cat busily using up her nine lives, but beneath the levity was a serious concern for her welfare. She had taken risks in the past, desperate to prove herself, and wound up in dangerous situations. Perhaps getting shot, even if it was only a shotgun pellet grazing her earlobe, had calmed her down a bit. She did seem a little less impetuous now and he hoped it would last. He was sure she would make an excellent detective. If she lived long enough.

The *Mexton Messenger* narrowly missed decapitating a pot plant as an incandescent Emma hurled it across the room.

'Who the fook talked to the press?' she demanded,

sounding more Yorkshire in her anger. 'You were all told to say nowt to these reptiles and look at the headline. "Mexton Terror Threat". The phone to the press office hasn't stopped ringing, the ACC wants to know who leaked and, worst of all, the terrorists know we're on to them. This could cost lives and it's gonna cost someone their job. And I'll charge them with misconduct in public office. So who was it?'

Expressions of disbelief and indignation greeted her outburst. Jack Vaughan spoke up.

'I'm sure it's none of us, guv. I know everyone in this room and they wouldn't be so stupid. I've seen the article and it's Jenny Pike again. She's screwed us over before and hates us 'cos she was for drink driving. She wants to be a superstar journalist but she's just a twat.'

Others nodded their agreement.

'So where did she get her information?'

'Reading between the lines, it looks like the paper was contacted by the old lady in the ground floor flat. The EHO was told to keep quiet, and I'm sure he did. We passed it off as a chemical leak and that's all there was on social media, until this morning. Now it's going crazy with terrorism and conspiracy theories. According to one nutcase, Jeremy Corbyn is behind it, and there are plenty of people blaming asylum seekers, immigrants or aliens. If Pike doesn't have enough facts, she makes them up and that seems to be what's happened here.'

Somewhat mollified, Emma took a deep breath and continued.

'OK. I hope you're right and no-one has leaked. We're holding a press conference at noon and DCI Gale wants me to take it. She has a sore throat, apparently.'

Mel snorted in disbelief.

'Remember what happened last time she faced Jenny Pike?' she whispered to Jack, who smiled grimly.

'We'll put out a statement and take a limited number of questions. Try to defuse the situation. No pun intended. So, leaving Pike aside for the moment, as most of you know, it is highly likely that we have a live bomb somewhere in Mexton. We don't know where it will be detonated or when. But we know Derek Farren and Michael Harris are involved.'

She paused to project images of the two men on the whiteboard.

'Both of these men have convictions for racially aggravated assault, and their social media posts and internet search histories are appalling. So, it's likely that the intended target is somewhere used by a large number of asylum seekers, Muslims or other members of the BAME community. I want you all to come up with likely sites and list them on the board. Start with the material we found on Duncan's flash drive.

'We need to know where Farren and Harris hang out, where they drink, everything you can find out about them, plus a list of their associates. Find out what vehicles they drive and see if you can find them on ANPR – assuming, that is, they're registered with DVLA. Of course, they may not be the ones planting the bomb, but we need to start with them.'

Several detectives started scribbling on notepads.

'Is this anything to do with Duncan Bennett's murder?' asked Karen.

'There is a link, yes. I am now allowed to tell you that Duncan was a CHIS for Counter-Terrorism, passing on information on far-right activity.

The team looked astonished.

'He volunteered to keep an eye on social media for them, posing as an extremist, but seems to have gone deeper than he was supposed to. Whether that got him killed we can't say. It could just have been that he spotted the drugs operation and had to be silenced.'

'So, are we still looking at that? Trying to find Duncan's murderer?'

'Not for the moment. All our resources must go on finding the bombers. DCI Gale is liaising with the security services and Counter-Terrorism. For the moment I'm still SIO, but that may change. For those of you who haven't met her, I'd like to introduce DS Angela Wilson from SO15. She will be our link person. Please make her welcome and give her every co-operation.'

DS Wilson, who had been sitting at the side of the room, stood up and smiled uncertainly.

'Let's hope co-operation goes both ways,' muttered Jack.

'We should be getting some additional help from SO15 in due course. Extra uniformed officers have been deployed to keep an eye out for suspicious activity, but they haven't been given the details yet. We're borrowing some sniffer dogs from other forces and they'll be used as soon as we get them. The only people who know about the extent of the threat are ourselves and senior officers. Let's keep it that way.'

'What about the Environmental Health bloke?' asked Addy.

'He doesn't know much and has been sworn to secrecy. He's signed the Official Secrets Act. He'll write his report up, describing a chemical smell that has now dissipated. So, crack on. We have to find these buggers before they kill a lot of people.'

Emma walked back to her office, her head spinning. She knew her team would do a good job, but how do you deal with a threat to an unknown target at an undetermined time, possibly from an unknown individual? They would need luck as well as skill and dedication. She recalled the famous IRA quote: *Remember we only have to be lucky once. You will have to be lucky always.*

She trembled as she closed her office door.

Chapter Thirty-Seven

JACK PUT THE PHONE DOWN, looking grim.

'Fancy a trip to Darley Woods, Mel? You're a tree lover, aren't you?'

'Ha, ha. What for?'

'Someone's reported a body and the DI's busy. Paramedics have confirmed death.'

'Sure. I'll get my coat.'

When the two detectives arrived at the scene, cordons were in place and SOCOs were already working. Mel remained behind while Jack suited up, signed in and followed the stepping plates to a tent amongst the trees. He pulled the flap aside and approached the body lying supine amongst twigs and rotting leaves, a dark hole in the middle of its forehead from which a small patch of blood had oozed.

'Oh shit,' he murmured, as he stared into the lifeless eyes of Anton Kominski.

He stepped out and spoke to a uniformed constable.

'Who reported the body?'

'A dog walker, Sarge,' PC Dawnay replied. 'She's sitting in the patrol car muttering something about never coming here again. Not surprised. It was her what found a dead body here last year.'

As Jack approached the car, he realised that this was the same part of the woods where a serious villain had been found hanging, a few months previously. He attempted to interview the unfortunate dog owner, but all he could get from her was that the dog had run into the bushes, barking, and she had followed, whereupon she had nearly fainted at the sight of Anton's body. Jack asked PC Dawnay to take her home and find someone to sit with her.

'We'll get her to make a formal statement in the morning, when she's recovered,' Jack told Mel, 'but I shouldn't think she'll have anything useful to add. She hasn't been here for a couple of days and I doubt she'll ever come back.'

Mel nodded sympathetically and the two officers returned to their car.

'So, what do you reckon to this Coronavirus threat, then?' Mel asked, as they drove back to the nick, hoping to catch Emma's press conference.

Jack frowned.

'I really don't know. Too early to tell, I guess. The government doesn't seem that worried. I suppose we'll be all right if people behave sensibly.'

Mel snorted.

'How long have you been a copper, Jack?'

'Getting on for twenty years. Why?'

'And what, in all your career, have you seen that suggests people will behave sensibly?'

Jack shrugged.

'Point taken, I suppose. But, if what some of the medics say is true, we're in for some very disturbing times. As usual, we'll deal with things when they happen.'

Chapter Thirty-Eight

THE REST of the morning was taken up by routine detective work. Lists of the suspects' haunts and associates were written on the whiteboards around the room. Any vehicles they were known to have access to were tracked through ANPR cameras and CCTV. Potential bomb targets were identified and aerial photos obtained. Uniformed patrols were stepped up in vulnerable areas but officers were not armed. Firearms officers patrolling the streets of Mexton, with their weapons on view, were unheard of and would only cause alarm. Beneath the bustle, the phone conversations and the tapping of keyboards, there was an undercurrent of fear. Fear that they would be too late to stop Mexton's first terrorist atrocity.

By eleven forty-five the press briefing room was packed with journalists holding mobile phones and cameras. Two TV crews had set up their equipment and the heat from the lights was stifling. The smells of sweat and a dozen mingling grooming products did little to improve the atmosphere. At precisely twelve noon, Emma entered the room, followed by DCI Gale and Chief Superintendent Herrick, the area commander. They sat behind a long table and Emma addressed the room.

'Good afternoon, ladies and gentlemen. I am DI Emma Thorpe and I am leading this investigation. I have a prepared statement that I will read, after which I will take a few questions.'

She cleared her throat.

'On Tuesday afternoon, following a report from a Council employee, officers attended premises in Coleridge Street. Various chemicals were found there, which led us to believe that someone had been unlawfully manufacturing explosives. No explosive devices were found. We need to trace the individuals responsible without delay and we would like your support in this. We would particularly like to talk to Mr Derek Farren and Mr Michael Harris, whose pictures appear on the screen behind me. You have copies. Anyone seeing them should call 999 immediately. The public must not approach these people. I would stress that, while there is a risk to the public, there is no need for panic. We would ask everyone to be alert to any suspicious activity and report it to us. We would rather have a hundred false alarms than miss a genuine one. If anyone sees a suspect package anywhere, on no account should they touch it. I am confident that police, in co-operation with the security services, will be able to deal with this potential threat and prevent a loss of life. Thank you.'

She had barely finished speaking when the room erupted with shouted questions.

'Is it Muslim terrorists?'

'What about the IRA?'

'Why did you say it was a chemical leak?'

'We have no reason to believe that ISIS or Al Qaeda are involved and we don't think the IRA is responsible,' replied Emma. 'The first call to the Council was about a chemical smell and it would have been inappropriate to speculate on matters before we had consulted experts. We would have preferred to apprehend the people responsible without causing a public panic. Unfortunately, the individuals we would like to talk to are now aware of our interest in them and will be difficult to find.'

Jenny Pike fired off a series of challenges 'Should we be scared? Are Mexton CID up to the job? What is MI5 doing?'.

'I repeat, Ms Pike, there is no need to panic. All our officers are concentrating on finding the suspects and preventing an incident. I have every confidence in them and would ask the public to co-operate and be vigilant. And, as you know, we never comment on the activities of the security services. Thank you everyone. That's all. We have an important job to do.'

Emma ignored a barrage of questions and accusations and strode out of the room, followed by the senior officers.

'Well done, Emma,' said the Chief Superintendent. DCI Gale nodded her approval, obviously glad that she hadn't had to face the press herself. I need a coffee, thought Emma, though a large drink would be preferable. That will have to wait. And I must change this sweat-soaked shirt.

'Thank you, sir. I think I'd rather face a riot than a baying horde of journalists. I just hope they don't make the situation worse.'

'In your dreams,' muttered DCI Gale.

Chapter Thirty-Nine

MEL COTTON HAD WATCHED Emma's performance at the press conference and was impressed with her. Here's a woman who can handle pressure, she thought. Good to work for.

'I'm off to get some lunch, Jack. OK?'

'Yep. But don't get into trouble.'

'I'm just going to the shopping mall for a slice of pizza. The only threat there is to my waistline.'

Jack grinned and refrained from pointing out that Mel didn't have an ounce of spare fat on her.

Pale sunlight penetrated the grubby glass enclosing the shopping mall, which was crowded with lunchtime shoppers and people looking for takeaway meals. Just the time to mount a terror attack, she thought mordantly. The sight of patrolling uniformed constables reassured her somewhat, but as she approached a falafel stall, with its queue stretching for several metres, she felt something was wrong. She tried to work out what, scanning the scene for anything that didn't look right. Then she focused on what was worrying her. Why, she thought, is that cleaner's trolley standing there with no-one using it? The bright yellow wheeled bin, with broom and scoop attached, was parked close to the stall and there was no sign of a cleaner.

She moved towards it, sweating and with a rising heart rate. Should she call it in, just on spec without checking it? That might be the sensible thing to do but she would look a complete tit if the operative had just nipped off for a leak. She remembered the mickey taken out of DI Thorpe over the replica pistol and decided to take a look.

Cautiously, she opened the lid. Her hopes that all she would find would be sweet wrappers, discarded coffee cups and general dirt were demolished when she saw the contents. A battery and an old-fashioned alarm clock were visible in a clear plastic box that seemed to be glued shut. She could see wires running from the battery to the clock and onwards to a large tub, passing through a hole in the lid. Oh fuck, fuck, fuck, she thought. What was she supposed to do now? She had never been so scared in all her life.

Waving to a passing pair of uniforms she showed her warrant card and asked them to move everyone away from the stall. She knew the shopping centre should be evacuated immediately so she ran to a fire alarm point and smashed the glass. Alarm bleeps and recorded messages came over loudspeakers, asking customers to leave in an orderly manner, which, of course, they didn't. The exits were rapidly jammed with panicking shoppers, and the screams and swearing of desperate people drowned out the instructions from the loudspeakers. A pushchair containing a toddler, knocked out of the mother's hands by a group of youths, was grabbed by a security guard, centimetres from the top of a flight of stairs, and the less able shoppers were brushed aside by younger, fitter individuals determined to escape.

Turning back to the bomb, Mel could see that the minute hand, to which a wire was attached, was moving ever closer to a screw fixed to the clock face next to the number twelve. She realised that, when they touched, the bomb would go off. And she had about two minutes left. No time to call in the bomb squad or anyone who knew anything about explosives. She would just have to deal with it herself.

All she knew about bombs was that they needed a timer, an electrical source such as a battery and a detonator to set off the explosive. She couldn't get at the battery or the clock to stop it and she had nothing to cut the wires with. So, could she remove the detonator? Gingerly she pulled on the wires, where they entered the plastic tub through the hole in the lid. Something moved and then stopped. It was too large to come out through the hole. Suppressing the urge to flee or vomit, she slowly eased the lid off the plastic tub, watching the clock all the time. It was filled with white crystals that smelt faintly of bleach. A slim brass tube, with one end crimped shut and the other wrapped in tape, with wires protruding, slid out of the crystals as she lifted the lid. The detonator. And there was less than a minute left. Staring around, she spotted a discarded drinks can. She lifted out the box with the clock and battery and grasped the detonator in the other hand, fearful that it might blow her fingers off any second. She moved as far from the trolley as she dared, slid the detonator into the empty can and covered it with her jacket. Then she ran.

Two seconds later there was a muffled crack and her jacket seemed to pulsate. Shiny shards of aluminium punctured the cloth and wisps of grey smoke seeped around the edges. Mel collapsed on the floor in relief as the two uniforms ran towards her. She could hear multiple sirens, as emergency vehicles approached the centre, and the screams of people still trying to escape, their panic intensifying by the second.

What she needed now, she thought, was a toilet and a very large drink. But she knew she would have to postpone the latter until she came off duty. That was likely to be a long time off. In the meantime, she would help the uniforms secure the scene, give a statement to Jack or DI Thorpe and write up her report. While she was sorting these jobs out in her mind, she didn't notice a spotty white youth, filming her on his phone, until she stood up. She moved towards him but he ran off, dodging through the evacuating shoppers and quickly disappearing. Just another social media vulture, she thought. Posting stuff on the internet in the hope it would make him famous. She shrugged and went to assist the uniforms.

Once the army bomb disposal unit had removed the tub of explosive and declared the area safe, police work could begin. The area was cordoned off into two sections, with an officer at the outer cordon logging anyone entering. Within the inner cordon, suited SOCOs gathered evidence for analysis by contract laboratories. The force fingerprint unit dusted the cleaner's trolley, and as they moved it, Mel saw a book on the floor beneath it.

'What's that?' she called.

A SOCO picked it up and examined it.

'There's Arabic writing on it. Wait a minute. It's the Koran.'

'OK, thanks. Can you try to get prints off it and send it for DNA?'

The SOCO complied and the book was soon in a plastic evidence bag. DI Thorpe arrived shortly after and, with nothing else on the scene needing her attention, Mel set off for the station.

Remembering she had missed her lunch, she pulled a bar of chocolate from her pocket. Despite her lost appetite, she forced herself to eat it, but as she dropped the wrapper into a rubbish bin, she noticed a small black cylinder jammed between the recycling and the general waste bins. It was pointing towards the bomb site, and she realised it was a miniature TV camera and transmitter. So the bastards wanted to film their atrocity, did they? Something to boast about on social media? She photographed the camera in situ with her phone, taking shots from several angles, and called to a SOCO who slipped it into a plastic evidence bag. Returning to the bomb site, she asked a fingerprint technician to dust the bins, although she didn't expect he would find anything useful. Even the stupidest criminals wear gloves.

Mel was met with cheers and whistles when she walked into the incident room. She blushed and tried to hide herself behind her laptop but Jack Vaughan called her over.

'You've done it again, haven't you? Taken a chance.'

She bristled.

'What the fuck was I supposed to have done? If I hadn't spotted the bomb, it would certainly have gone off. It was too late to get everyone far enough away. I don't know how powerful these things are, but dozens of people could have been killed and perhaps hundreds injured. The place was full of families with children, for Christ's sake. I had no choice but to try and defuse it.'

'It's OK.' Jack held up his hands in a placatory gesture. 'I'm not having a go at you. But if you were a cat, you'd have lost at least three of your nine lives in that business last year. Please try not to lose the other six.'

Mel smiled, appeased.

'I'll do my best. But I guess I'd rather go out with a bang, doing something useful, than whimpering my days away in a care home.'

Jack winced at the mangled reference.

'Get yourself a coffee. DI Thorpe wants to see you in her office. You can write up your statement afterwards. Then it's the pub.'

'OK, Jack.'

Emma looked up and smiled when Mel knocked on her half-open door.

'Come in and sit down, lass. I hear you were very brave this lunchtime.'

'I didn't have time to think about being brave, guv. There was no alternative. But saving lives is what we do.'

'Yes, but perhaps not so many all at once. We're really proud of you. How did you know how to tackle it?'

'I just knew that if you could pull the detonator out, the main charge wouldn't go off. I only hoped there wasn't a second one concealed somewhere. Or a booby trap. A lucky guess, I suppose.'

'I think it's the shoppers who were lucky. Anyway, I wanted to congratulate you.'

'Thanks, boss.'

Emma reached into her handbag and pulled out some notes.

'Put these behind the bar and make sure you all get drinks. I'll join you later. I've got a conference call with the ACC and the Chief Super at five but it shouldn't take too long. The White Hart?'

'Yes, guv. Thanks again.'

Chapter Forty

A<small>FTER SHE HAD WRITTEN</small> her statement, and before she went to the pub, Mel knew she had a phone call to make. She picked up her mobile and dialled.

'Hi Dad. It's me. Have you seen the news?'

'Too bloody right I have. What the hell's going on down there?'

'We've got some trouble with racists. They planted a bomb in the shopping centre. I ended up defusing it.'

Mel's tone was nonchalant but inside she knew that her father must have been horrified when he saw the TV reports.

'But you're not a bomb expert. Why didn't you leave it to someone who does that sort of thing?'

'No time. There were just two minutes left on the clock when I found it. We couldn't evacuate or wait for the army. I just crossed my fingers and did the job. Fortunately, there were no booby traps. It was fine.'

'One of these days, love, you're going to give me a heart attack. I can see you had no choice. In all my years of coppering, I never did anything like that. I'm so proud of you.'

'Well, I don't want to make habit of it. I thought I'd better let you know I'm OK. I know you worry.'

'Glad you did. And when are you going to bring young Tom up to meet me?'

'Soon, I promise. But we're really busy. You know how it is, especially after the cuts.'

'I understand. But don't leave it too long, eh.'

'I won't. Gotta go. Love you.'

'Bye, love. Take care.'

<hr/>

'Drinks are on the guv'nor,' called Mel, as the detectives piled into the pub after work. Cheers ensued and ten minutes later they were sitting around tables in a corner, pints in front of them, some distance from the other patrons.

'So you're a heroine now,' teased Martin Rowse, holding up a copy of the evening edition of the *Messenger,* which bore the headline 'Girl Cop Saves Shoppers'.

'Just for the day,' grinned Mel. 'They'll find something else to write about tomorrow. And I'm not so keen on the "Girl" bit. I haven't been a girl since I took my A-levels.'

The others chuckled.

'Yes, but it's good to see the rag saying something nice about us for a change. That Jenny Pike is always slagging us off for one thing or another,' Jack said.

'She still hasn't got her licence back after we did her for drink-driving,' replied Martin. 'She can't have enjoyed riding a pushbike and using the buses over the winter.'

'Serves the bitch right,' someone muttered. The others laughed.

As the others drank with enthusiasm, Mel sipped her beer

slowly. She was mentally and physically exhausted and all she really wanted to do was go home to Tom, have a bath and drink a large glass of wine. She let her gaze roam around the pub, idly wondering if any of the drinkers had been in the shopping centre that lunchtime. She noticed a group of burly, shaven-headed men at the far end of the pub who kept glancing in their direction. Eventually, one of them dragged himself to his feet and lurched over, clutching a half-empty glass of lager, clearly not his first.

'Behind you, Martin,' murmured Mel. 'Could be trouble.'

Martin turned, but before he could stand up the man put his hand on the back of his chair.

'I wanna just say,' began the man, in the carefully articulated phrasing of the seriously drunk, 'that you did good, girl. Stoppin' those terrorist bastards from killin' English people.'

'What do you mean?' asked Mel, puzzled.

'It's you, innit. Boom! Shopping centre. You stopped the ISIS bomb. Brave girl. Showed these fuckers where they can stick their Koran.'

'But I've never...'

'That's all right, Mel,' interjected Emma, who had just appeared. 'I'll explain in a moment. I'll just see this gentleman back to his friends.'

Emma steered the drunk back to his table and shook her head at the barman, indicating that the man shouldn't be served any more drink.

'It's this,' she said, switching on her phone as she sat down.

The screen showed a blurred picture of Mel at the shopping centre with the caption 'White Heroin Girl Foils Muslim Bomb.' It went on to say how hundreds of lives had been saved by a brave English copper who defused an Islamic bomb just in time. The post continued to stir up racial hatred, called for all

Muslims to be deported and continued in the same vein for several paragraphs. It had already received hundreds of likes and approving comments, despite having been up for only two hours.

'Bollocks. Utter bollocks,' said Mel. 'It was Derek Farren and his nasty mates behind it. What makes these idiots think it was ISIS?'

'Because they left a copy of the Koran under the bomb to implicate Muslims.'

'That's crap,' interjected Martin. 'A Muslim wouldn't let the Koran touch the floor, let alone blow it up. It's their holy book. My next door neighbour is a Muslim and we've had some interesting chats.'

'Of course,' replied Emma. 'But these clowns, with the collective intellect of a dog turd, will believe anything, however clumsy the set up. They can't even spell "heroine". We thought Farren and co. would be targeting ethnic minorities, when, in fact, they were setting up the Muslim community and trying to provoke a race riot. DSup Gorman is meeting the local Imam to explain the situation tomorrow. Right, I'm getting myself a drink. Anyone else want one?'

Those who weren't driving accepted but Mel declined and sat back in her seat, thinking. When Emma returned, with a pint of Theakston's for herself and several Scotches for the others, Mel spoke up.

'The camera they left by the bins wouldn't have picked me up. I suppose it was just there to transmit pictures of the scene during and after the explosion. But I was filmed by some spotty little oik who ran off. I didn't recognise him but I'll do an e-fit tomorrow. He wouldn't have seen the Koran so the mention of it clearly came from Farren's crew. If we can find out who posted this shite, we may be able to trace him.'

'IT are working on it now,' replied Emma. 'But it's taking time. And we don't know if the buggers have another bombing planned. I've heard about your whizz-kid partner in cyber-crime. D'you think he would help?'

Mel smiled at the thought of Tom.

'I'll ask him, though it might be better if a request went through official channels.'

'Yes, but that takes time. I'll try, though,' replied Emma.

'I'd better go home, anyway,' said Mel. 'He was shit scared when he heard what happened and he's desperate to have me back in one piece. Thanks for the drink, guv. Night all.'

The others chorused their goodbyes and turned back to their drinks. Jack left at the same time, to take part in a pub quiz with his wife. Mel shivered as she stepped into the chilly night air and walked briskly back to her flat, leaving her car in the station car park. The exercise would do her good and help to clear her head, she thought. She didn't notice the shadowy figure that kept pace with her a few dozen metres behind, turning back only when she reached the flat and fumbled for her keys.

Chapter Forty-One

Day 30, Friday

WEAK SUNSHINE FILTERED through the grime on the incident room windows as the detectives gathered for the morning briefing. One or two of them looked as though they had made a night of it in the pub, and the smell of strong coffee masked the usual odour of sweat and toiletries.

'OK everyone,' began Emma. 'DI Morton has a few things to say about yesterday's bomb.'

'Thank you, Emma. The device was quite crude. Fortunately for DC Cotton, there were no anti-handling features, like the IRA incorporated in many of their bombs, so she was able to disarm it without it going off. It was a smart move to shove the detonator in the can and muffle it. If it had exploded too close to the main charge the shock might have set it off.

'The charge itself was TATP, which was what we expected from the chemicals found in that basement. The tub also contained half a kilo of nails and ball bearings. The sides of the trolley had been weakened with cuts, so the blast would have spread outwards in all directions. Had the device detonated as planned, and given the number of people in the vicinity at the time, deaths could have run into three figures. There would have been hundreds of horrific injuries from flying metal and window glass.'

He paused to let his words sink in. Several detectives went white and one crossed herself.

'Surely Farren didn't make it himself?' queried Jack. 'He's not a chemist. He's just a violent thug.'

'I'm sure you're right. Making TATP is a dangerous process. It needs skill and steady hands. He could have been taught how to carry the device reasonably safely, but that's all.'

'So, do we have any idea who made it?' asked Mel?

Emma replied, 'There's no-one on the list of Farren's associates with any scientific training, as far as we can see, apart from deceased Duncan, that is. Their particular set of skills comprises drinking lager, shouting abuse and putting the boot in. There were no fingerprints on the device, apart from Farren's and Harris', and no recoverable DNA. The person who pushed the cleaning trolley into position hid his or her face and was wearing bulky clothes, but it looks as though it could have been Harris. There was no trace evidence on the Koran.'

'And MI5 have no knowledge of a rogue chemist in the area, either,' added DI Morton.

'Do you think there's another bomb in play, sir?' Karen asked.

'That we don't know. Our scientists looked at the empty bottles in the basement and compared them with the amount of explosive used. It's possible there could be more TATP out there – not as much as the last lot, but they can't be sure. It would depend on the skill of the chemist.'

Jack Vaughan shuddered.

'We do have one possible lead, though,' said Emma. 'There was a small piece of broken glass in the basement with a trace of blood on it. The lab sent a report through this morning. It doesn't belong to Farren or Harris and it isn't on file.'

'Useless, then,' someone called.

'Not quite. We've got a familial match. The donor is closely related to a Barry Marsden. He was convicted of assault seven years ago, when he was eighteen, and, for some reason, only received a conditional discharge.'

'The magistrates must have had a good lunch that day,' whispered Mel to Martin, who grinned in response.

'Right then, Mel,' continued Emma, 'I want you to find Barry Marsden and talk to him about his relatives. I guess we're looking at brothers, sisters, parents, maybe cousins. If he has any children, they'll still be pre-teens so we can rule them out. The rest of you, please keep looking for the suspects. You know the drill. Oh, Martin, can you try and find out where the chemicals came from? There's a list on the whiteboard with the manufacturers' names. The batch numbers seem to have been scratched out.'

'Will do, guv. By the way, we've traced Farren's brother, courtesy of the Met. Another charming specimen. He lives in London and said he hasn't seen his brother since last spring. He was released from the Scrubs yesterday, after doing six months for aggravated burglary. He's solidly alibied for what's been happening down here.'

'Useful to know. Thank you everyone. Report developments to me as soon as they happen. And don't forget to keep DS Wilson in the loop.'

The officers and civilian staff dispersed to their desks, each one looking thoughtful, and an air of quiet industry settled over the room.

Chapter Forty-Two

'Guv. I've got something on Barry Marsden,' said Mel, standing outside Emma's office.

'Well, come in, lass. Spit it out.'

'It's not good news, I'm afraid. He's dead.'

'How?'

'He was in the army and died in an IED explosion in Afghanistan. There was a piece in the *Messenger* – local hero killed by ISIS bomb. They printed a photo of him in his uniform. It was his first tour overseas and, looking at the dates, it was a month after his conviction for assault.

'Looks like that's why he got off with a conditional discharge. He was due to go out there and the bench didn't want to ruin his career. They didn't do him any favours, did they?'

'S'pose not. Anyway, there's more. His mother died shortly afterwards but his father, Philip, is still alive. And he's a chemistry lecturer at the local college. He was also in the army, some years previously. There's a sister, but she's married and lives in Exeter, so the father looks like the best lead.'

'Well, I think we need a serious talk with Philip Marsden. We've got grounds for arrest but I'd like to do this quietly. Let's pick him up when he finishes work. Phone the college and see what time he leaves. And get his car number and address in case we miss him. Also, Afghanistan keeps coming up. Can you find out if any of these people served together?'

'OK, boss. Who do you want to pick up Marsden?'

'You can do the honours since you did the work. Well done, by the way. Take Martin and let Jack know.'

'Should we have armed backup?'

'I'll ask for a unit to tactically relocate to the area, just in case. It shouldn't be necessary. He's a lecturer, not a commando. Good luck.'

Philip Marsden looked up from his desk in the chemistry laboratory as two students approached. They were not the brightest in the group but they worked hard and he had high hopes that they would achieve good enough A-level grades to get into university.

'How can I help?' he asked the two girls.

'It's the transition metals, Mr Marsden. We still don't get why they form coloured compounds. We know you tried to explain, but some lads behind us were whispering and we didn't catch it.'

'OK. It is a bit tricky. I'll send you a link to a really useful animated video on this site that explains it. Take a look and come back to me with any questions. All right?'

'Yes, thank you, Mr Marsden,' one of the girls replied, while the other smiled her appreciation.

As they left, Marsden glanced at the clock on the wall.

Time to pack up and go. Back to the emptiness of his flat with nothing but marking, a ready meal and tedious television to look forward to. He missed his wife and son so much. He had had such high hopes for his son's career, and his wife had been his soulmate for nearly thirty years. Those murdering bastards had taken them away from him, directly and indirectly, and he had yearned for payback ever since.

He was furious at those idiots for screwing up. Perhaps he should have done the job himself, but it was a long time since he'd been a man of action. What if they talked? He couldn't stand the thought of prison, although he was, effectively, in a prison of his own grief already. He had a cottage in the country he could escape to, at least for a while, and a means of holding off the police if they came for him. He fingered the jar in his pocket as he switched off the lights and left the lab, a feeling of deep foreboding added to his melancholy.

Mel drove the unmarked police car into the college car park, jolting as they crossed the speed bumps, and parked just inside the entrance.

'Five o'clock, you said he left, didn't you?' asked Martin.

'Yep. And it's five past. Look – that's him. The college secretary emailed me the photo on his ID. And there's his car. We're on.'

The two officers walked casually over to the bespectacled man of about fifty-five, who was approaching a Ford Fiesta, car keys in his hand.

'Mr Marsden?' called Mel. 'Can we have chat? We're from the police.'

'Ah. Yes,' he replied. 'The office said you were asking for me. What's this about?'

Mel silently cursed the secretary. This was supposed to have been an unannounced visit.

'It's related to the death of your son. I'm very sorry for your loss.'

'But those bastards killed him seven years ago. Why do you need to discuss it now?'

'I'm afraid something's come up. We'd like to talk to you at the police station, if you don't mind. You're not under arrest but it is important we talk.'

'Well, if it's really necessary. Just let me put my briefcase in the car.'

'That's all right, sir,' said Martin. 'I'll hold it for you.'

Marsden looked nervous, then a resolute expression spread across his face. He shoved the briefcase at Martin and reached into the pocket of his overcoat. His hand came out holding a jam jar. White crystals were just visible, glittering under the car park lights. Mel and Martin recoiled, suspecting that the jar's contents were lethal.

'I'm sorry. I'm not going with you. I know why you're here. Those idiots were supposed to blow up the mosque but tried to be clever.'

Mel and Martin backed off slowly and let Marsden get into his car, reaching for their radios simultaneously. They watched as he put the jar on the seat, closed the door and accelerated towards the gate, clearly panicking and driving erratically.

'Get down,' shouted Martin, pulling Mel to the ground. 'Speed bumps.'

The Fiesta hit the speed bumps at around thirty miles an hour. The jar flew off the seat and hit the floor. A fearsome explosion echoed around the car park and a plume of glass and blood shot out of the shattered offside window. The windscreen was catapulted three metres down the road and the car began to burn as ruptured fuel lines spilled their contents onto ignited plastic. Screams from staff and the few remaining students echoed round the car park, complemented by the blare of car alarms, while Mel and Martin gingerly picked themselves up.

'Oh fuck. So much for a quiet collar,' cursed Mel, brushing glass fragments from her hair.

'Oh fuck,' echoed Martin, reaching for his phone.

Then the car's petrol tank exploded.

The detectives ushered college staff and students away from the scene, cordoning it off with blue and white tape. The fire and rescue service arrived shortly afterwards and extinguished the flames from the burning car. Drivers were busily photographing the damage caused to their vehicles by flying debris, but many had to make their way home by other means, their vehicles retained in the car park for the SOCOs to process. Insurance claims were likely to be astronomical.

'Another of your lives lost, was it?'

Jack Vaughan approached as Mel was sitting in the damaged police car, eating a bar of chocolate to calm her nerves. She could only just hear him over the ringing in her ears.'

'Not really. We weren't going to rush him. Not with a bomb in his hand. Even I'm not that crazy.'

'Glad to hear it, Mel. Glad to hear it. Now go home, pour

yourself a drink, and write your report up in the morning. The DI will want to see you first thing.'

Mel smiled and thought longingly about curling up with Tom in front of a film. But not one with explosions in it.

Chapter Forty-Three

Day 33, Monday

'LET'S SUM UP, SHALL WE?' Detective Superintendent Gorman addressed DCI Gale and DI Emma Thorpe as they sat round the conference table with DI Steve Morton.

'A major incident has been averted, thanks to a brave and quick-thinking DC. The chemist behind the bomb is dead, killed by his own explosives, and, as far as we know, there is no more explosive out there and no means of anyone making more, since the lab has been closed down. Correct so far?'

'That's right, sir' replied DI Morton. We believe Mexton's safe from these particular terrorists, at least for the time being.'

'On the other hand,' continued DSup Gorman, 'our prime suspects are still at large. We still have to find Duncan Bennett's murderer and, if possible, take down the drugs gang. There is also the ongoing threat to public order posed by these far-right extremists, who will be all the keener to stir up racial tension now their plot to frame the Muslim community has failed.'

'Agreed,' said DCI Gale. The others nodded their assent.

'So how do you see SO15 and the security services being involved from now on, DI Morton?'

'I think what's needed now is normal policing, sir. You've clearly got a competent team of officers here and I'm more than happy to leave things in your hands. My guv'nor agrees. I'd like to leave DS Wilson with you, in case anything sensitive comes up. I'm sure you can use an extra pair of hands.'

Emma smiled at this.

'DS Wilson will keep me informed and I'll pass anything relevant on to Five. So that's me done, I think. Thank you for your efforts. And please pass on my appreciation to DC Cotton. I haven't had a chance to thank her personally, but she was really impressive.'

Morton stood up, shook hands with the others and left the room. For the rest of the morning the senior officers discussed how the case would proceed and what resources could be made available.

'We need another press conference,' said DSup Gorman. 'The public needs to be reassured that the threat is over. Can you do that, Fiona?'

'I will, of course,' replied DCI Gale. 'But as it's Emma's team that worked so hard, shouldn't she get the chance to break the good news?'

'I'm happy to, sir,' said Emma, now well aware of DCI Gale's antipathy towards the press.

'Good. One o'clock then. I'll inform the Press Office.'

DSup Gorman left the room and DCI Gale smiled gratefully at Emma.

'So, it's back to how we were before. You'll remain SIO and I'll keep a hands-off watching brief. Don't hesitate to come to me if you need anything.'

'Yes. ma'am. Thank you. I'll call the troops together and let them know what's happening.'

―――――――

'Right, settle down everyone.' Emma tapped her pen on a coffee mug to get the team's attention.

'First of all, the Super has asked me to convey his thanks for all your hard work on the bomb threat. There's a few loose ends to tie up. First of all, Marsden. It seems he became so embittered at the loss of his son in Afghanistan that he developed a pathological hatred of Muslims. He wasn't a man of action himself, any more, but he offered his services as a bomb maker to the local racist nutters. He'd worked on bomb disposal in Northern Ireland for a while so he knew how these devices worked. From what Mel and Martin said, he wanted them to blow up a mosque but they decided it would be better to frame the Muslim community.'

'I've been wondering about that,' interjected Mel. 'Isn't that a bit subtle for Derek Farren? By all accounts, he's thick as pigshit and thinks with his fists.'

'Are you suggesting someone else is behind it? SO15 are content that we've identified those responsible.'

DS Wilson, sitting next to Emma, nodded.

'I'm not sure,' replied Mel. 'It doesn't sit quite right. Perhaps I'm overthinking. He might be bright enough.'

'Hmmm. I'll keep an open mind and we'll see what turns up. Hopefully, we'll be able to question Farren and his mates soon and he may let something slip. Anyway, did you get anywhere with the chemicals, Martin?'

'Yes, guv. The hydrogen peroxide is used to add oxygen to polluted rivers and lakes in an emergency. It was stolen from a shed near the Thames in Berkshire, a few months ago. The theft was reported to the Home Office but the information never reached us, though I suppose it wouldn't as it's not on our patch. Marsden stole some nitric acid from the college, but as he's head of chemistry there, he covered it up easily. He also ordered bottles of acetone on the school's account that never reached the stores. I asked the technician to check invoices and stock, and the shortfall is accounted for by the empty bottles we found in the basement.'

'Thanks, Martin. How about the kid who filmed you at the scene, Mel?'

'I got some help from Tom. He used his lunch hour to track down the IP address of the computer that uploaded the file. It's an internet cafe in the centre of Mexton. We know it was posted around half past three in the afternoon but they don't keep records of who uses the machines, and there's no CCTV. Uniform showed the proprietor the e-fit I provided and he remembered a kid of about seventeen who rushed in and paid cash for a half hour session.'

'Have we put a name to the face?'

'Not yet, but I'm going through footage of racial disturbances to see if it crops up. We may get a clearer picture of him, which we could use in an appeal if necessary.'

'Good thinking. Keep looking. We've still got to find Farren and Harris, so keep on them please. I've got a press conference this lunchtime and we'll put out another appeal, with their mug shots.

Emma changed the subject.

'That's enough on the bombing for the moment. We have two other priorities. Finding Duncan Bennett's killer and breaking up the drugs racket. Where have we got with these, Jack?'

'Not very far, boss, for obvious reasons. Mel had an unfortunate encounter with a lorry driver, parked near a Maybrick and Cream van in a motorway services, when she was on her day's leave. It confirmed that something dodgy was going on.'

Emma raised her eyebrows but said nothing.

'Did you give the Border Force the reg number?' continued Jack.

'Not yet. I'll do it this afternoon.'

'No. Hold off on that,' Emma said, thoughtfully. 'I'll have a chat with DS Palmer and see if we can use it ourselves. When's my appointment with the MP, Addy?'

'Tomorrow at ten,' replied Addy.

'Good. And you can come with me. Anything more on the Bennett murder?'

'Still waiting for forensics on the concrete, boss,' replied Jack. 'And the suspects have gone to ground. It's only a matter of time before one of them shows themself.'

'Well, we know Farren was at the murder scene,' said Emma, 'so we'll talk to him about that as well. When we find him. One more thing. We've got the results of Kominski's PM. Shot once in the head with a 9mm round. He was a serious cocaine user, judging by the state of his nose. We also found cocaine in his flat, so we can assume the gang kept him sweet with supplies of marching powder. We found nothing political there, so his links with them are solely the drug. His family in Wroclaw is being notified.'

'Right, I've a press conference to prepare for. Thanks, everybody. Meet up again tomorrow morning.'

After an uneventful press conference at which, for a change, Jenny Pike was not slagging off the police, Emma spent half the afternoon preparing for a crucial meeting. She was determined to overcome DCI Gale's reluctance to raid the drugs gang and knew she would need to have all her arguments bulletproof. Her fingers crossed, and feeling more than slightly nervous, she stepped into the video conference room where her senior colleagues were waiting.

Chapter Forty-Four

'So, WE CAN REALLY DO IT?' Emma beamed excitedly at the conclusion of the two-hour meeting. Officers from the drugs squad, the Border Force and the National Crime Agency had conferred with Mexton CID, in person and via videolink, to work out how they could organise a raid, in Mexton rather than Hampshire.

'Yes, we can,' replied DCI Gale. 'All we need is an officer with an HGV licence who can put on a convincing Belgian accent. Preferably one who isn't local, in case he's recognised. We'll have the team ready and our European colleagues will let us know when the truck is on the move. We've got two days to put this together. Wednesday seems to be the day they do it.'

'I'll arrange the RIPA authorisations,' said DSup Gorman, 'and leave you to find the driver. Thank you, everyone.'

Emma returned to her office, her head buzzing. Where could she find an HGV driver? Then she remembered. A former colleague in Sheffield used to drive a lorry before a major accident on the M1 prompted him to join the police, determined to improve driving standards. Jaded by the daily carnage, and driver stupidity, he later transferred to CID from traffic. She picked up her phone and dialled Sheffield central police station, from memory.

'DS Knowles, please.'

'CID.' The familiar voice at the end of the line brought back memories.

'Hiya Grassy. How're you doing, lad? It's Emma Thorpe.'

'Blimey, it's ET. Are you calling home? Missing us up here and yearning for our balmy climate?'

Emma chuckled.

'I'm after a favour. Do you still have your HGV licence?'

'Yeah. I never let it lapse. Why? Do you need a removals van?'

'No, I want you to drive something a bit bigger. An op we've got running down here. Can your guv'nor spare you for a couple of days?'

'I should think so, if you ask him nicely. It's DCI Outhwaite. He was a DI when you left. He's OK.'

'Right. I'll have a word with him when we've finished. Can you pack some stuff and get down here tonight? You can stay with me and Mike. Oh, and practise your Belgian accent, will you?'

'Bien sûr,' he replied, although it sounded like 'Ben shore.'

'That's awful.' Emma laughed and gave him her address before she rang off, looking forward to seeing an old colleague.

With permission granted for DS Knowles to help, she phoned her husband to alert him to the unexpected guest. She got herself a coffee and called a few select members of her team together.

'OK, folks,' she began, once they had settled down. 'We're running a sting on the drugs gang, working with several other agencies. On Wednesday we expect there'll be another drugs run, from Belgium via France and through the channel tunnel. We have the reg number of the Belgian HGV Mel spotted, and the Border Force will intercept it at Folkestone. We're assuming the same vehicle is used each time. Reasonable, given that many drivers stick to the same truck and personalise it. If there are drugs on board, we'll arrest the driver and put surveillance devices in some of the boxes. The bugs will broadcast a signal we can track and also a video feed when the boxes are opened. An old colleague of mine, from up north, will drive the truck to the service station and hand over the goods as usual. We'll track them to Mexton, and when the recipients open the boxes, we've got them. They won't be able to pretend they didn't know what was in them. So, jobs. Addy – I want you to track the Maybrick and Cream van from Mexton to the services and back again using ANPR. Martin, I want you to track the devices in the load, cross-checking with Addy in case they split the consignment.

'Assuming the van comes back to the Maybrick and Cream warehouse, we'll raid it there once they open the boxes. If they go somewhere else, we'll have to improvise. Mel, you can have the pleasure of joining the strike team. Armed officers will go in first, though, since firearms may be involved. Any questions?'

'Would it be worth tracking the packages to the next dealers down the line?' asked Jack.

'The drugs squad thinks not. There are probably too many. Anyway, they'll have spotted the bugs by then. But if the motorcyclists arrive before we hit them, we may get them as well. Oh, and I must emphasise, no-one talks about this outside the room. We'll bring in other people as and when we need them.

'OK. That's Wednesday sorted for the moment. There'll be further briefings nearer the time. Any progress to report on your other tasks?'

'There's something, boss,' said Martin. 'We've had a few suggestions as to the identity of the kid who filmed Mel. A Jason Finney, aged 17, seems the most likely. He's got previous for shoplifting and nicking pushbikes. Nothing violent though. Lives in Priestley House on the Eastside with his mum, a smackhead. Dad's inside, doing five for dealing and GBH. Lovely family.'

'OK. Let's pick him up and have a chat. Jack, can you organise an arrest? Get Mel to look at his mug shot first, to confirm identity. Take plenty of uniform and make sure you seize any phones on the premises. Perhaps he'll lead us to Harris or know where Farren was living.'

'Yes, guv. Sparrowfart tomorrow?'

'Aye. And organise an appropriate adult in case his mum's not fit to join us.'

As the team returned to their desks Emma walked back to her office, her brow furrowed in thought. Being involved in a major op like this one was challenging but exciting. She knew she and her team would only be a part of it, but a success would certainly help her standing in Mexton. No-one was hostile to her; on the contrary, she had been made welcome, but she felt she still had to prove herself. And this was an opportunity she couldn't afford to miss.

'Mike, this is Gerry Knowles, known as Grassy, for obvious reasons. Gerry, this is Mike.'

Emma's husband looked puzzled, as he shook hands with the slim fair-haired detective, until the penny dropped.

'Pleased to meet you. I gather you worked with Emma in Sheffield.'

'That's right. Nice to meet you, too. We had some great times up there together. We were all sorry when she decided to move south. Still, Sheffield's loss, Mexton's gain. Thanks for putting me up, by the way.'

'No problem. Fancy a beer?'

'You bet. It was a thirsty drive.'

Mike retrieved three bottles of Theakston's Old Peculier from the pantry and poured their contents into pint glasses.

'Cheers!'

The others echoed his toast and they sat sipping the ale until their takeaway meal arrived.

'Ahhh,' sighed Grassy. 'This stuff reminds me of the time when we were staking out the cemetery off Loxley Road. We were both DCs. We'd knocked off and were having a beer when we got the call to come back in. A notorious pervert had been spotted and they needed everyone available. We'd only had a pint each, so we were fit for duty, but it was all of a rush and we didn't have time for a pee. An hour later, while we were sitting in the car waiting for the Sheffield Flasher to make his appearance, you were desperate. So you nipped behind a gravestone and you'd just got your...'

'Food's here,' interrupted Emma as the doorbell rang, preventing any embarrassing revelations. 'Perhaps continue this later?'

Mike looked intrigued and slightly disappointed. Grassy grinned.

The rest of the evening passed pleasantly, with the detectives swapping war stories, both humorous and grim, many of which were new to Mike. He retired early, looking somewhat overwhelmed, leaving Emma to reminisce with her ex-colleague until late.

'OK, Grassy. Serious for a moment. Are you OK with this gig?'

'Course. It'd be good to drive a truck again. It might take me a little while to get used to it, though. They've got more sophisticated since I last took the wheel. But a few turns round the car park and I'll be fine. And I can pose as a Belgian. We've holidayed in Bruges a couple of times, so that'll be no problem. As long as I know where I'm supposed to have come from, in case anyone asks.'

'Yeah. We can find that out. I'm really grateful for this, Grassy.'

'Glad to help. Reminds me of the old days.'

There was something wistful in his eyes that Emma preferred not to think about.

Chapter Forty-Five

MEL AND TOM had just finished their evening meal in front of the television, and Robbie was in the shower, when the doorbell rang.

'I'll get it,' said Mel. 'I need some more water anyway.'

She got up and opened the door on the newly installed chain. She recognised the caller instantly. Before she could push the door shut, it burst open, ripping the chain out of the jamb and knocking her to the floor. Derek Farren charged in, a leer on his face and a Walther P38 semi-automatic in his hand.

'Got you, you bitch.'

Mel lay on the floor groaning and Tom stood up. Farren glared at him.

'Stay where you are, twat. Or I'll drill you now.'

Tom held up his hands in a placatory gesture and moved towards the gunman.

'I said stay,' snarled Farren, aiming the weapon over Tom's shoulder. He fired and hit a framed photo of Mel and Tom receiving commendations. The glass exploded, the 9mm bullet cratering the wall behind it.

Mel staggered to her feet and faced the gunman, moving towards the other side of the room from Tom. Her face was flushed and her pulse raced but, furious as she was, she knew she shouldn't antagonise her attacker.

'Come on, Derek.' She kept her voice as calm as she could. 'Threatening police officers is a really bad idea. Everyone's looking for you. And with a firearm involved it's bound to end badly for you.'

'See, that's where you're wrong, bitch. The boss said to teach you a lesson. You fucked up our plan, you meddling cow. You're a traitor. So, you're gonna pay. And your boyfriend is a bonus.'

Mel trembled, mentally searching the room for a possible weapon she could use against Farren. But there was nothing she could reach in time. Tom remained impassive.

'Put the gun down and leave,' he said. 'You've one chance to escape. The guy upstairs will have heard the shot and I estimate you've got seven minutes before a firearms unit arrives.'

'Plenty of time to kill both of you fuckers. And online it'll say that a bloke in one of them Muslim frocks was seen running away.'

'Don't be stupid. No-one will believe you.'

'Enough will. And you won't be saying anything different. So, who's first?'

He levelled the pistol at Mel and grinned venomously. As his finger tightened on the trigger a silver laptop flew across the room, a two thousand quid frisbee, and hit him on the side of the head. He staggered but remained upright. The pistol fired, narrowly missing Mel and shattering a mirror. Before he could aim again, Tom's foot lashed out in a Tae Kwan Do strike and caught him in the groin. Farren doubled over in agony and dropped the weapon, clutching at his crushed testicles. His

bulky frame collapsed and Mel and Tom piled on top of him. He bucked and thrashed until Tom got his arm around his neck and put him in a chokehold, and Mel sat on his legs.

Mel looked up to see a stark-naked Robbie, dripping from the shower, the expression on his face a mixture of excitement and fear.

'I got him. I got him.' Then his face fell. 'But what about my laptop?'

'Never mind that, Robbie,' she said. 'In the drawer of the hall table there's a pair of handcuffs. Chuck them over, would you? And then you might want to put some clothes on. Well done, mate. Well done.'

With Farren handcuffed and Tom standing over him, his foot menacingly close to the thug's groin, Mel informed him he was under arrest and recited the caution in case he let slip anything they could use in evidence. Farren said nothing. Ten minutes later two marked police cars arrived, blues and twos going, followed by Jack Vaughan in his own vehicle. Farren was bundled into a police car, kicking and cursing all the time, while an AFO made the weapon safe and boxed it up for removal to the ballistics lab. When the commotion had died down, Mel, Tom and Robbie started on a bottle of brandy.

'How many lives is it now, Mel?' Jack asked.

'Oh, come on, Jack. It wasn't my fault this time.'

'Yeah. I know. Who's this?'

He turned to look at Robbie, who, now dressed, was tinkering anxiously with his laptop.

'That's Robbie. He's a friend who's staying with us. He saved our lives by flinging his laptop at Farren.'

Robbie smiled uncertainly and turned back to his computer.

'OK you two,' said Jack. 'There's no point treating this as a

crime scene, as we know what happened and we've got the attacker. I'll get a SOCO to dig the bullets out of the wall. We'll ask NABIS to compare the weapon with the bullet that killed Anton Kominski. I wouldn't be surprised to find they match. If so, we may have Farren for Kominski's murder as well.'

'Even if they match, we can't prove he killed Kominski, though, can we?' observed Mel. 'It doesn't mean he fired the weapon.'

'True, but we'll look for phone evidence, vehicle movements and other circumstantial stuff. We may be able to build a strong enough case to satisfy the CPS. You never know. Anyway, you'll need to provide full statements in the morning. You too, Robbie. And heartfelt thanks to you. We don't want to lose these guys.' He smiled.

After Jack had left, and with a measure of calm restored, Mel and Tom hugged Robbie.

'We owe you big time, mate,' said Tom. 'More than we can say.'

''S OK,' replied Robbie, looking slightly embarrassed. 'By the way, why didn't you kick the gun out of his hand like they do in the movies? You did karate or something on him, didn't you?'

'Yeah. Tae Kwan Do, in fact. I needed the distraction you provided before I could do anything. And someone once said "Never go for the gun or knife hand". It's a small, moving target.'

''Oh. Who was that?'

'Modesty Blaise.'

'Who?'

'A character in a series of books I used to read. But it's abso-

lutely true. Now, we're knackered and need to go to bed, though I doubt we'll sleep much. Thanks again Robbie. Good night.'

Chapter Forty-Six

Day 34, Tuesday

THE EARLY HINTS of spring that appeared in other parts of Mexton seemed to have bypassed the Eastside. Where buds were forming on trees elsewhere in the town, those on the estate that had not been torn down, for bonfires or weapons, seemed to be refusing to recognise the season, perhaps in protest at their dismal surroundings. Jack and six uniforms, clad in stab vests and shivering as the dawn struggled to brighten the grey, stained concrete of Priestley House, crept steadily towards the building. No-one noticed their approach, many of the residents having only recently gone to bed after a busy night's thieving, fighting, dealing and scoring.

'Watch out for needles, lads,' called Jack. 'And don't step in any pools of liquid.'

'As if we didn't know,' muttered one PC, all too familiar with the conditions in Priestley House.

The officers climbed the stairs to the first floor and tapped on the door of number twelve.

After repeated knocking produced no response, PC Halligan pushed open the letterbox and shouted, 'Police. Open up.'

The blade of a kitchen knife flashed through the opening, narrowly missing his nose.

'In,' shouted Jack, and Halligan used the Big Door Key to smash open the door.

A gaunt woman in a filthy dressing gown dropped the knife and fell to the floor as the door came off its hinges. She staggered to her feet cursing.

'What the fuck do you lot want?' she yelled. 'And who's gonna fix my fuckin' door?'

'Calm down, Mrs. Finney,' said Jack, trying in vain to defuse the situation. 'We just want a word with your Jason.'

'Can't you bastards leave 'im alone? Always on 'is case you are.'

'We need to speak to him about a serious offence. I'm not at liberty to say any more, I'm afraid. So where is he?'

'Not 'ere.'

'What is it, Mum?' came a tremulous voice from a room at the back of the flat.

'The filth. What you been up to now?'

'Nothin'. Honest. Who do they want?'

'Honest,' scoffed Jack. 'You're as honest as the day is square. I'm asking you to come with us voluntarily, but if you don't, we'll have to arrest you. Mrs Finney, are you prepared to come along as an appropriate adult, since Jason's under eighteen?'

'I ain't going near no fuckin' police station. They give me the creeps.'

'Very well. We'll find someone else.' As Jack turned away a thought struck him.

'What did you mean when you asked who we wanted, Jason?'

'Nothin'.' Jason paled, his acne standing out like red traffic lights, and started to shake.

'Is there anyone else in there who we might want to talk to?'

'No. Course not. Just me.'

'All right, but I think we'll take a look while you get your coat. Oh, and we have authority to seize any mobile phones on the premises. Here's the search warrant.'

Jason and his mother ignored the piece of paper as the officers piled in. A quick search turned up a dozen mobile phones, of various ages, but no other humans. They were just about to leave when PC Halligan heard a muffled sneeze from the main bedroom. It still seemed empty, but when he pulled a filthy mattress off the bed, a skinny figure leapt out of the hollowed-out divan, brandishing a knife wildly. Halligan's baton cracked across the man's forearm, sending the knife flying and prompting a torrent of 'fucks'.

'Look who's been playing hide and seek, Sarge,' called Halligan. 'It's our friend Mr Harris.'

'We want a word with you, Michael,' grinned Jack. 'And I'm arresting you for assaulting a police officer in the course of his duty.'

'But I never touched him, you bastard.'

'It doesn't matter. Trying counts as attempted ABH. And if you had injured him seriously, you'd be looking at GBH. So shut the fuck up and come along.'

A muttering Harris, still nursing his aching arm, was hand-cuffed and escorted out of the flat.

'Who's gonna look after me and get me my gear?' shouted Mrs Finney. 'And what about my door?'

'We'll put in an emergency call to Social Services,' said Jack. 'But they probably won't help you score.'

Cries of 'bastards', 'filth' and other insults followed them as they led Jason and Harris down the stairs and into the cars.

Chapter Forty-Seven

AT THE STATION, Michael Harris was booked into custody and left in a cell to reflect on his fate. Jason Finney was put in an interview room and offered tea, pending the arrival of Sharon Bowles, a social worker who had agreed to act as the appropriate adult. When the duty solicitor arrived, an hour later, Karen joined them.

'Jason,' began Mel, the caution having been delivered by Karen and introductions made for the recording. 'Why were you filming me in the shopping centre where the bomb was?'

'Cos you're a fit bird, innit?'

'Nice of you to say so, Jason, but I don't believe it. I don't know what your solicitor has told you, and, of course, it's confidential, but there is such a thing as conspiracy to commit a terrorist act, which can mean twenty-five years. And you don't even have to handle the bomb or the explosives.'

Jason's cocky demeanour faded away and he looked petrified.

'Is she right?' He glared at the solicitor, who simply nodded.

'But I never did nothin'. Mickey said to go and film the foreign food stall and send the pictures to 'im live, like. Then I 'ad to put them on the internet. He gave me the phone to do it. He said their food was polluting white people and 'e wanted to see who was buyin' it, so's he could 'ave a word with them. Persuade them not to or summink. He gave me fifty quid.'

'So you didn't know about the bomb?'

'No. I never. Honest.'

'If the bomb had gone off, Jason, it would have almost certainly killed you at that distance. You would never have spent the fifty quid.'

Jason went white and threw up over the table. After he had been cleaned up, and spent time with the solicitor, the interview resumed in a different room.

'Before we start, Jason, we are not charging you with conspiracy. I believe you,' Mel reassured him. 'But it's essential you tell us everything you know.'

OK. I ain't a grass but I don't owe these bastards anythin'. An' it looks like you saved my life. Ta.'

'That's OK. So how did you know Michael Harris?'

''E gets gear for my mum sometimes. 'E used to give her one, until she started to look too old and 'e lost interest. I went with 'im to a couple of meetings where they said we was bein' taken over by immigrants and foreigners. I sort of agreed with 'im. I'm English and proud of it.'

He pushed out his bony chest and attempted to look patriotic. If this grotty specimen of racist English manhood was the future, thought Mel, then heaven help us. She said nothing.

'Anyway. Mickey said I could help the cause. I did a bit of tagging on some walls. "Britain first, Polish go home", that sort of thing. Then he offered me fifty quid to do the filming, like I said. I never knew nothin' about bombs, I swear.'

Jason began to sob and Sharon asked him if he wanted to take a break, looking pointedly at Mel.

'No. It's all right. I don't know nothin' more.'

'OK, Jason. You can go in a minute. We may want to talk to you about those phones but they're not important at the moment. One last thing: do you know where Michael Harris and Derek Farren live?'

Jason flinched at the mention of Farren's name, saying only that Harris had been squatting somewhere on the Eastside and he thought Farren had a bedsit near the High Street, which he'd never visited.

'OK. Thanks, Jason. I'm sorry this has been so scary for you. Would you like a lift home?'

'No thanks. I can't be seen getting out of a cop car on the Eastside. I remember what 'appened to Billy Peel.'

Mel recalled Billy's slashed body draped over a swing in a playground, killed because somebody mistakenly thought he was a grass.

'It's all right, Detective Constable,' said Sharon. 'I'll drop him nearby on my way home.'

Mel nodded her thanks and guided the three individuals to reception.

'Thanks, again, Jason,' she said. 'I think you've been used by some unscrupulous people. You might want to choose your mates a bit more carefully in future.'

Jason shrugged. 'Where I live, you don't get much choice.'

'The callous shits,' seethed Mel, as she reported back to Jack. 'And if you say calm down, dear, I'll bloody well deck you.'

Jack smiled. 'I would never say that to you. Or to anyone else, for that matter. So what's got to you?'

'They set him up. They gave him fifty quid to live stream the bomb going off, knowing he'd be killed. What type of scum does that?'

Jack thought for a bit.

'I've a nasty feeling about this. You said Farren mentioned "the boss". There's clearly someone pulling the strings, co-ordinating things. We know who made the bomb but Farren's too thick to plan this all out. He might have come up with the crude attempt to frame the Muslim community but the rest of it is way beyond him. I'll ask the guv'nor if we can have a brainstorming session, or whatever it's called now. We need everyone's ideas, however daft.'

'What about the counter-terrorism lot?'

'We should involve them, I know. But they can be as tight as a frog's fanny when it comes to sharing info. I'll see what the DI says. It sounds as though you handled that interview well. No complaints from the solicitor, anyway.'

'I know. I don't think he did much, in truth. He must have realised Jason wasn't really involved and going "No comment" would only have made things worse.'

'Hmm. Makes a change. Some of them collect a fee for telling a suspect to shut up, which they would have done anyway.'

'How about Harris?'

'He's going "No comment" for the moment. We're pretty sure he's the one who placed the bomb, but we've got no real evidence.'

'Some DNA would be useful.'

Yeah. Wouldn't it? We've got his phone, though, and we can track it. Trouble is, we can only place him at the shopping centre, not where he was within it. He'll claim he was going to buy a burger or trainers or something.'

'So there's nothing actually placing him at the scene?'

'Not as far as I know. But the SOCOs were getting excited about a hi-vis jacket and a baseball cap a PC found in a bin inside the shopping centre car park. Could be a link, if they can process it in time.'

Chapter Forty-Eight

FOR MUCH OF THE MORNING, Tom and Mel were occupied with giving formal statements. Derek Farren, after the forensic physician had declared him fit to be detained, had been locked up overnight and was left to stew in a cell until after lunch, when his solicitor was summoned. After a brief consultation, the solicitor indicated that his client was ready to be questioned. Martin and Jack conducted the interview, which proved singularly unproductive. To every question, Farren replied with his own version of 'No comment', namely, 'Fuck off'.

After an hour, the two detectives halted the interview, sent Farren back to his cell and conferred.

'So what have we got, Jack? Will the CPS run with the terror charges, do you think?' Emma had been watching the interview on a video screen.

'We've got his fingerprints from the basement, which shows he was there,' Jack replied. 'We also got some prints on a couple of twenty pound notes found in Marsden's flat. Those in Marsden's wallet were largely melted, but parts of the serial numbers were visible and they were in the same sequence. We still don't know where Farren has been staying, so we can't look for traces of explosives on his clothing. There was nothing on the things he was wearing when he came in, apart from gunshot residue, which is totally different. I don't think it's enough, unless we can place him at the scene. There's some CCTV from the mall, but the guy pushing the trolley doesn't look like him.'

'We've got motive, though. His posts on social media, for a start.'

'Yeah. There's that,' Jack agreed. 'But thousands of other far-right arseholes have the same motive and post the same shite.' Emma nodded her agreement.

'What about the stolen hydrogen peroxide?' she asked. 'Was there any evidence at the break-in?'

'I'll check with Thames Valley. If there's anything to suggest he was involved in the theft, we might be able to get him on conspiracy.'

'One other thing. I noticed he was constantly fiddling with a scar on his hand. Did you see it?'

'Yes. Looks like a badly healed dog bite. A nasty one.'

'OK. Thanks, Jack. I'll talk to DCI Gale and the CPS. I've an appointment with the MP now. We'll all meet up at two.'

Emma walked briskly back to her office, wondering how she would tackle the MP. She hadn't been particularly political in the past, even though the repercussions of the miners' strike were still being felt in Yorkshire while she was a child. Since austerity, however, she had become much more aware of inequality and knew she would have to keep her feelings in check when talking to him. But she was a professional and could overlay her native bluntness with diplomacy and charm.

'Good morning, Detective Inspector.'

Maxwell Arden's voice oozed an oily charm and his hand-shake, though firm, was damp. His well-cut suit didn't quite hide the evidence of substantial subsidised meals in the House of Commons plus, no doubt, expensive dining elsewhere. A slight flicker of distaste crossed his face when he saw DC Adeyemo.

'How can I help the police?'

Emma looked around his comfortable office. Photos of the Prime Minister, Margaret Thatcher and the Queen adorned the walls, while a whisky decanter and several cut-glass tumblers stood on a side table. A new-looking laptop and a pro-Brexit coffee mug, containing a couple of pens, were the only items on an antique desk. Two comfortable-looking armchairs faced the desk, contrasting with the high-tech office chair behind it. Perhaps he has back trouble, thought Emma. She was sure that any constituents wishing to see their MP were met elsewhere. Arden didn't invite the police officers to sit down.

'I'd offer you coffee but I'm afraid my secretary's out running an errand at the moment.'

'That's quite all right, sir. We won't keep you long. It's about your directorship of Carter's Commercial Vehicle Hire.'

'What about it?' A wary look passed fleetingly across his face. 'I'm afraid I don't have anything to do with the day-to-day running of the firm. Why do you ask?'

'Several days ago, a police officer was kidnapped and falsely imprisoned at the premises leased by your firm. Had help not arrived in time, the officer would have almost certainly been murdered.'

'Well, I'm shocked, Inspector. Completely shocked. I do hope she is all right. Obviously, I know nothing about these terrible events.'

Arden's manner verged on bluster but it could have been genuine outrage. However, the expression in his eyes told Emma he was hiding something, and he was clearly uncomfortable.

'How did you get involved with the company, sir?'

'Well, it was George Meredith suggested I get on board. He does my accounts and we were having drinks at the club when he asked if I'd join. It's quite useful to have an MP on the headed notepaper, you know. Prestige and all that.'

Arden was almost preening.

'And, no doubt, you receive a fee for this?'

'There are, of course, directors' emoluments, but the nature of these is none of your business.' A hint of steel had crept into his voice.

'And what do you understand the company's business to be?'

'Hiring out vehicles to anyone who wants them. I believe we have a contract with a major confectionery distributor. Some warehousing services as well, I think. You'll have to talk to George or perhaps the manager. A chap called Lorde. A bit uncouth but he seems efficient.'

Lorde's role with Carter's was news to Emma. How could he work for two firms at the same time?

'And where would we find Mr Lorde?' asked Addy.

'I've no idea,' replied Arden, barely looking at him. 'At the depot, I suppose. I don't keep track of the staff in a company with which I have little involvement.'

'That's unfortunate, sir,' said Emma. 'You see, Mr Lorde is

wanted for a number of offences and hasn't been seen for some days. Are you sure you don't have an address for him?'

'I've already told you, officer. Now I'm afraid I must terminate this interview. I have constituency business to attend to.' His eyes flickered towards the whisky decanter. 'Can you see yourself out?'

'Yes, of course. Just one more thing. Does the name Derek Farren mean anything to you?'

At this, Arden's complexion paled.

'No, Inspector. It doesn't ring a bell. Now, I must get on.'

'Thank you for your time, sir. We may have more questions for you later on. Good day.'

Arden waved her out, ignoring Addy, and the two detectives lingered behind the closed door. A glass clinked and Emma heard Arden using his phone. She could just make out a few words.

'Fucking idiot... Get back to me... You've had it... Keep out of sight... Screwed up... Last chance... They won't like it...'

Emma and Addy slipped out of the building, closing the door silently.

'Ma'am,' began Addy, hesitantly. 'Did you bring me along just to piss him off? Only he looked at me as if I was a dog turd on his posh carpet.'

'No Addy. I wouldn't do that. I'm sorry he made you uncomfortable. I suspected he was a shit but I didn't know he would be that overt. But please don't quote me.'

Addy looked somewhat mollified but his eyes reflected years of racial prejudice, both in and out of uniform.

Chapter Forty-Nine

'LADIES AND GENTLEMEN,' began Emma, as the team settled down with coffee in the incident room. 'I've been in touch with the CPS and there's good news and bad. The bad news is we don't have enough to charge Farren over the bombing. The CPS said it doesn't meet the threshold.'

Emma's announcement provoked a variety of profanities and expressions of contempt from the team.

'The good news is we've authority to charge Farren with the attempted murder of two police officers and the possession of a prohibited firearm. He won't get bail. The bastard's going nowhere.'

Although this news was hardly unexpected, the team cheered.

'But we mustn't give up,' continued Emma. 'There must be more evidence out there, linking him to the conspiracy, and we need to find it. Mel, go through Marsden's flat, now the SOCOs and the labs have finished with it. Take a look at his locker at the college as well. They may have missed something significant.'

'Yes, guv.'

'Martin, go through everything we found on Farren. Look for takeaway receipts, bills, anything that pinpoints where he's been. You know what to do. We know he hasn't lived at his registered address for some time but maybe there's something on his bank account, or credit card statements, that could help. I'll arrange a warrant to search online. It's vital we track down his current address.' Martin looked slightly uneasy.

'One more thing. Addy and I went to see our esteemed Member of Parliament. His racist leanings were obvious from his behaviour and he was far from honest with us. On the off-chance, I asked him if he knew Farren's name. He denied it but was clearly lying. He also denied all knowledge of the events at Carter's and appeared to be shocked. The interesting point is that when I mentioned that a police officer was kidnapped and falsely imprisoned on the premises, he said he hoped she's all right. I didn't mention Lorna's name or gender. So, he obviously knew something about it. Not enough to pull him in, I'm afraid.'

Just as Emma was about to conclude the briefing, her phone rang.

'DI Thorpe,' she answered. 'Yes. That's right.' A sharp intake of breath.

'That's very helpful. Very helpful indeed. I'll look forward to your report. Thank you greatly.'

She turned to her team, her eyes gleaming and excitement in her voice.

'That was the lab. They managed to amplify a tiny amount of DNA in some skin cells on the lump of concrete that killed Duncan Bennett. It's Farren's. We've got the bastard for murder.'

Once the excitement had died down, Emma continued.

'Jack, I want you working with me to build a case for the CPS. We've got Duncan's photo of Farren showing time and place, plus the DNA. We have to make it watertight and we're starting now.

'Finally, before you get lunch, Michael Harris is saying nothing but he's obviously worried. We've filmed him walking up and down the corridor, so our consultant can compare his gait with the CCTV of the bloke pushing the cleaner's cart. Seems a bit sketchy though. We may get some forensic, from the cart itself and a jacket found near the scene. But nothing is coming back in the next twenty-four hours, so the Super has authorised an extension of custody to thirty-six hours. Beyond that, we'll apply to the magistrates for a warrant of further detention but, with his prints at the bomb factory, that shouldn't be a problem. So, when you've refuelled, concentrate all your efforts on finding out where Harris was living – and also Derek Farren. Not that he'll tell you. Meanwhile, the digital forensics lab is looking at the phones Jason Finney had in his possession. There may be something on them, though I suspect they are mainly burners used for drug deals. Oh, we recovered an unregistered phone in Marsden's place that may link to Farren. The PC who found it switched it on, despite strict protocols, and may have FUBARed it. The lab will have a look, anyway.'

'FUBAR?' queried Addy.

'Fucked Up Beyond All Recovery. Used by paramedics at road accidents. Here it refers to damage to digital information. Some devices have a kill code that wipes data if they're not opened correctly. We're hoping that this lot aren't that sophisticated. If they are, we're screwed. And so is the PC who fiddled with the phone. So, that's your afternoons sorted. Those of you involved in the drugs op, please meet me in my office at three.'

With coffee mugs refilled, Mel, Jack, Martin, Grassy and Addy were joined in Emma's office by DCI Gale.

'It looks like we're on,' began Emma. 'We've had word from our colleagues in Belgium that the lorry in question is booked on a train tomorrow morning. Border Force will stop it and DS Knowles will be there to plant the trackers – assuming, that is, there are drugs on board. Better get moving, Grassy.'

She handed him a rucksack.

'The kit's all in here, plus details of the B&B we've booked you into. Liaise with Barry Hallett, our Border Force contact, as soon as you get there. Good luck – and be careful.'

Her tone was professional but she smiled as she spoke. She realised the job was dangerous and hated the thought of her friend getting hurt. But she also knew he was tough and resourceful.

'Don't worry,' he replied. 'I've been on dodgier jobs than this. At least we're not expecting firearms.'

'I know. But there'll be discreet armed backup at the handover, just in case.'

Grassy grinned and made his farewells.

'See you in the pub tomorrow night,' he called, as the door closed behind him.

'OK. The rest of you,' Emma continued. 'We'll go live as soon as Grassy gets on board the truck, tracking him every metre of the way. Mel, you'll come with me on the raid. Keep yourself ready from early afternoon onwards, in case the van goes somewhere else.'

'OK, guv.'

'That's all for now. Back to work, but don't stay too late. You need to be sharp tomorrow.'

Before the detectives could disperse, DCI Gale spoke up, for the first time in the meeting.

'This has been a difficult operation to set up, given the different organisations involved, and I give full credit to DI Thorpe for doing it in such a short time. Good luck to you all. I'm sure you'll do her proud.'

With that she left Emma's office.

'What was that? A pat on the head for the guv'nor?' Jack muttered with irritation. 'Why on earth was she there?'

'I heard that, sergeant,' said Emma, coolly, although there was a twinkle in her eye. 'DCI Gale is simply exercising the proper oversight. If things go tits up, she'll get part of the blame.'

'Well, she can't 'ave that, can she?' whispered Jack to Martin.

'No, she can't, Jack,' he replied. The two grinned.

The rest of the afternoon was taken up with routine police work, the unglamorous bread and butter of detection. Just before he left for the day, Martin's phone rang. He listened thoughtfully then called over to Mel.

'We've got a sighting for Michael Harris two days ago. A couple of uniforms went to serve a warrant on the Eastside and they reckon they saw him coming out of a flat in Rutherford House. And guess whose flat?'

'No idea. But Rutherford House is familiar.'

'Billy Peel's mum's.'

'You're shitting me.'

'Nope. We'll tell the DI and go round there tomorrow

morning, with a couple of uniforms. We might find something linking him with the bomb.'

'Who's Billy Peel?' asked Karen.

'A kid from the Eastside who died last year,' Martin replied.

'Oh yes. I remember. Before I joined CID.'

Mel was less than enthusiastic about returning to Rutherford House. The last time she went, she had to deliver the death message to Mrs Peel and was met with total indifference at the loss of the woman's son. But the prospect of tracing Harris' movements was enticing. Martin and Mel caught Emma as she was leaving. Martin briefed her on the sighting and on the Peel household. She quickly gave permission for them to call on Mrs Peel before the drugs operation began, promising SOCO backup if needed.

'Are you sure you're up to this, Martin?' asked Mel. 'You're not fully recovered, are you?'

'As good as. I can't leave all the hairier jobs to you lot, can I?'

Mel shrugged.

'If you're sure. But stay in the car if things look like turning nasty.'

'Not sure I'd be any safer, on the Eastside,' grinned Martin. 'But don't worry. I'll be OK. We've got uniform as well.'

Chapter Fifty

Day 35, Wednesday

Eɪɢʜт ᴀ.ᴍ. on the Eastside and little appeared to be happening. This didn't mean that the police presence had gone unnoticed. An estate like that operated a jungle telegraph system, warning of intrusion by the authorities. As she looked around, Mel saw the occasional twitched curtain, a face appearing at a window or a door opening a fraction and closing again, as the sketchier inhabitants prepared to hide, dump or flush incriminating items. She shivered.

Mel knocked on the door of flat six but the door offered little resistance and swung open.

'Mrs Peel. It's the police. Can we come in?'

A familiar foul smell wafted through the opening and Mel's senses were immediately on alert. She expected tobacco fumes and the stench of decaying food. The flat, she knew, was a stranger to cleaning products. But there was another, sickly-sweet, component of the odour battery, which worried her. She called again.

'Mrs Peel. It's DC Cotton. We met last year. Are you OK?'

Fearing the worst, she put on a pair of nitrile gloves and stepped into the ice cold flat. Mrs Peel sat slumped in her armchair, her oxygen mask dangling from her neck and a syringe sticking out of her stick-thin forearm. Her skin was mottled greenish black, which Mel knew meant she had been dead for some time.

'Great,' muttered Mel. 'I just love the smell of corpses in the morning.'

'Nasty,' said Martin, who had followed her in while the uniforms kept watch for local opposition to their presence. 'Overdose, you reckon?'

'Could be, but let's not jump to conclusions. She's been a user for years so she's not likely to overdose by accident, unless there's something wrong with the gear. I'll call it in and we'd better treat the flat as a crime scene, much as I'd like to have a rummage around. It's clearly suspicious, so we'll have to wait for the SOCOs to do their bit.'

Mel phoned Emma and brought her up to speed, then turned to Martin.

'We'll have to leave Mrs Peel. We're needed back at the station. Jack and paramedics are on their way.'

She asked the two PCs to keep the scene secure and the detectives returned to their car, which someone had pelted with a couple of eggs. Wiping the mess off the windscreen, Mel wondered whether she would ever visit the Eastside without something unpleasant happening.

When Mel and Martin returned to the station, the incident room was buzzing.

'Some good news,' said Emma, as they grabbed coffee and opened their sandwiches, appetites undiminished by their grisly find.

'We've got a DNA match on the cap and coat found in the bin by the shopping centre. Hairs and skin cells from Michael Harris. We've got the bugger.'

Emma grinned triumphantly.

'Have we charged him?' asked Martin.

'Not yet. We'll disclose the new information to his solicitor and question him again. He may still go "No comment" but the CPS will give us authority to charge, as and when we want to. I'd like to get something from him, though. Find out more about who's involved and especially where Farren's been living.'

'What about Mrs Peel?' asked Mel.

'We won't get anything until the PM tomorrow. But you think it's a suspicious death?'

Martin and Mel looked at each other and Martin replied.

'Junkies don't usually overdose unless there's something wrong with the heroin. It's too pure, or it's been laced with fentanyl or another drug. I've not seen any reports of this happening in Mexton so I was suspicious.'

Mel nodded her agreement.

'OK. Well, we can put it to Harris that she's been found dead in suspicious circumstances and see how he reacts. Worth a try. I'll interview him this afternoon, before things kick off on the drugs front.'

Harris' solicitor, Gordon Cranford, pursed his lips when presented with the evidence against his client, although Emma held back the information about Mrs Peel's death.

'I'll need to discuss matters with Mr Harris, of course,' he said.

'We need to talk to him urgently,' replied Emma. 'So I'd be grateful if you would prepare him as soon as possible.'

'Detective Inspector,' he said, snottily, 'I will take as long as I need and I will not be pressured by the police. I will let you know when my client is ready.'

'Of course.'

Emma and Addy left the room seething.

'Prick,' she muttered. 'No, not you, Addy. That brief. He must know we've nailed Harris, so why should he be so obstructive?'

'Probably sees it as his job, ma'am.'

'I suppose so. Oh, and please call me guv or boss, not ma'am.'

The interview was not going well. After stating his name during the formalities at the start, Harris had said little, denying all knowledge of the bombing or Derek Farren. Cranford had clearly advised him to go 'No comment', advice that he followed assiduously. Emma was becoming increasingly frustrated.

'Michael,' she said, 'we have evidence that places you at the shopping centre at the time of the bombing. A jacket and a distinctive baseball cap bearing your DNA were found and linked to the clothing seen on CCTV recordings of the suspect placing the bomb. Would you like to say anything about that?'

'No comment.'

'We consulted an expert in gait analysis who compared the

gait of the person planting the bomb with yours. His opinion is that you are that person.'

The solicitor interrupted.

'Detective Inspector. You should know that gait analysis is an uncertain procedure. Indeed, in 2017 the Royal Society published a primer for the courts on the subject, stating that it is not evidentially reliable.'

'Be that as it may, I think we'll let the jury decide.' Emma knew there was an element of bluff involved, but hoped it would prompt Harris into talking.

'Oh, and one other thing. You were recently seen coming out of a flat in Rutherford House.'

Harris shrugged.

'You may be interested to know that the tenant, Mrs Peel, died in suspicious circumstances a few days ago. A post mortem examination is being carried out tomorrow morning and we will need to talk to you about her death once we have the results.'

Harris paled and looked scared.

'No comment.'

'Do you have anything at all to say? This is your last chance. I should remind you that you are looking at a very long sentence when you are convicted.'

'If, Inspector. If,' interjected the solicitor.

'No comment,' muttered Harris, clearly terrified.

'OK. In that case, subject to CPS approval, you will be charged with conspiracy to commit an act of terrorism, attempted murder, possession of explosives and assaulting a police officer. Take him back to his cell, Addy. He'll go before the magistrates tomorrow morning.'

Chapter Fifty-One

Grassy Knowles climbed up to the cab of the Belgian lorry, forgetting that it was left-hand drive and provoking smirks from the Border Force officers, there to see him off. As predicted, two boxes of cocaine, disguised as chocolates, had been discovered in the back and the driver was now in custody.

The driver's sweaty overalls, bearing the logo of the Belgian haulage company, hung loosely over Grassy's slim frame, held in place with a belt. Their owner must have been at least a stone heavier, but Grassy had insisted on wearing them. British clothing could attract suspicion. He phoned Emma to let her know he was on the move, then switched his phone off and hid it under the passenger seat. Despite the riskiness of the operation, he was pleased to be driving a truck again and the rumble of the engine lifted his spirits. He waved at the Border Force officers, put the artic in gear and headed towards the motorway, quietly singing the song *I like trucking* as the road unfolded before him.

The journey west was uneventful. He knew there would be police vehicles following him but he couldn't spot any. But that was the point. You weren't supposed to spot them. By the time he pulled into the services on the M3, he was aching from holding his arms in an unfamiliar position for so long and needed the toilet. There was no van there to meet him so he went off to relieve himself. When he returned to the truck an aggressive, stocky man with a shaven head challenged him.

'Where the fuck you been, then?'

'Piss,' replied Grassy, putting on a thick accent and hoping to keep conversation to a minimum.

'You're not the usual bloke. Where is he?'

'Jan is sick. Much beer last night. They sent me.'

'They didn't say.'

Grassy shrugged, forcing himself to look indifferent.

'You want I should go away?'

The man thought for a moment.

'No. You're all right. Help me unload.'

Grassy obliged, keeping conversation to grunts and mono-syllables where he could. As the van doors were closed the stocky man addressed Grassy.

'See you next time?'

'No. Jan next time. No more beer.'

He chuckled and the other man attempted a thin smile.

'Mind how you go,' he said.

Grassy grunted and swung himself up to the cab, this time on the correct side. As he pulled out of the services, heading for a police compound where the truck would be kept pending further examination, he whooped with relief. He called Emma to update her and set off along the motorway, simply enjoying the drive.

Chapter Fifty-Two

'Yessss!' exclaimed Emma when she ended Grassy's call. 'No problems at the handover and Grassy's on his way to the compound.'

Excitement in the room heightened as the Maybrick and Cream van was tracked on CCTV, leaving the services and heading back towards Mexton. A slowly moving red dot on the map, projected on the whiteboard, showed the progress of the trackers placed in the boxes and confirmed the van's route.

'Right, people, let's get ready to welcome them back. Mel – with me. And wear your stab vest. We'll join the strike team near the warehouse. Keep phones and radios silent unless the van looks like going somewhere else, in which case I need to know immediately. Let's go.'

The maze of small roads in the industrial estate provided plenty of places for the watching vehicles to lurk unnoticed. By seven o'clock there was little activity. Any premises still in business had shut down for the evening, leaving just rats, foxes and the occasional security guard to patrol the estate. The strike team arrived an hour before the van was expected and kept communications, on the dedicated Airwave channel, to a minimum. The Armed Response Unit, in the disguised Tube Alloys van, was parked almost opposite the Maybrick and Cream warehouse, while Emma's car and the other police vehicles were hidden slightly further away. A plain van covered the back entrance to the premises.

The team monitoring the tracker watched the red dot move closer to Mexton, hardly daring to breathe. Martin kept up a running commentary over the Airwave and Emma listened intently.

'Coming off the ring road now... Approaching the industrial estate... Four hundred metres from the warehouse... You should have eyeball any second.'

The strike team tensed as the van appeared and parked outside the Maybrick and Cream building. Someone inside raised the roller shutter, the van was driven in and the shutter was lowered.

'Ready to go, DI Thorpe?' the Tactical Firearms Commander queried.

'Not yet. We need them to open the boxes. Otherwise, they could claim they didn't know what was inside. They're monitoring the cameras back at the station and they'll give us the word.'

For twenty minutes Emma sat gripping the Airwave set, hardly daring to breathe. Two things happened almost simultaneously. A couple of motorbikes appeared and approached the warehouse. The roller shutter was raised to let them in. Then Martin's voice came over the air.

'They've opened a box and spotted the camera. You're good to go.'

Emma nodded.

'Strike! Strike! Strike!' yelled the TLC and the armed response van hurtled towards the warehouse and hit the descending roller shutter, preventing it from closing. Black-clad officers poured out, carbines at the ready.

'Armed police. Show us your hands. Armed police. Hands, now.'

The shouts echoed through the loading bay and its occupants looked around in terror.

No-one fired a weapon but one of the motorcyclists attempted to squeeze his bike between the ARU van and the wall of the warehouse. The handlebars carved a deep scratch in the van's side. Just as the biker got free, Emma's car pulled up in front of him. Mel leapt out and dragged him off the bike, wrestling him to the ground. He swore and struggled, his helmet catching Mel in the face and setting off a spectacular nosebleed. She brought her knee up between his legs. He groaned in agony and suddenly became docile. Mel handcuffed him, switched off the bike's engine and dragged her captive to a waiting police van.

'I ain't done nothin',' the biker protested. 'I was just collecting sweets for my dad's shop. You can't nick me for that.'

'No, but I can for resisting arrest, assaulting a police officer and damaging police property. Now shut up and get in the van.'

Three men, including the second motorcyclist, were arrested inside the warehouse and a fourth was caught trying to escape through a back entrance. Once it was clear that there were no firearms on the premises, the scene was secured until SOCOs were able to attend.

'I hope you're not going to bleed all over my car, Mel,' said Emma, grinning and handing her some tissues.

'It's all right, guv. It'll stop soon enough. I've had a ball. Well, two, really.'

'Nice job, lass, anyway.'

Mel smiled as Emma whisked them away to the police station.

'Well done, guys,' beamed Emma as the detectives assembled in the incident room.

'A really neat op with no-one hurt, apart from a twerp who inadvisably took on Mel. And Mel's nose. By the way Mel, why are you wearing a Grateful Dead T-shirt?'

'It's tradition, boss. Last year DC Tom Ferris got a bloody nose in the line of duty and his shirt was covered with blood. This was the only thing in the clothing store that fitted him. So now, if anyone is bleeding and needs a clean top, they have to wear this. Tom is the Keeper of the T-shirt and has to wash it before it goes back to the office.'

'I see,' said Emma. 'And they say us northerners are odd.'

The team laughed.

'Anyway,' Emma continued. 'It's off to the pub in a moment and DCI Gale has given us some money to put behind the bar, as she won't be able to join us. Before we go, there's some more good news. One of the suspects we arrested is Darren Lorde. This is a really good result and we'll have a serious talk with him in the morning. The others are minor nuisances, well known to us. We'll deal with them tomorrow as well. So, off we go. Theakston's for me.'

Chapter Fifty-Three

THE FOUR MEN sat around a table in the repurposed cellar of the Maldon Club. Ostensibly closed, after the company that owned it had been dissolved the previous year, the building was still used by a select few. A very select few. Substantial bribes in the right places had kept it off the market and maintained its anonymity. Although dingy, the room was clean and warmed by a series of electric heaters. A whisky bottle and glasses sat on the table and, at the far end, there was small bed, a playpen full of new-looking toys and a video camera on a tripod.

'It's a bloody disaster,' ranted Paul Black, the owner of several nightclubs in the Mexton area. The broken veins in his drinker's face stood out angrily and he spilled whisky down the front of the expensive, tailored shirt that stretched across his midriff. 'A total bloody disaster. Where did you dredge up those two idiots? They were supposed to take out the mosque and they went off piste, screwing everything up.'

'I know, Paul, and no-one is more disappointed than I am,' replied Maxwell Arden. 'The operatives were carefully chosen and paid well. I was assured they were up to the task and would do as they were told. It's unfortunate that they have both been arrested. Derek Farren won't say a word – he's tough. The other one might talk and measures are being taken. That'll stiffen Farren's resolve as well.'

'What measures?' asked Peter Horrocks, a retired army officer.

'You don't need to know.'

'So where does that leave the campaign?'

'Unfortunately, our explosives source is dead. His car blew up after the police approached him. So, we'll have to leave the more dramatic aspects aside until we can find another bomb expert.'

'I'll have a sniff around,' said Horrocks. 'Some of the chaps who were with me in Afghanistan could be interested. A good few of them bear grudges and might have brought home souvenirs. A pistol or the odd grenade, perhaps.'

'Well, be careful. We don't want any more cock-ups.' Arden took a gulp of his whisky. 'The other aspects of our campaign are still on track, however. We have a surprise in store on Friday for lunchtime shoppers in the centre. This will be followed by posters put up around town and an explosion of activity on social media. It will all build up to the planned riots in the third week of March. If we can fit in a bomb beforehand, all well and good. If not, it may not matter. Also, our funds are healthy. So, we've had a setback, gentlemen, but not a fatal one. And the police have no idea what's happening.'

'Do you know where they are with the investigation?' The fourth man, Gordon Lewis, a town councillor with thin sandy hair, a weasely demeanour and a skinny frame, licked his lips nervously.

'I had a visit from a detective woman,' replied Arden.

'Inspector Thorpe. Had the cheek to bring a black man with her. Shouldn't let them in the force. They were looking into a company I'm involved with. A separate issue. She knows nothing.'

'And what about the other thing? The prize?' The man's gaze flickered towards the end of the room.

'Don't worry, Gordon. I'll need to find someone else to claim it. But we will have entertainment soon.'

Lewis looked relieved and a lascivious grin spread across his face.

'Any problems on the horizon?' Horrocks asked, glaring at Arden.

'There's a hacker snooping around on the internet, looking at sites we might have used. We know who he is. He hasn't got close yet, but I'm concerned he might find out something. Again, measures are being taken, at some financial cost, I might add. They might dampen the enthusiasm of a couple of nosy police officers as well. Something of a bonus.'

Arden crossed his fingers under the table and hoped that Farren's contact in Glasgow would deliver. Using a US contractor was risky, and expensive, but at least there would be no direct link to him.

'Just make bloody sure nothing gets back to us,' Horrocks snorted.

'It won't. Suffice it to say that professional services have been engaged and you need to know nothing more.'

The men chatted for a few more minutes, finished their drinks and left, separately and unobtrusively. Maxwell Arden sighed with relief and looked forward to his next encounter with Shona. She always made him feel better.

Chapter Fifty-Four

Day 36, Thursday

THE CONTRACTOR STRETCHED his arms and flexed his fingers, taking care to avoid being seen through the half-open window of the office building. A stroke of luck, he thought. An empty building overlooking the police station car park, with easy access to the rear and little traffic likely in the vicinity. He rested the rifle barrel on the window sill and adjusted the sights. He had calculated the distance between him and the target zone, taking into account the angle, and had included the drop of the bullet in flight.

The rifle was nothing special – a .308 hunting weapon, stolen from a country house in Scotland and handed to him in a Glasgow car park. It was fine for the job. He didn't need a Barrett sniper rifle for a kill over this distance. He had checked the round loaded into the chamber for imperfections and had a couple of spares in case he needed them. Not that he thought he would. He prided himself on needing only one shot. And in these calm conditions, with clear morning light, one shot should be enough. Easier than shooting deer in Vermont. All he had to do now was wait.

As Michael Harris was being taken out of the back entrance of the police station, towards the car that would take him to the magistrates court, he had no idea that this morning was supposed to be his last on earth. Neither did the officers escorting him. He had a blanket over his head to hide his face, in case there were journalists looking to photograph him, but the car park was deserted. Some 100 metres away, as the bullet flies, the hitman decided that a head shot was too risky and chose to go for the heart. At this range, and with this weapon, the result would be the same.

As Harris moved towards the car, the shooter's finger tightened on the trigger. A motorbike backfiring in the street below him failed to distract him. He was used to working in noisy surroundings, after all. But it did disturb a small flock of pigeons on a ledge below him. As the birds flew upwards, he fired, and the bullet hit one unfortunate bird, virtually exploding it. Now, deflected slightly, the bullet continued its flight but instead of hitting Harris in the heart it slammed into his leg, breaking his femur but miraculously missing his femoral artery. Harris screamed and fell. One of the escorting officers had the presence of mind to drag him behind the car and clamp his hand over the wound. He called for an ambulance and firearms backup, all the while maintaining pressure on Harris' thigh. Harris yelled like a tortured hyena and eventually passed out.

The contractor cursed. Not just because he had missed his target, but because his unblemished record, 100% success, was now spoilt. Reputation was all, in his business. Realising he wouldn't get a second shot, he gathered up the rifle and spare rounds, pelted down the stairs and dashed to his car. Twenty minutes later he had rotated a file inside the barrel of the rifle, to prevent it matching the bullet that had hit Harris, and thrown it in the river. He had an awkward phone call to make to his employer, but before he did so, he would put a couple of hundred miles between him and Mexton. That would be later. He had another job to do in the town before he could head back to the airport and home, and this time he wouldn't fail.

Within ten minutes an ambulance arrived and paramedics took over, glancing nervously around in case another bullet was on its way. Harris was loaded into the ambulance on a stretcher, and the blood-soaked PC accompanied him after radioing in to his sergeant. By the time the Armed Response Unit arrived, the only evidence of the attempted murder was a pool of blood on the tarmac and a dent in the door of a police car where the bullet had ended up.

'The Chief Constable won't be pleased,' said one of the firearms officers. 'His car's gonna have to remain behind the cordon until the SOCOs have finished. He'll have to take the bus!'

His mate laughed and they returned to the van, while officers wound police tape around the scene.

Chapter Fifty-Five

Emma Thorpe began a late morning briefing with an update on Michael Harris' condition.

'He's out of emergency surgery and still heavily sedated, in a separate room with an armed guard twenty-four/seven. He would be in tremendous pain if it weren't for the morphine. Nobody cheer, please. He will need several more operations to put his leg back together again.'

'Yeah. And the NHS is paying for the little shit,' somebody spat.

Emma ignored him and continued.

'He was shot with a .308 hunting rifle, we think, from a disused building about a hundred metres away, which we searched. It looks like an attempted professional hit. There were shoe marks in the dirt, which had been scuffed over, and there was no empty cartridge case at the scene. I doubt very much that SOCOs will recover any DNA.'

'Do we know why he was shot, boss?' asked Karen.

'Not as yet. Perhaps to stop him talking. It'll be a long time before we can interview him and, as we've charged him, we can't press him on any of the matters concerned. But he may choose to make a voluntary statement, which would help us enormously. He'll be shit scared at what's happened and any loyalty may have evaporated. We'll see. But it's clear we're not just dealing with a few drug-pushing racists with a penchant for planting bombs. There's someone serious behind it all. So, I want you to be careful in your daily lives. I understand that several of you were targeted last year and I don't want it happening again.'

No-one spoke, as an air of disquiet settled over the room.

'Right. To other matters. The kid on the bike we nicked trying to leave the warehouse is going "No comment", but we've sent his phone to digital forensics and we may be able to track where it's been. He'll get bail since he hadn't taken possession of Class A drugs, although a small amount of cannabis was found in his bedsit. He had a hidden burner phone, which we left there. We may be able to track it, if he's daft enough not to dump it. His name's Shane Morris. He's got previous for assault and affray but seems to have avoided prison. So far.'

'What about known associates?' asked Martin.

'A couple of youths from the Eastside were arrested at the same time as him, on the affray charge. They were subsequently charged with racially aggravated assault when they attacked a Muslim woman in the street and ripped off her hijab. They got three months each. Apart from those two we've no other links in the database. Addy – could you look at footage of right-wing demonstrations and see if his face crops up?'

'Yes, guv.'

'How about the others we grabbed during the raid?' asked Trevor.

'Apart from Lorde, they're much like that biker. Low-level nuisances with a few convictions, all going "No comment".'

'Anything on Farren's address?' asked Mel.

'Digital forensics have tracked some phone calls from a burner found in Harris' place to an unknown number that we think could be Farren's. They've narrowed down a possible location to three or four streets. We're sending uniforms door-to-door with his photo. Someone must recognise him and know where he lives. That's all for now. I'm sure you've got things to be getting on with. If you're at a loose end, ask Jack. And I can't emphasise it enough. Be careful out there.'

'How are you getting on, Addy?' Emma stuck her head round the door of the video viewing room, late in the afternoon. 'Any joy on Shane Morris?'

'A couple of possibles, boss. Someone looking like him was involved in a disturbance outside the mosque and it could be him throwing a bottle. Also, he's definitely here at a demo in support of Tommy Robinson, when Robinson was in court in London. Shane's standing next to a male who looks like Farren. It's hard to be sure but I'm eighty percent confident it's him. I've still got a couple more recordings to go through.'

'Thanks. Good lad. So, we know that he's not just a drug courier but a racist twat as well.'

Addy nodded, his distaste obvious on his face.

Emma walked back to her office, wondering just how deep racism ran in Mexton. Since the Brexit vote, it seemed to have got worse everywhere and the thought depressed her enormously. As she reached her desk, her phone rang.

'Yes. Thank you. Great work. Where?'

She reached for a pen and a scrap of paper and scribbled down an address. Then she called Jack.

'We've got a location for Farren's flat. A neighbour recognised him from the photo. Can you send someone round to have a rummage? His keys are in the seized property store.'

Derek Farren's flat smelt sour. The carpet was sticky underfoot, its original pattern obscured by dirt. Cobwebs and mould lurked in the corners of the walls, which looked as though they had been painted using a Pekinese on a stick, rather than a paintbrush. Stale lager, sweaty trainers and takeaway curry containers combined to fill the air with the stench of neglect. Funny how so many of these racists seemed to like Indian food, thought Mel, as she and Martin put on nitrile gloves to search the premises.

'Lovely decor,' she called to Martin, pointing to a flag of St George with a picture of Tommy Robinson fixed to the centre. It was pinned up above an old Victorian fireplace, heaped high with crushed beer cans and empty vapes. 'I've often wondered,' she continued, 'why a posh boy wanting to change his identity to look like a man of the people should choose the name of the bloke who sang Glad to be Gay.'

Martin grinned and continued opening drawers and cupboards in the kitchen.

'Got his laptop,' Mel said, sliding the item into a plastic evidence bag and sealing it. 'It was under his bed. And there's a burner phone here as well. Have you found anything?'

'There's an empty box for 9mm ammunition here. No live rounds and I haven't found a weapon.'

Mel winced. 'Probably the one he tried to shoot me and

Tom with.'

The officers continued searching, bagging up documents, flash drives and SIM cards, of which there were several in an envelope stuck to the back of a drawer. They were just about to leave when Martin glanced back at the flag.

'Is there something behind that photo?' he speculated. 'Let's take a look.'

Mel unpinned Robinson's smug image from the flag.

'Bingo! There's an envelope here.'

She slid a folded sheet of paper from inside and opened it up.

'Oh shit. Look at these.'

She showed the paper to Martin, who whistled.

'Dates and places. Top of the list is the shopping centre with the date of the bombing next to it. Then there's the mosque, the halal supermarket, the Green Party and Labour Party offices. All with dates in the next couple of weeks next to them. Your bomb was only the first. We'd better get this to the guv'nor pronto.'

The two officers locked up and left the flat at speed, both dreading the prospect of more bombings.

Fifteen minutes later Mel and Martin were in Emma's office, having collected Angela Wilson, now a regular attendee at team meetings, from her desk on the way. Emma put DCI Gale on speakerphone and asked her officers to relate what they had found.

'It's a list of targets, guv. With dates. And the next one's two days away. The shopping centre was only the first.'

'But I thought you already had a list, from Bennett?' DCI

Gale's disembodied voice sounded puzzled.

'Yes, we did,' replied Emma. 'But that was pretty speculative. This is much firmer. And there are weights in kilograms next to each target.'

'They could be the amounts of explosive they're planning to use,' interjected Angela. 'If so, the devastation would be horrific.'

Everyone was quiet for a few moments, considering the implications of the SO15 officer's words.

'Hold on a minute,' said Mel. 'We've shut down their lab and their chemist is dead. Doesn't that mean they won't be able to make more bombs?'

'If we're lucky,' replied Angela. 'But they may have other sources. There could be stockpiled bombs. Another cell making TATP. And we don't know how many people are involved. Until Harris was shot, it looked like they were amateurs with a tame chemist in tow. Now, it seems as though there's a bigger network to worry about. Even without explosives they can still cause serious grief. Arson, shootings and beating people up are all in their toolbox. Petrol bombs can be just as deadly as explosives if used in crowded buildings.

'It looks like a sustained campaign is underway, and we need to stop it before there's a horrendous loss of life. I'll contact my boss and he'll liaise with the Home Office and the security services. Your team knows Mexton, so you'll take the lead. Can you warn the owners of the premises on the list and step up uniformed patrols? We'll give you all the help we can. Now I must make a phone call.'

Angela left the room leaving the others stunned and scared.

'So what the fuck do we do now?' asked Mel. Nobody answered.

Chapter Fifty-Six

MEL NIPPED home at lunchtime to collect the salad she had left in the fridge. She frowned when she saw a stocky figure, carrying a small rucksack, leaving the building furtively, his face covered by a scarf and a baseball cap pulled down low. She didn't feel she had grounds to challenge him but she memorised the number of the silver hatchback in which he drove away. Probably nothing, she thought, but she still had an uneasy feeling when she entered the flat.

There were no obvious signs of an intruder inside but something didn't feel quite right. Tom's parrots seemed nervous in their big cage and there was an unfamiliar odour of sweat in the hall. She grabbed her lunch, took a final look around and was just about to leave when something clicked into focus. There were indentations on the living room carpet below the central light fitting. Someone had obviously put a chair there, presumably to change the light bulb. But she remembered changing it less than a week ago, so there was no way it needed replacing. Mel pulled out her phone and dialled.

'Tom, have you changed the bulb in the living room light?'

'No. Why would I?'

'Well, it looks as though someone's been fiddling with the light fitting. Where's Robbie?'

'He's gone to see a mate, I think. Said something about research. Can you take a closer look at the light? And whatever you do, don't turn it on.'

Mel climbed on a chair and moved the lampshade aside. The bulb was an old-style tungsten type. There were several in a cupboard in the flat when she moved in and she hadn't got round to replacing them with energy-saving alternatives. Looking closely, she could see a layer of whitish powder in the bottom of the bulb, which seemed a little larger than the one she had installed a few days ago. She described what she saw to Tom, who almost screamed down the phone.

'Don't touch it. Turn the power off at the fuse box and get out of the flat. It looks like some kind of device intended to go off when the light's turned on. I'm calling bomb disposal.'

'OK. OK. I'm not an idiot. I didn't need telling. I'll wait in the car until they arrive. Are you coming home?'

'As soon as I can. Don't worry. And, just in case, could you take Bruce and Sheila out?'

Mel grimaced at the thought of sharing the car with Tom's two eclectus parrots, which could be extremely noisy, but transferred them to their travel cages and put them in the car. Sheila, a parrot rescued by Tom from dire circumstances, was reluctant to be caught, but Bruce, bought from a parrot rehoming centre to keep her company, was more amenable. She also collected Ernie, her tortoise. All the time, her heart was beating nineteen to the dozen, but she reassured herself that, whatever was in the flat, it couldn't do anything without power.

Forty minutes later, an army Land Rover pulled up and a lieutenant, accompanied by a couple of corporals, climbed out.

'Good afternoon. I gather you've got an oddity for us.'

The officer looked positively excited at the prospect. Mel described what she had seen and where it was. The lieutenant thought for a moment then conferred with one of his men, who lifted a large box out of the vehicle and carried it towards the house.

'Just wait here, if you would. Shan't be a tick.'

Mel sat impatiently in the car, wishing she had brought the salad out with her. She had briefed Jack about the situation and he'd sighed, muttering something about another life going. Twenty minutes later, the soldiers came out of the building, a corporal gingerly carrying the large box.

'Got it,' said the officer. 'It's definitely nasty, designed to do something horrible when the light's switched on. I'm not sure what the powder is. Probably explosive. We'll get our boffins to take a shufti when we get back to base. We've had a look round and couldn't find anything else suspicious. You can go back in now. Cheerio.'

Mel thanked the soldiers and went back inside with the pets. 'Tom can clean the bloody parrot shit off the car seats,' she thought to herself. 'How they managed to get it through the bars was a mystery. And it's time we moved to somewhere with more space for them. Letting them out of their cages to fly around the room and crap everywhere isn't good enough. Tom's trying to get them to fly to him from their perches. Recall training, he calls it. It's OK at the moment but he'll need much more space before long.'

She'd lost her appetite and picked desultorily at the salad, giving much of it to Ernie. The thought of SOCOs rummaging through the flat, now a crime scene, depressed her but she realised it was necessary. She waited for them and handed over a spare set of keys before returning to the station, haunted by flashbacks of the time she was kidnapped and two colleagues were nearly killed.

Chapter Fifty-Seven

DI Thorpe called Mel into her office late that afternoon. Her expression was grave as she invited Mel to sit.

'You've had a lucky escape, Mel. I've had a call from the lieutenant who removed the device from your flat. The bulb contained an explosive mixture of propane and air. It's lucky you went home in daylight and didn't need to switch the light on.'

Mel looked puzzled.

'It wouldn't make that much of a bang, surely? Just a bit of gas?'

'More worrying,' continued Emma, 'was the powder in the bottom. The army helicoptered it to Porton Down as they were suspicious. Porton Down did a rush identification and found that the powder was ricin. If the bulb had exploded, ricin would have been spread around the flat. Anybody inside would have inhaled a fatal dose and the poison would have filled the place. In short, you would have had a major chemical incident inside your flat.'

Mel felt sick.

'Did the SOCOs find anything?'she asked.

'Nothing,' replied Emma. 'No prints on the bulb or light fitting. They've taken swabs for DNA but aren't optimistic. We'll need to get elimination samples from the soldiers if anything turns up. Your locks were opened without damaging them. Again, no prints. Can you remember anything about the man you saw leaving the building?'

Mel shrugged. 'No. He was well covered up. Generic dark clothing, baseball cap pulled low. Stocky build, no hair visible. And I didn't see his face. I ran the number plate on the car he drove off in. It's registered to a Doctor Stephen Cattermole in Leeds. I tried to contact him but he died three months ago.'

'Cloned plate, then.'

'Looks like it.'

'OK. Ask Addy to follow it though ANPR.'

'I already did. It entered Michaelwood Services on the M5 and didn't leave. So, either the driver changed plates or switched to a different vehicle. Addy was going to check with the car park operators. If it's still there we might get some forensic from it.'

Emma looked increasingly frustrated.

'Don't hold your breath, lass. What's worrying me is that this all looks very professional. It's miles away from Derek Farren going after you with a World War Two pistol. So, why should a couple of DCs, in a medium-sized English town, be targeted by a professional killer?'

'I've no idea, boss. But frankly I'm shit scared. I've never had anything to do with anti-terrorism work until now and the drugs and racism mob aren't sophisticated enough to pull a stunt like this. The only really intelligent one we've come across is the chemist and he's dead.'

'You're right. Preparing ricin without poisoning yourself is difficult, I'm told, and you need a fair amount of skill. But there must be some link. We presume Harris was supposed to be killed, in case he talked. So, there's something major going on that we don't know about. Unless the incidents are separate, which seems unlikely.'

'No. It is the same person, I'm sure, guv. The silver hatchback was picked up by ANPR cameras, not far from the back of the nick, ten minutes after the shooting. They must be connected. After all, a hitman is unlikely to advertise that he had a spare hour in Mexton, in case somebody wanted a mark taken out.'

'Could your partner have been the target?' Emma asked.

'I talked to Tom last night. He's looking at a range of internet scams on pensioners run by arseholes pretending to be from their banks. They're based in Ukraine and have no idea Tom's working the case. And cybercrime doesn't usually involve murder.'

'So, what do you want to do? Take leave and go and stay somewhere else? With your dad perhaps? He must be worried sick.'

'You know my dad?'

'Yes, I worked with him when I was starting out. An inspiration. And I know he keeps an eye on you, through his contacts who are still serving.'

Mel felt slightly uncomfortable at this, although Emma's appreciation of her father pleased her.

'I don't see the point. If a professional killer wants to get me, I've not got much chance, wherever I am. A bullet could come from a building anywhere and bombs could be planted in vehicles or buildings without me spotting them. No, I'll stay on the job.'

'That's what I expected you to say,' Emma smiled. 'Both of

you must take strict precautions from now on. Vary your routes home. Break routines. I'll get you a pair of those mirrors on sticks so you can both check under your cars for devices. Don't open any strange packages. And if you see anything suspicious in your flat, get out at once.'

'Yes, boss. I've already asked a security company to fit better locks and an alarm at the flat.'

Mel was comforted by Emma's concern but also felt slightly irritated. These were basic measures she would have taken anyway. Of course, she would have to warn Robbie when he returned from his mate's. He would be terrified at the thought of what might have happened if Mel hadn't gone home on a sunny afternoon, instead of the usual dark evening.

Robbie. Oh shit, she thought. Suppose the target was Robbie? He would need to be warned and told to take precautions as well. She kept her suspicions to herself and left Emma's office deep in thought. She needed to talk to Tom urgently. Perhaps they could meet for coffee in the canteen. Whether or not they were the intended targets this time, the experience had scared her. What with the attacks last year, this attempted poisoning and Farren's murderous invasion, she was beginning to feel unsafe at home. Perhaps another reason for moving.

Chapter Fifty-Eight

Day 37, Friday

NEXT MORNING BEGAN with limited news of the vehicle used by the suspect in the attack on Mel and Tom's flat.

'No joy on the car, guv,' called Addy. 'Theoretically, it's still at the services. It arrived late yesterday afternoon and never left. When I got the attendant to look for it, it wasn't there. The driver must have changed the plates, or covered them with mud so the number wouldn't be picked up, before he left.'

'Get on to the operators again and see if they've a record of a car leaving that never entered the site, or two cars with the same plates. Or an unreadable plate, for that matter.'

'I thought of that. There was a silver hatchback with the plate obscured.'

'OK, well done. Contact the Gloucestershire and West Mercia forces. See if their motorway patrols stopped a silver hatchback with dirty plates. Ask Gwent Police as well, in case he took the M50 into Wales. They probably wouldn't have done a motorway stop just for a dirty plate, but you never know.'

'I did, boss. I didn't go home until I'd sorted it. An unmarked patrol signalled a silver hatchback with dirty plates to pull off the M5 at Junction 11 northbound, yesterday evening. It had a faulty brake light as well. But, as they slowed for the junction, an Audi TT shot past at over 90 so they followed in pursuit, prioritising the more serious offence. No-one else saw the suspect's car.'

'Presumably he changed the plates after that. So, basically, he's in the wind.'

''Fraid so, guv.'

'Obviously a professional. And thanks for all your efforts, Addy.' Emma smiled at him. 'We'll not get anywhere looking for him now,' she continued, 'though it might be worth asking the National Crime Agency if they know of anyone with those skills. But we still don't know what's so important about Mexton that it's worth employing a hitman to shoot a suspect and launch a chemical weapon attack on police officers.'

Mel spoke up. 'It might not have been us, boss. The guy who's staying with us has annoyed a lot of people. He's helped to expose dozens of paedophiles, although his methods were a bit dubious. He may have angered someone enough to want to kill him.'

'But these nonces aren't likely to be professional killers,' argued Emma. 'They wouldn't use murder to cover up their vile activities, surely?' She looked thoughtful. 'If your theory about your lodger is correct, there's a link between a local drug operation, far-right terrorists and a bunch of kiddy fiddlers? Come on, lass, it's a bit far-fetched.'

'Yes, it is, boss, but that doesn't mean it's impossible.'

'Well, we've hit a brick wall at the moment, so if you want

to take some time to look into it, I suppose it's OK. Don't forget we've other cases on the go. Talk to vice and CEOP – see what they think. But don't spend too long.'

'Thanks, boss.'

As the meeting broke up, Mel was deeply worried. She had discussed things with Tom at length last night, and he had agreed that Robbie was a possible target. They had debated trying to find him a safe house but both felt that senior officers would probably not regard him as a high enough priority, given that such premises were limited in number. Mel resolved to have a long talk with Robbie when she returned home. In the meantime, she had some very nasty stones to turn over in her attempts to link the Mexton events to organised paedophiles. She was not looking forward to it and knew Tom felt the same about that type of offence.

Chapter Fifty-Nine

PETE FRY, duty manager at the Mexton shopping centre, pushed open the door to his office with his shoulder, taking care not to spill the lunchtime coffee he'd just bought. The coffee didn't last long. He dropped it as soon as he felt the point of a knife under his ear.

'Turn and face the wall,' a voice hissed. 'Don't look at me and don't make a sound.'

His legs shaking, Pete complied. He cringed as a hood was shoved over his head and he was pushed to the floor. His assailant fixed his wrists to a section of pipework and warned him, again, to stay silent. For the next few minutes, he could hear someone fiddling with the equipment on the table next to his desk. It sounded like a DVD was being loaded into the player. He didn't understand but refrained from asking. Then, without further communication, the attacker left the room, leaving Pete unable to see or move. He managed to get the hood off, by repeatedly rubbing his head on the wall, and when his eyes focused on the video monitor, he couldn't believe what he was seeing.

Steve Walsh plonked a tray of burgers, fries and Cokes on the table in front of his wife, Josie, and daughter, Kayleigh. Tired from a morning's arduous clothes shopping, which featured much discussion but little actual expenditure, the family were refuelling in the food court before the second round. Idly glancing at a video screen, which normally featured ads for the shops trading in the centre, he dropped his burger in horror and covered his daughter's eyes.

'What is it, Steve? His wife looked perplexed.

'That screen. Look. Don't look. It's horrible.'

Josie looked up and just caught the sight of someone's head, severed by a Middle Eastern man with a sword, dropping onto the sand. She screamed. The image was followed by flashing English text, condemning ISIS and demanding that all Muslims be deported from Britain. Films of the 9/11 atrocity, Islamic extremists ranting and a subtitled speech by Nick Griffin followed, punctuated by the same message. Cries of horror and disgust drowned out the muzak played over the shopping centre's PA and several people rushed towards the toilets, clearly on the point of throwing up. The same images were repeated, on a loop, until the screens suddenly went dark. Shocked by what they had seen, shoppers deserted the centre in droves, leaving half-eaten meals in the food court and dropped coffee staining the floors.

In the manager's office, a quick-thinking security guard switched off the video relay system simply by pulling the equipment's plug out the socket. He freed Pete with the aid of a pair of scissors and helped him to his feet, at which point Pete broadcast a message over the PA system, apologising to shoppers for the distressing images they had seen. He called the police and had the sense to leave the intruder's DVD in the player, in case there were any forensic traces on it. Then he rushed to the staff toilets to be sick.

Chapter Sixty

Day 38, Saturday

WHEN COLONEL HORROCKS contacted Charlie Horgan, he was only too pleased to help. His honourable discharge, military medal and army pension were small compensation for lungs full of shrapnel and the loss of his leg to an IED in Afghanistan. When he joined up, he had had no particular animosity towards Muslims, or any other group for that matter. He just fancied the excitement and the camaraderie. But he had harboured a burning grudge since his injury and bitterly regretted that he was unable to continue fighting. His old CO had kept in touch with him, and when he offered Charlie an opportunity to strike back, he jumped at it. He had smuggled a hand grenade back from Afghanistan, partly as a souvenir and also as a possible way of ending his pain if it became intolerable. No-one thought to check the kit of an injured soldier. They just bundled it all on the aircraft that took him back home. His brother, who took charge of his belongings when he returned, kept quiet about the lethal object. Now it would be useful.

Charlie had driven past the halal supermarket four times before he saw his chance. He pulled in as a delivery lorry drew away, three metres from the entrance. His gorge rose as he saw women in hijabs and burkas, as well as men in loose robes and kufis, entering and leaving the store. He hated them all. He put the car into first gear and kept the clutch depressed, ready to drive off as soon as his job was done. Reaching into his jacket pocket he grasped the grenade and pulled out the pin. His heart raced as he wound down the window. Confined as his arm was by the roof of the car, he knew that he could hurl the bomb into the store and be away before it exploded.

Dominic Williamson had enjoyed a good lunch. He felt he had deserved it, as he'd just finalised the sale of a substantial property on the outskirts of Mexton, the former residence of a now-deceased drug dealer. It wasn't often that his estate agency was in line for a £30,000 commission so he felt justified in splashing fifty quid on a bottle of fine burgundy. OK, he was a bit fuddled, but he was sure he could drive safely. He'd been driving over the limit for years and never had any trouble. Spotting a florist, and a parking place behind a stationary car with a disabled sticker in the back window, he pulled in, thinking it would be nice to buy his wife some flowers. He might even get lucky tonight. But his luck was out when his foot slipped off the brake and caught the accelerator. He was dimly aware of bumping the car in front and seeing the occupant drop an apple-shaped object. Three and half seconds later his life ended.

The crash of the grenade exploding was muffled slightly by the body of the car. Shrapnel, and bits of Charlie, were propelled out of the open window and struck passers-by, causing several serious injuries and smashing a row of shop windows, while shards of glass and bits of bodywork scythed across the street, damaging vehicles and people alike. The explosion blew apart Charlie's petrol tank, and the burning petrol turned Dominic's BMW into an incinerator. For a second or two the street was silent, as a black cloud of smoke roiled upwards and falling glass tinkled on the road surface. Then the screaming started.

Within ten minutes, three ambulances, two fire engines and a couple of police cars arrived and paramedics began the grim business of triaging the victims, ferrying the living but seriously injured to hospital immediately. Minor injuries were then treated on site, for out-patient follow-up if necessary.

Witnesses hadn't noticed anything until the grenade went off, so attempts by the police to take statements proved largely fruitless. The fire and rescue service quickly doused the flames from the two cars but remained on standby in case anything flared up again. It was fortunate that Dominic's car ran on diesel, so his fuel tank hadn't caught fire.

When Emma arrived, accompanied by Angela and Martin, uninjured people were still being cleared from the scene. Officers were recording their names and addresses as they left in case further statements were required. The street resembled a war zone. Debris was scattered over a wide area and foam covered the vehicles, from which steam was rising. They would be taken away for forensic examination when it was safe to do so. The stench of burning plastic and petrol smoke hung heavily in the air. A large section of the street was cordoned off, with uniformed officers standing guard, much to the annoyance of shopkeepers who had been evacuated and prevented from returning to their premises.

As Emma got out of her car and waited behind the outer cordon, two scientific services vans arrived and SOCOs piled out. Jackie Thorne, the Crime Scene Manager, looked around, grinned ruefully and addressed Emma.

'It'll be days sorting this lot out,' she said. 'There's bits scattered all along the street, to say nothing of stuff blown into shops. There's no point you being here, really.'

'I agree, replied Emma, 'but I just wanted to take a look at the scene. I've not gone through the cordon. Can you let me have some photos as soon as possible for the briefing?'

'Will do. An hour or so?'

'Great. Thanks. Can you contact your colleagues in Counter-Terrorism, Angela?' she asked. 'I'll call the team together for a briefing in an hour.'

Then Emma drove away, sick at heart.

Chapter Sixty-One

'OK, everyone. Pay attention please. Sorry to call you in on a Saturday evening.'

The incident room quietened, waiting for Emma to speak.

'As you know, we had a terrorist atrocity this afternoon. Two people are dead, including the perpetrator. Four people remain in hospital, one of whom is on life support as a result of a heart attack, and there are dozens of minor injuries. Damage to property will run into hundreds of thousands of pounds. The target could have been the halal supermarket, but the explosion occurred in a car parked outside.'

'Do we know what caused the explosion?' asked Martin.

'SOCOs picked up fragments of what looks like a hand grenade. The army ordnance guys are looking at them. They should be able to tell us its provenance.'

'Who did it?' asked Mel.

'It looks like it was Charles Eric Horgan, an army veteran discharged after losing a leg in Afghanistan. The car was registered to him. It's possible that he intended to throw the grenade into the store but dropped it. The BMW behind him appears to have bumped into his car so that could be the reason why.'

'Motivation?' Jack queried.

'Revenge, I assume. But it's been seven years since he came back from Afghanistan so he's taken his time.'

'Is there any link with Farren and his scummy mates, or Barry Marsden?' Mel asked.

'Not that we've found so far, although digital forensics have the bits of his phone. If they can get the IMEI number we can see if he's had any calls from persons of interest. Of course, it could just be that the publicity over the shopping centre bomb prompted him to take action himself. We have no way of knowing.'

DCI Gale, who was sitting quietly in the corner of the incident room, stood up.

'I think we must assume that the two events are linked. It's too much of a coincidence otherwise. And I fear there may be others. We haven't talked to the press yet, and I don't think we will until we need to, but MI5 have categorised the threat level in Mexton as severe. In other words, another attack is highly likely. Please bear that in mind in everything that you do. Keep your eyes open, talk to informants and take care of yourselves.'

DCI Gale returned to her office, leaving Emma to allocate actions.

'Martin, go round to Horgan's address with Mel and see if you can find anything linking him to these far-right nutters. Talk to his neighbours. Has he had any visitors? What was he like as a person? You know what to ask. Addy, see if digital forensics have a number for the phone yet. When they get one, track its movements and get a list of calls, incoming and outgoing. Jack, contact the MoD and see if there's anything useful in his army records. Also, find out who his mates were and look for next of kin. If he has any living relatives, someone will have to deliver the death message. Probably me, if they are local. Uniform will deal with the relatives of the deceased BMW driver. Karen and Trevor, you're on ANPR and CCTV. Find out where his car's been and try to track his movements on foot. I'll borrow a uniform to give you a hand. Everyone else, please drop what you were doing before this shitshow. Jack will find you something to do. Thank you everyone. This is top priority and I know you'll all do your best. Angela, can I have a word with you?'

Angela followed Emma into her office and the two women sat down.

'Did SO15 have any idea something like this was going to happen?' Emma began.

'No. Not at all, ma'am. I know MI5 and the MoD keep an eye on discharged forces personnel who may bear a grudge, but I checked with them and they had nothing about Horgan on their radar. There doesn't seem to be any kind of national campaign to recruit disaffected soldiers, so the consensus is that this is just a Mexton problem. The trouble with anti-terrorism work is that we can monitor organised groups with the usual methods, but the rogue individual, or emerging small cell, can slip by. Look at the Shoe Bomber.'

'Bloody great, isn't it?' Emma groaned and Angela smiled sympathetically. 'Well, please keep in touch with your colleagues in London and report anything you find directly to me. You'd best work on your own ideas, alongside the rest of the team. If you need anyone to help, let me know. We've got some good folks here who'll be happy to lend a hand.

'Yes, ma'am. Will do.'

'Oh – and please call me Emma. Like Helen Mirren said, I'm not the bloody Queen.'

Chapter Sixty-Two

Day 39, Sunday

'So, what's it like, working in counter-terrorism, Angela?' asked Mel, as they waited to use the coffee machine before the morning briefing.

Angela seemed pleasantly surprised that someone wanted to engage her in conversation. Since she had been in Mexton, hardly anyone had spoken to her, unless it was to discuss the case.

'Well, I suppose most of it is much like normal CID work. Gathering information, following leads, undertaking surveillance, searching databases. Occasionally making arrests. I suppose the main difference is that the stakes can be higher. When you stop something dreadful, like you did, the feeling's incomparable. But if a bomber slips through, it's devastating to morale, even if we could have done nothing to prevent it. Why, are you interested in joining us?'

'Maybe,' replied Mel. 'I've not been in CID that long and I love it. But I'm not sure where I want my career to go. I don't want to end up like the DCI, stuck behind a desk and worrying about budgets all the time. I wouldn't mind leading a major inquiry, as SIO, though. But that's a long way down the road. Is it hard to get in to?'

'Not really. I think the vetting is a bit stricter, but we're all normal people. I know some people resent it when we take over a case, but we're not poaching or trying to steal the glory. It's just that we have a specialised remit. Some people here looked at us as though we're vampires.'

Mel nodded sympathetically.

'How about MI5? D'you get on OK with them?'

'I've never come across any problems. If there are rivalries at higher levels, I wouldn't know. But communication seems to be OK. They have a bit of a mystique, though. None of them looks like Daniel Craig, I'm afraid.'

The two women laughed.

'If you do decide you're interested, later on, please give me a ring. I'd be happy to chat some more.'

'Thanks, Angela, I will. And don't forget that invitations to the pub do include you.'

'Firstly, thanks to everyone who worked late yesterday night,' began Emma as the team settled down for the briefing. 'We've got some results and you'll be pleased to know that the Super has authorised overtime payments.'

Several officers smiled and an unknown voice muttered, 'About time.'

'Martin and Mel went round to Horgan's flat. Can you fill us all in, one of you?'

Martin spoke up.

'It was sparsely furnished and tidy, as if he was still in the army, so it didn't take long to search it. There were no explosives or weapons, apart from a rather vicious combat knife. He had some heavy-duty painkillers, which didn't appear to have been prescribed, but he probably needed them. There was also a small amount of cannabis. The only item of significance was a notepad by a burner phone. The top copy was probably burned – there was some debris in an ashtray and he didn't smoke. I could just make out the impression of the writing on the second sheet. ESDA will confirm it, but it looked like the address of the bombed supermarket, the word Muslim and the three letters COL.'

'So, we're looking for a Colin or a colonel, presumably,' said Emma. Did the MoD say who his commanding officer was in Afghanistan, Jack? We need to talk to him urgently.'

'They said they'd get back to me, but it may take until tomorrow morning.'

'Right. Thanks. Any luck with the phone, Addy?'

'No, guv. We couldn't get the IMEI number or anything else from the bits. Sorry.'

'OK. Not your fault.'

'It looked as if he'd just received it,' said Martin. 'There was an empty box and mailing envelope in the bin under his desk. Forensics are looking at them now.'

'So probably a burner. How about his neighbours, Mel?'

'They hardly knew him. He said hello if he met them inside the building but otherwise kept himself to himself. He never had visitors, didn't play music and his TV was usually quiet. He rarely had any post, apart from junk mail and the odd official-looking document. Sounds a bloody miserable existence to me. You'd think the country owed him more than this.'

'Now, now, Mel. You're almost sounding sympathetic. He is a terrorist,' Jack said, reprovingly.

Mel shrugged. 'Just saying.'

'Karen – anything on ANPR and CCTV?' Emma asked.

'Still getting CCTV images, guv, but he seems to go most places by car. Mainly the shops and the hospital. He doesn't seem to visit pubs or restaurants. No private individuals, apart from the occasional trip to his brother's place. Absolutely nothing of interest to us.'

'Thanks, Karen. Keep at it. OK, everybody. You've all got things to do. We're getting a couple of extra bodies from Counter-Terrorism tomorrow, which should help. Meanwhile, we've still got to work up the case against Farren and co. We'll meet again tomorrow.'

———

'Guv,' Mel called, knocking on Emma's open door. 'Digital forensics found something nasty on Farren's laptop. And you'll never guess what they found on his burner phone.'

'Don't muck about, lass. Give.'

'First of all, they found a load of indecent images of children on the laptop. The worst category, in folders labelled birthday and Christmas presents. They're still working on some encrypted stuff.'

'The filthy bugger. We'll charge him with that as well. That should worsen his time inside. What about the phone?'

'There's not much on it. Some texts to Harris and Jason Finney. Darren Lorde's number is in his contacts, plus a few other males known to us for racial offences. More significant is the number for a certain Maxwell Arden.'

'I'm not surprised,' said Emma. 'I knew he was a shit as

soon as I met him in his office. But what's the link with Farren? The pornography or the bombing?'

'Don't know. There are no texts and he's only used that number a couple of times. I'm surprised Arden let him. I'm sure he wasn't contacting his MP to complain about the library closures. Farren was stupid to store it in his phone, but then again, we never had him down as an intellectual.'

'Right. We need to go carefully here. I don't want to question Arden about this yet, for fear of scaring him off. Farren will continue to go "No comment" and if we ask him, word might get out that we're looking at Arden. We'll not get a RIPA warrant for direct surveillance on Arden at this stage but it would be useful later on. I'll ask Angela to find out if the security services have any suspicions about him. They may have picked up something, if the link is through far-right activism.

'Can you do some background work on him, Mel? Speeches, social media posts, press reports and so on? Run a PNC check to be on the safe side but I expect he'll come up squeaky clean. Keep quiet about it for the moment – we don't want gossip spreading.'

'Of course, guv. There's no-one likely to leak deliberately, but careless tongues and all that.'

'Precisely.'

Once Mel had left, Emma sat for a while at her desk, deep in thought. She hadn't expected anything like this when she applied to work in Mexton, a move prompted by Mike's offer of a permanent teaching post at the nearby university. After Sheffield, she had expected a relatively easy ride, but she soon found out that Mexton had plenty of problems of its own.

Its manufacturing industry, never huge but still significant, had been out-competed by China and austerity had hit the town hard, putting the gap between rich and poor in the national top twenty. Crime, especially drug-related offences, had increased sharply and the Eastside estate was almost a no-go area for the police. Now she had to deal with racial violence, which was steadily increasing, and terrorism. And what of the MP? She was well aware that Members of Parliament had their foibles, just like anyone else. She tried not to let the man's racist views colour her judgement but she had the distinct impression that he was up to something rather more serious than fiddling expenses.

She had always welcomed a challenge, although, at the moment, she was beginning to feel stretched. But, in the short time she had been in Mexton, she had come to realise that her team was enthusiastic and dedicated, in contrast to her rather lacklustre DCI. And that gave her a feeling of considerable confidence.

Chapter Sixty-Three

EMMA OFTEN WENT for a drive or a cycle ride to clear her head. She told Jack she was going out for a while and took her Golf for a tour of the town. As well as helping her to think, the drive improved her knowledge of the local geography, something on which she still had to work.

Merchant Street, formerly a commercial centre but now dilapidated, was punctuated by roadworks as utilities installed and upgraded pipes and cables, so traffic was slow. Emma began to regret taking this route. As she looked around, once more trapped in stationary traffic, her attention was caught by a man stepping furtively out of a betting shop, with a hat pulled over his face and wearing sunglasses. Sunglasses. On a rainy afternoon in February. Now that was odd.

Acting on instinct, she decided to have a word with the man, but by the time she found a place to park, he had vanished. Emma dashed from her car and rushed up to the betting shop's counter, which was staffed by a bored-looking young woman working her way through a doughnut.

'Police.' Emma pulled out her warrant card. 'Can I see your CCTV for the past ten minutes, please?'

The woman called the manager, who emerged from the back room, brushing crumbs from his grease-stained shirt. He pointed to a grubby chair, but Emma preferred to stand as she fast forwarded through the recording.

She almost whooped with excitement when the image of the man, minus sunglasses, came on screen. No doubt about it. Her instincts had been right. It was Mark Dickens.

He must be daft, thought Emma. Risking capture just to place a bet. Why didn't he do it by phone? She phoned Jack.

'I've spotted Dickens. He came out of Leach's Bookmakers on Merchant Street five minutes ago, heading towards the railway station. I want everyone available on the streets looking for him. Check pubs and bars, especially the dodgy ones. If he's daft enough to go to the bookies he may want to drown his sorrows or celebrate. But no blues and twos – I don't want him spooked. He's wearing a grey hoodie, a black baseball cap, dark joggers, white trainers and sunglasses. I'll look at street CCTV when I get back.'

She ended the call and returned to her car, waving away a traffic warden who was about to give her a ticket. She drove back to the station, excited at the prospect of catching Dickens and confident that Jack would have the troops on the ground within minutes.

Mark Dickens kept his head down as he passed the CCTV camera outside the bookies, his senses on full alert. Was that a police car on the other side on the road? No, an ambulance car. He breathed again. But was the guy sitting in the cafe opposite watching him? And why did that VW suddenly pull in from the traffic stream and park on double yellows? Being a fugitive was getting to him, he realised, but he had been desperate to get out of that cramped squat where he was staying. He'd needed to place a bet. Well, several. Not that he'd won anything. Even the horses were suspicious of him.

The hat and glasses were OK at concealing his face, but they looked a bit obvious. Perhaps he could wear a hijab instead? He'd heard of some bloke fleeing the country dressed as a Muslim woman. But he wouldn't know where to get one and couldn't stand the thought of looking like one of 'them' anyway. He would just have to keep out of sight as much as possible, skulking in the shadows like an assassin, and hoping no-one recognised him. The pictures put out on TV and social media were not particularly accurate and were yesterday's news. Only the police would still be watching for him and there weren't that many on the streets these days.

With that in mind, he decided to risk a pint. He made his way to the Fife and Drum, using back alleys where possible, and slipped in the back door, away from the CCTV camera in the car park. He ordered a pint of Stella, found himself a table at the back of the pub and pretended to read an old copy of the *Racing Post* that someone had left behind. Fuck, but that lager tasted good!

Karen and Addy pulled up outside the Fife and Drum, the last call on their list. No-one in the pubs they had already visited recognised the photo of Mark Dickens and they didn't expect much from the clientele of this one. The police were never welcome and talking to them could get you barred.

'Go on Addy. It's your turn. I need the Ladies,' Karen said.

'I'd hang on, if I were you. Unless you want to catch something horrible.' Addy grinned.

'Needs must, mate,' she replied and followed the smell to the toilets.

Addy walked up to the bar with Dickens' photo in his hand.

'Have you seen this man in the last half hour?'

Predictably, the barman denied all knowledge, but his eyes flicked towards the corner of the pub and his body language gave the lie to his words. Addy glanced round, spotted the man behind the *Racing Post* and called over to him.

'Excuse me,' he began, his words drowning out the faint click of a safety catch being released. He saw the paper fall and found himself staring at the muzzle of a Walther PPK semi-automatic, three metres away.

Addy ducked. Dickens fired. The bullet narrowly missed Addy's head before smashing a bottle of vodka behind the bar. Addy dived for cover but there was nowhere to hide. Dickens fired again, this time hitting a fruit machine, which gave an electronic squawk and disgorged a pile of coins. The other customers, roused from an alcoholic haze by the gunshots, hid behind various bits of furniture and the barman ducked behind the counter. Dickens pulled the trigger a third time, at close range, but nothing happened. The weapon had jammed.

Addy hauled himself upright and lunged at Dickens, who tipped a table over in front of the police officer. He tried to dodge past, but Addy caught hold of his wrist and put him in an arm lock, forcing him to the floor. Dickens lurched backwards, catching Addy's face with his head and breaking his nose. Almost blinded by the pain, Addy managed to handcuff Dickens before he could do any more damage and sat on him until Karen returned. No-one offered to help. That's not what people did in the Fife and Drum.

'Blimey. I turn my back on you for two minutes and look what happens,' joked Karen. 'Seriously, are you OK?'

'Yeth. Fine. But I think my nothe ith broken,' Addy mumbled. 'And my shirth's ruined.'

'Never mind. There's a special T-shirt back at the station you can wear. I'll get this shite into the car and call the boss.'

'Right. I'll move the gun so ith not pointing at anyone in cathe ith's a hang fire. But we need an AFO.'

Fifteen minutes later, Jack arrived with two PCs in a marked police car.

'Nice collar, Addy,' he said. 'We'll take Dickens back to the station and you, Karen, can take Addy to A&E.' He turned to Addy. 'No arguments. You could be concussed.'

Jack told the barman to close the pub and left a PC to guard the scene until SOCOs and a firearms officer arrived.

Chapter Sixty-Four

'WHAT'S THE MATTER, TOM?'

Mel dropped her keys on a side table and looked at him, hunched on the sofa looking as white as a bled corpse and just as cheerful.

'It's work. They've got me looking at a paedophile's laptop, trying to find who he's been in contact with. And I feel totally and utterly sick. Just looking at some of the images makes me want to stand in the shower and scrub myself for hours. And I've found nothing on the fucking bastard's filthy mates.'

'So why are you doing it? I thought you were dealing with scams and financial crimes. Christ, I know how you feel about this type of thing and I'm surprised you agreed.'

'I didn't have much choice. We've got three people off, CEOP is overloaded, partly because of Robbie's efforts, and they said I was the best. Flattering sods.'

Mel thought for a moment.

'Do you know the owner's name?'

'No. I've just got a case number,' replied Tom.

'Is there anything else dodgy on it?'

'A load of racist stuff, rants about Muslims, gays and feminists. That sort of thing.'

'Then I think I know whose it is. Derek Farren's,' said Mel, a note of excitement in her voice.

'What? The arsehole who tried to shoot us?' Tom sounded outraged.

'The same. A very unpleasant gentleman, linked to the bomb in the shopping centre.'

'Yes, I know. That's why he was after you. But a nonce as well?'

'So it seems. Have you found anything else?'

'Nothing digital yet, apart from a search history showing the vile sites he looks at. But on one video, and I can't bear to tell you what was happening, someone was careless.' Tom's voice trembled. 'There's a man's hand in shot for a few seconds, with what looks like a healed dog bite across a network of rather distinctive veins. My guv'nor reckons it could be used to identify him, if we ever get hold of him.'

'Yes, I've heard of identification by hand veins. There was this court case where a girl filmed her father on her laptop and accused him of abusing her. The vein evidence was accepted by the judge, but the jury didn't believe her as she didn't cry enough in court, according to a barrister. He got off. Poor kid. There've been convictions since, though.'

Tom looked shocked.

'Hang on a bit,' Mel continued. 'When we interviewed Farren, Jack said he was fiddling with a scar from a dog bite. We'll take another look at him. It could confirm his involvement and we'll have an additional serious charge to bring.'

'Well, that would be a bonus. I'm glad it's not me interviewing him.'

'Are you going to carry on with it?' Mel asked.

'Of course. Especially now I know whose machine it is. There's still a couple of encrypted files I'll get into tomorrow.'

Mel snuggled up to him. 'I'm glad you're not one of those hard-bitten blokes who take it all in their stride. I think if you lose your humanity, you're not fit to be a copper.'

She kissed him.

'I'm not sure they really exist, love. Underneath, I expect they're just as much of a mess as those who show their emotions. Any chance of a drink?'

Mel poured them both a large brandy and they sat there in companionable silence, each exploring their own demons, until Robbie came back bearing pizzas.

Two hours later, their stomachs full of food and their heads still woozy from the brandy, Tom and Mel sat watching the local TV news, as Robbie dozed in an armchair.

'Look at that twat,' snorted Mel, as the local MP's face filled the screen. 'He's opening a community centre, but judging by the make-up of the crowd, he hates half the people likely to use it. Bloody hypocrite.'

'Why's that?' queried Tom.

'He's a raving racist. We're looking into him 'cos Farren had his number on a burner phone. It's just me at the moment, not quite official and only using easily accessible sources. We haven't got enough for a warrant and we don't want to alarm him. I'd love to know who he's been phoning and contacting through his computer, though.'

'Wish I could help. Anyone in contact with that shit Farren is up to something, as far as I'm concerned. When you get a RIPA warrant, let me know and I'll pitch in.'

'Thanks. I guessed you would. Still feeling bad?'

'It's like a foul taste in my mouth I can't shake. It'll probably be there until we get a conviction.'

'Well let's get to bed and forget about Farren and his fellow sewer rats.'

Mel turned off the TV and they left the room, both knowing that sleep wouldn't come easily, leaving Robbie in the armchair, still apparently asleep. But his eyelids flickered as they left.

'Mike,' began Emma, as they sat in front of a log fire, drinking their coffee with the dinner dishes soaking in the sink. 'Do you think it was a mistake to come down here?'

'Not from my point of view,' his comforting voice rumbled. 'My job's fine, the students are great and we've a decent house. Are you having second thoughts? I know teaching English is different from police work, but I thought you liked it in Mexton.'

'No, not really. I miss Yorkshire a bit, I suppose, but the job is proving more challenging than I expected.'

'Come on, lass. You've never wanted it easy, have you? And you've got a good team, even though your boss isn't up to much.'

'True. It's just the past few weeks have been traumatic, what with terrorism, racial hate, child pornography, a hitman and attacks on fellow officers. It makes some of the Sheffield scrotes look like fluffy bunnies.'

'Well, we could always go back up north if you need to,' Mike said, a trifle hesitantly.

'No. Of course not. I'll deal with whatever Mexton throws at me. Don't worry. I'm just a bit stressed.'

'Well come and sit in front of me and I'll rub your neck.'

Within minutes, Mike's expert kneading had drained away

Emma's tension and, soon after, she fell asleep with her head resting against his knees. He looked down at her, watching a few tendrils of her hair fluttering each time she exhaled, concern and admiration fighting for control of his thoughts. He knew, without a doubt, that he was lucky beyond his dreams. And he would follow her anywhere.

Chapter Sixty-Five

Day 40, Monday

'WELL, if that idiot is typical of your regiment, Peter, I'm surprised the Taliban didn't piss all over you.'

Horrocks bridled at Arden's insult.

'It wasn't his fault. My source tells me that the car behind bumped him and probably made him drop the grenade, before he could throw it. When you've been in combat and taken fire, you can criticise my men. Until then, keep your bloody mouth shut.'

Arden, whose experience of conflict was confined to the cricket pitch at his public school and the local election hustings, muttered an apology.

'So where does that leave us?' he asked.

'I don't want to involve anyone else from the army. I'm already lying low in case the police link Horgan with me and I don't want to attract any more attention. How about your unsavoury contacts? Don't you have a fire-raiser among the drug pushers and petty thieves?'

'I don't know them personally, you fool,' Arden snapped. 'All this was done through Farren and now he's been arrested it's a lot more difficult. Perhaps his solicitor could get a name or two out of Farren during a professional visit.'

'Would he do that? Hardly ethical, is it?'

'We know things about him. He'll co-operate. A fire bomb at the mosque is just what we need now. And we need someone to acquire the "entertainment". I know Farren had someone in mind, so perhaps the same people could do both jobs.'

'Well get a bloody move on,' Horrocks grumbled. 'People are waiting.'

Arden grinned.

'Don't worry. It will be worth the wait. Pink or blue, do you think?'

'Whatever's easiest, Max. Whatever's easiest.'

The two men left the Maldon Club separately. Horrocks stepped out briskly with a military gait, his features concealed by a hat and scarf, while Arden shambled out a few minutes later. To his fury, he saw a traffic warden fixing a parking ticket to the windscreen of his Jaguar.

'What the hell do you think you're doing?'

'You're parked on double yellow lines. I'm giving you a ticket.'

'How dare you? Do you know who I am?'

The officer, who fancied himself as something of a comedian, replied, 'No sir, but if we can find your carer, I'm sure they'll remind you of your name.'

'I'm Maxwell Arden. Member of Parliament. I'll park where I bloody well like. And I've got your number. I'll be demanding you're sacked.'

'I'm afraid being an MP doesn't entitle you to do that. Now

please stop harassing me and be on your way. You can use the appeals procedure if you believe the ticket is wrong. Good morning.'

The warden walked off with a satisfied smile on his face, while Arden stood there fuming. He would get that smug bastard, one way or another.

Arden returned to his office to prepare for his surgery. This was the part of being an MP that he hated. Constituents. They seemed to think that he had some sort of magic wand, which he could wave to solve all their problems. He knew he was in for two hours of complaints from people who had got themselves evicted or had no money. Largely their own faults, in his opinion.

Looking at the list of appointments he could see some familiar names. Jason Davis, complaining that his Universal Credit wasn't enough to live on. Work-shy scrounger, he thought. Should try harder to get a job. Arthritis was no excuse. And Mrs Amin, whingeing that the landlord refused to carry out repairs and her children were always coughing and getting ill. Shouldn't have so many kids, and shouldn't even be in this country. Oh God, there was that hippy woman again. Wanting him to stop a prestige housing development that would mean filling in a pond. People needed houses more than Great Crested Newts. Anyway, he had shares in the building company. He was practised at dispensing smooth words and promises to look into things that he had no intention of keeping. He had enough supporters, from the well-off parts of the constituency, to ensure he would never lose his seat. He reasoned that nobody on the Eastside would be bothered to vote for anyone, let alone his opponents.

While he waited for the surgery to start, he checked his emails. Most of them were from the public and he would get his secretary to answer them, using the standard replies he had prepared when he was first elected, tweaking them slightly where necessary.

The only email of interest was one under a Buckingham Palace address with Garden Party in the subject line. He couldn't believe it. At last. He opened the email and clicked on the attachment marked 'Invitation'. His screen flickered briefly and a message appeared: 'Attachment unavailable. Please try again later.' Annoyed, he resolved to ask his secretary to chase it up. Downing a swift Scotch to fortify himself, he waddled to the outer office to see the first constituent, smug at the prospect of sharing sandwiches with the Queen.

Chapter Sixty-Six

'OK, folks. First off, Addy's OK. He had slight concussion and they've sent him home for twenty-four hours' rest. He should be back tomorrow.' Emma addressed the team, who audibly expressed relief. 'Have you heard anything from the MoD, Jack?'

'Yes, guv. Horgan's CO in Afghanistan was Colonel Peter Horrocks. He retired a couple of years ago and lives in a country house just outside Mexton.'

'Good stuff. Get someone round there as soon as the briefing's over. See what he knows about Horgan. Send some uniform as well, just in case.'

'Will do.'

'We've had something back from NABIS,' Emma went on. 'The Walther PPK that Mark Dickens used was stolen in a burglary in Surrey a year ago, as was Farren's P38. They belonged to a military historian who collects Nazi memorabilia and we believe the raid was targeted. They knew what they were after. The weapons had been deactivated, and were held legally, but an underworld armourer has clearly reactivated them. Another pistol, a Walther PP, is also missing.'

'What's a PP?' asked a civilian researcher. 'The PPK is the James Bond gun, isn't it? I read it in *Doctor No*.'

'That's right. And it's the same make of weapon that jammed when Princess Anne's bodyguard tried to fire at armed would-be kidnappers in London in 1974. The officer chased after the gunman and ended up with a gunshot wound and a George Medal. Brave guy. Luckily for Addy, Dickens' PPK jammed as well. The PP is slightly bigger and takes a larger round. Nine millimetre.'

'What about Bennett's Luger?' Mel asked.

'That was a replica. Completely harmless. He bought it himself – there was a receipt in his flat.'

'Did Harris have a weapon too?'

'Not that we've been able to find. And he's still in hospital, under guard and semi-conscious. We can ask him, if he's willing to talk to us, but, honestly, I wouldn't trust him with a firearm. He's not bright enough.'

Several detectives chuckled.

'Don't laugh. There's another Walther in circulation, possibly in Mexton. So watch yourselves. Jack, can you check whether any of the local sources have heard anything about handguns in town? A long shot, but someone may have picked up something.'

'OK boss. I'll put the word out.'

'Oh, there's something else. We've had another brown envelope. Printouts of emails, a list of websites visited, and the titles of some encrypted files on a laptop. And guess whose laptop it is.'

Apart from a few facetious remarks about the top brass,

Prince Andrew and government ministers, no-one had any suggestions.

'Maxwell Arden's,' said Emma. 'And we can't use any of it. It's clearly been obtained illegally.'

'Oh fuck,' spat Jack. 'Surely we can use it to get a RIPA warrant?'

'Unfortunately not. We need evidence to apply for one and this isn't admissible. It's the same as the last load of anonymous data we received. At least that gave us some ideas of where to look. Someone's obviously trying to do us a favour but he or she could be compromising the investigation.'

'Can't we do the same with this lot?' Mel asked.

'I'm not sure I can condone the use of material obtained illegally from a Member of Parliament. I'll have to take advice.'

She threw the envelope on the desk in front of her and appeared not to notice it sliding to the floor.

'By the way, Maybrick and Cream's IT person, Jeannie McLeod, seems to have disappeared. The office manager phoned in and said that she's not been into work for several days and isn't answering her phone. I've passed it onto uniform and they'll go round to her home.'

With that Emma returned to her desk. As soon as she had left the room, Mel pounced on the envelope on the floor.

'You never know,' she said to Jack. 'There may be something we can use. Point us in the right direction.'

Jack appeared not to hear.

Chapter Sixty-Seven

THIS IS A GOLDMINE, thought Mel, as she leafed through the anonymous printouts in the women's toilets. An absolute goldmine. But how could she use it without getting into trouble? She knew that if she ran a trace on the mobile numbers, it would leave a digital record and she might have to explain what she was doing. But she could make a note of them and see if they came up anywhere else in the investigation. One of them did look vaguely familiar. She would have to check the number of Derek Farren's burner.

The emails she could look at later. At first glance, they seemed to relate mainly to constituency business and party matters, with a few social engagements thrown in. There were some that looked more interesting and she would photocopy them for later perusal. The websites were a problem. If they were illegal, she couldn't attempt to access them from work without a good reason, which she didn't have. She certainly couldn't try from home. Then a thought occurred to her. She speed-dialled a number.

'Tom. Can you help me with something?'

'What is it?' Tom sounded guarded.

'I need to know what's on a few websites and I suspect it's filth. I'm not supposed to have the details and I can't access them myself. Do you have a list of suspect sites you can look them up on?'

'No, I don't. But I have a mate in CEOP who might. Give me the addresses. What have you got yourself into now?'

'Nothing. I mean, I'll explain at home. Don't worry.'

Mel gave him the details of four sites and he promised to get back to her.

'Thanks, love. You're a star.'

Mel slipped back into the office and waited until there was no-one near the photocopier. She copied the emails that interested her, put all the papers back in the brown envelope and walked briskly to Emma's office.

'You dropped, these, guv,' she said.

'Oh, thank you Mel,' Emma replied, smiling slightly. 'I don't suppose we know who's sending them and why he should sign himself "Cheap Goat"?'

Mel suppressed a chuckle. 'We've no evidence as to who it is. And he's having a laugh. It's a rhyme. Deep Throat was a source of leaked information during the Watergate scandal back in the seventies. Brought down a president. So Cheap Goat is a...'

'Yes, yes. I know who Deep Throat was,' interrupted Emma. 'I'm not so green as I'm cabbage looking. But if he's caught, this hacker could end up inside.'

'Yes, guv. I realise that.'

Mel left Emma's office knowing full well who Cheap Goat was. The poor, stupid sweetie, she thought to herself. She really must warn him off before he found himself in a shit-storm. And if he was caught, she and Tom could also be under suspicion as accomplices. She uttered a silent prayer to the goddess of hackers and determined to speak to him as soon as she got home.

'Horrocks has done a runner,' reported Martin when he returned to the office. 'His housekeeper said he took off in a hurry when he heard the report of the explosion on the radio. He grabbed a holdall, jumped into his car and drove off without saying where he was going.'

'Shit. We really need to talk to him,' cursed Emma. 'It's obvious he's involved somehow, otherwise he wouldn't have bolted. I'll organise a search team to go over his place. It shouldn't be hard to get a warrant. In the meantime, find out if he owns any other properties. See if you can get a photo from the MoD we can circulate and put out an alert. And ask Trevor or Karen to look for his car on ANPR. Thanks, Martin.'

Chapter Sixty-Eight

MAXWELL ARDEN FONDLED the cool steel of the Walther lovingly. He admired the engineering, even though it was German. For him it represented power. He had wanted a real gun ever since he was a boy, dissatisfied with the low-powered air pistol that his father had bought him. When he realised that the private ownership of handguns had been outlawed following the Dunblane shootings, he was furious. So when the chance came to acquire one, via Derek Farren, he seized the opportunity. Peter Horrocks could wave his old army Browning around, he thought, but he wasn't the only one with a weapon.

He had spent several happy hours firing the pistol, at birds and squirrels, in deserted woods. He'd never hit anything. He had soon realised that handguns were not as accurate as they seemed on TV. He also enjoyed cleaning and oiling the piece. But what he wanted to do most of all was use it for real. Perhaps on that bloody traffic warden? A fantasy, he knew. But there was the question of clearing up after the 'entertainment' was over. Horrocks had always organised that but perhaps he could be involved? He would keep the gun with him at the club, in future. Just in case.

Karen Groves sipped her wine morosely. She had been drinking rather a lot since her meeting with her blackmailer, and the modest contribution to her finances couldn't compensate for her feelings of shame. So far, she hadn't been asked to do anything. But what would happen when she was? Could she remain in the police? Or would she be forced to take decisive action against her nemesis? She drained her glass and stumbled to the fridge for yet another solitary ready meal. As she waited for the microwave to ping, she wondered desperately whether she would ever be able to recover some semblance of honour.

Chapter Sixty-Nine

Day 41, Tuesday

DI Thorpe started the morning briefing with a summary of progress, or, rather, the lack of it.

'Dickens' phone had a few familiar numbers on it – Darren Lorde's and a burner that we've come across before. It was on Farren's phone as well. The phone we recovered from the fleeing biker during the raid had Lorde's number on it, plus a few old ones belonging to people in the Maldobourne street dealer network, which you dismantled last year. Some of them may be back in business, or could have passed their phones on to someone else.'

'Do you think Lorde's the boss, guv?' Mel asked.

'No, he reports to someone else. A male. Lorna heard him referred to when she was kidnapped. And we've no idea who he is.'

'So, who's behind the posters?' Addy asked.

'Yes. I was coming to those. For those of you who haven't seen them, the town centre and areas where there are substantial populations of BAME residents have been flooded with racist posters calling for Muslims to be deported, Afro-Caribbeans to be sent home and people from Eastern Europe to be chucked out. Some are advocating the murder of Muslims and Jews. We don't know who's behind this vile infestation. One kid was arrested in the process of pasting some up but said he was just given fifty quid by "some bloke in a van" to do the job. He could barely read and didn't understand much of the content.

'The posters appeared after the video screens in the shopping centre were hacked when, for half an hour, disgusting anti-Muslim videos were shown. They were followed by days of Islamophobic hate-speak, spewing out over social media.'

Jack spoke up.

'I'm seriously worried, guv. It looks like an orchestrated hate campaign, what with the bombings, the videos at the shopping centre and now the posters. We've already seen an increase in racially aggravated assaults and it's barely the end of winter. Where's it going to end? Are we looking at riots when the weather's warmer?'

'Quite possibly, Jack. And it scares me shitless. But until we can identify the players involved, we can't do much to stop it. I'll get on to the Home Office and ask Angela to talk to her contacts. See if they know of anything similar happening elsewhere.

'A couple of loose ends cleared up,' continued Emma. 'The pistol fired at Mel and Tom also fired the bullet that killed Anton Kominski, so it looks like Farren was responsible. Hard to prove, without additional evidence, but we're still looking for forensic links between the two men. Also, it looks like Mrs Peel simply overdosed. The traces of heroin found in her syringe were unusually pure, which means the dealer hadn't cut it as much as usual.'

'I dunno know what the world's comin' to, when you can't trust yer dealer to put rubbish in yer gear,' said Mel, in a mock cockney accent.

Several people laughed.

'Finally,' frowned Emma, 'there's no sign of Colonel Horrocks. Apart from his country estate, he owns no other properties and his car hasn't been seen since it headed into Mexton after the attack. It's probably in a multi-storey some-where, possibly with false plates. Uniform are keeping an eye out. The search team found nothing of use at his home. His laptop and phone had been taken. It's vital we track him down and the counter-terrorism guys are working on that. That's all for now. Thank you everyone.'

Emma walked back to her office with frown lines etched on her face that threatened to become permanent. Mel copied down the phone numbers on the whiteboard and refilled her coffee mug on the way back to her desk.

Chapter Seventy

AT LUNCHTIME, when half her colleagues were either queuing for sandwiches in the canteen or seeking better sustenance elsewhere, Mel turned her attention to the phone numbers she'd copied down from Robbie's list. Lorde's was on it, as was Derek Farren's. Some others she recognised, such as Arden's party headquarters, the Town Hall and his constituency office, but several were unfamiliar, including one that was called frequently. She was determined to identify the unknown numbers. Grabbing her coat, she stuffed the list into her pocket and left the office, heading for a café in town. With a coffee and a bacon roll in front of her, she started dialling.

Most of the numbers belonged to companies, restaurants or organisations relevant to Arden's work as an MP. Her efforts also identified two massage parlours, one in Mexton and one in London, a couple of B&Bs and a private club, the location of which she couldn't ascertain. Half her calls went to voicemail or were simply not answered, but the last one was more productive.

'Horrocks,' a voice barked, when the phone was answered.

And horrocks to you too, she thought, as she killed the call. She rushed to find Emma, uncertain how her senior officer would react to her discovery. She had found a link, albeit a tenuous one, between the Home Secretary's brother and an attempted terrorist atrocity in Mexton. OK, it was indirect. The two men could have known each other perfectly innocently, through a club or a fundraising event. And there was no proof, yet, that Horrocks had been in contact with Horgan, although his behaviour was highly suspicious. But it was significant. It could have been evidence, if it had been obtained legitimately. She now had a number for Horrocks' phone, which could be tracked, with the DSup's approval.

Emma's feelings were clearly mixed.

'I take it Cheap Goat is behind this,' she said when Mel outlined her discoveries. 'It's useful stuff and reinforces our belief that Horrocks is involved, but I don't know how we can use it. We certainly can't disclose it when we interview him, assuming we can find the bugger, that is. I'll ask for his phone to be tracked as a priority, though. Let's hope it's still switched on. This is a tricky area, Mel. Maxwell Arden's brother is immensely popular with his party and much of the public. The youngest Home Secretary for decades. The *Daily Mail* loves him. We'll have to go carefully.'

As Mel left Emma, feeling somewhat deflated, her phone rang.

'Hi Tom. I'm in the office. And there's something we need to talk about.'

'You bet there is,' he answered. 'Those sites you gave me. They're child pornography. Among the worst CEOP have encountered. We really do need to talk. Tonight.'

Chapter Seventy-One

Jeannie McLeod pulled on her knickers and slipped from under the duvet without waking the snoring form beside her. The trouble with most men, she thought, as she wriggled into a T-shirt, is that they over-estimate their competence, especially in bed. Not that she'd mention it to her companion, of course. With his privileged background and position of, albeit minor, power he was used to being buttered up and told he was wonderful. Perhaps she'd shatter that illusion one day. But not yet. He was still useful. Her end game was not complete and she would need him.

The flatulent walrus beside her would want to see the money from the drug dealing used to advance his cause, but he really had no clue about the size of the income the operation had generated. She intended to keep it that way. She had plans for the money. He was furious about the loss of the last load and she had to work especially hard to keep him sweet. Men!

When Jeannie returned from the shower, enveloped in a towel, Maxwell Arden was sitting up in bed, his over-lunched stomach flopping over his waist like the head of a toadstool.

'Fancy coming back to bed?'

His attempt at charm failed, the leer on his face just as unappealing as his pasty body.

'Sorry, Max,' she replied. 'I've got things to do. I won't bother with breakfast.'

'Where are you going?'

'Around and about.'

She had no intention of telling him what she was planning or where she would be staying that night.

'When will I see you again?'

'Soon. I'll be in touch.'

'Well, don't wait too long this time.'

'Course not. You know I can't keep away from you.'

Her smile looked genuine but was as real as the plastic palms in the hotel lobby.

'By the way, what's that brother of yours up to these days?' she asked casually.

'Still busy being Home Secretary. I haven't heard from him for a couple of days. Apparently, he's coming down to visit the Mexton mosque. His PA sent me an email. So I've got to smile and stand next to him, shaking the hand of some greasy Arab.'

'Poor you. Anyway, I'm off.'

She blew him a kiss.

She strode to her car, an unobtrusive white hatchback registered to a deceased social worker in Northampton, and drove around the streets of Mexton looking for an unsecured wi-fi network. It didn't take her long, and within half an hour she was online using an alias, shifting money around from the Carter account to several of her own.

Before she shut down, she had a thought. Suppose it wasn't just Lorde who had screwed up. She knew he wasn't the shiniest spanner in the toolbox but he'd always been reliable. Could someone have been checking the routes of the vans?

She'd persuaded the office manager to let go the youngster who designed the system, just to make sure he didn't find out anything. But perhaps Duncan Bennett had been sniffing around. She logged on to the Maybrick and Cream system, through a back door she'd installed, and scanned the list of users accessing the transport files. She recognised most of the names as legitimate but one was unfamiliar. Emeraldchalice2019. She resolved to find out more, but this would take more time than she had available at the moment. But, sooner or later, Emeraldchalice2019, whoever he or she was, would be answering some uncomfortable questions.

Chapter Seventy-Two

Day 42, Wednesday | 12.05 a.m.

DCI FIONA GALE sat in her flat and brooded. The turbulent events over the past few weeks had rekindled her feelings of self-doubt. The prospect of running a major inquiry had daunted her, even though she had successfully done so the previous year. That was why she had put Emma Thorpe in charge – an experienced DI who was obviously going places and could be trusted to do a decent job.

She was good at management, that she knew, but the pressure of intensive police work was getting to be too much for her. And she was lonely. Since splitting up from her partner some years ago, she had been out of the dating scene, although one or two fellow officers had made overtures on occasions. Sometimes she regretted not responding. She could scrub up OK, she believed, so why not take the plunge? Assuming, that was, a potential partner wouldn't be scared off by the prospect of going out with a senior police officer. There must be more to life than takeaway meals, historical drama DVDs and solitary gin-and-tonics?

Maybe she could get a new job, outside the police? Or resign, travel and see what came up? It was all too difficult, when she thought about it. Perhaps she should just get a cat. Realising that she was in danger of becoming maudlin, she decided to go for a walk. Fitness. Now that was another option. Years behind a desk, and an unsatisfactory diet, had added more than a few pounds. Maybe she would feel better about life if she was slimmer and fitter.

Her midnight walk took her through parts of Mexton she had once patrolled as a uniformed constable. But everything had changed. Interesting local shops had been supplanted by clone stores, some of which had been replaced, in turn, by tattoo parlours, vape vendors and second-hand phone shops, which, she knew, were fronts for money laundering. A disused Wesleyan chapel had been converted into a mosque, by the addition of a dome and a minaret, which, in DCI Gale's opinion, added some interest to the architecturally drab side street in which it was located.

The odour of overheated grease from takeaways drifted down the street, almost obscuring the hoppy smell from an elusive cannabis farm. Walking past the mosque, she noticed two men unloading pallets from a van and carrying them down a side alley beside the building. It looked odd. Her police instincts kicking in, she phoned control, gave the officer on duty the registration number of the van and asked for someone to investigate. After ten minutes, the promised patrol car had not arrived so she walked over to the van, confident that back-up would arrive soon. Several jerry cans were stacked inside and the smell of petrol wafted from the alley.

'Get away from there,' a voice shouted, followed by the

sound of footsteps running from the alley towards her. A stocky man grabbed the front of her jacket and glared at her, the smells of stale lager and halitosis assaulting her nose.

'Who the fuck are you?' he snarled.

'Police. Detective Chief Inspector Gale. And what are you doing?'

'None of your fucking business, filth.'

'Let go of me or I'll do you for assaulting a police...'

DCI Gale never finished the sentence. The man's fist smashed into her face and knocked her to the ground. Dazed and confused, she tried to reach for her phone. But which pocket? She was dimly aware of a blue flashing light at the end of the street, but the last things she heard were a whoomph from petrol igniting in the alley, the slamming of the van's doors and the revving of its engine coming ever closer. She didn't have time to register the crunch as it drove over her rib cage, sending splintered bones into her heart and killing her within seconds.

'You complete tosser. You've bloody killed a copper,' Tony Evans screamed at the driver. 'This was supposed to be a simple torching job. Not murder.'

'Tough shit,' spat Johnny Wallace. She'd have got us nicked. At least we got out before the filth arrived. And the fire's going nicely. It's all good. We'll still get paid.'

'No, it fucking isn't. What if she got the van's number?'

'The plates are false. I'll ditch them in a moment. And my mate Gav'll respray it in the morning. I'll put it through a car wash to get rid of the blood. We'll be fine.'

'We'd fucking better be, you moron.'

The two continued their journey in angry silence, reaching the Eastside within fifteen minutes.

PC Dave Jordan, recently returned to duty following an injury at work, swerved and braked sharply when he saw the body in the road. Ignoring the smoke pouring out of the alley, he leapt out of the car and ran to the crumpled form on the ground while his partner phoned the fire service.

'Ambulance, Joe,' he shouted. 'This one's in a bad way. He felt the woman's neck, with the forlorn hope of finding a pulse, and suddenly realised who she was.

'Shit. It's one of ours. DCI Gale.'

By now, flames were leaping up the side of the mosque and black smoke carried sparkling cinders over the rooftops. Two fire appliances and the ambulance arrived within minutes, followed by three more police cars, and the area around DCI Gale's body was cordoned off. Emma Thorpe arrived in an unmarked car, consulted the paramedic who had pronounced life extinct and declared the area a murder scene. SOCOs were summoned and attempted to process it, their efforts hampered by the streams of water flooding out of the alley as the fire service extinguished the blaze.

As dawn broke, DCI Gale's body had been removed and all traces of her blood had been washed away. Police tape fluttered in the morning breeze, keeping what was left of the scene secure, with a uniformed PC standing guard. The alley reeked of charred wood and half-burnt petrol. A ten metre high soot stain on the mosque wall bore witness to the failed arson attempt. A stray cat investigated the pool of dirty water that flooded the alleyway and decided it was unfit to drink. And Emma Thorpe, sick to her stomach, returned home for a shower and coffee before going into work, a dreadful day ahead of her.

Chapter Seventy-Three

'GOOD MORNING, EVERYONE.' Emma addressed a sombre gathering of detectives and civilian support staff at the eight o'clock briefing. 'In the early hours of today, we lost one of our own. DCI Gale was run down, undoubtedly deliberately, outside Mexton mosque. Let's just take a minute's silence to remember our colleague.'

For a change, even the heating system was silent as officers and civilian staff bowed their heads, some of them crying and others praying. DCI Gale might not have been particularly popular but the loss of a fellow officer struck deep. Every person in the room was appalled and grieving. And more than a few were reminded of situations they had been in themselves.

Emma continued, in calm, respectful tones.

'We don't know what she was doing there. Perhaps she was just going for a walk, but at half past midnight she phoned the station to request police attendance. We assume that she accosted someone who was acting suspiciously. By the time a patrol arrived, she was dead, a fire was blazing beside the mosque and the killer, or killers, had disappeared.

'According to the fire service, if it hadn't been for her call, the damage to the mosque would have been extensive, if not total. The Imam has sent his thanks and condolences.'

Emma's voice became angrier.

'We have the number of the white van that we believe was involved, so tracking that vehicle is our priority. We've already checked ANPR but we need to look at private CCTV when the owners' premises open. Doorbell camera footage, witness statements – we need everything we can to trace the bastards who did this. Unfortunately, we won't get much forensic but the SOCOs are doing their best. The fire service put out the blaze before it could spread inside the mosque but, in doing so, wrecked the crime scene. Unless we can get some traces from our colleague's body, pretty much all we've got is the van number. The Chief Super has said that we can have as much overtime as we need. I know you'll give this your all, so get to it.'

The officers dispersed, some to knock on doors and others to check out CCTV cameras near the scene. Notice boards were put up in the street, asking for witnesses, and local grasses were contacted in case anyone had heard anything. Officers pounded the streets, talking to rough sleepers, night bus drivers and anyone else who might have been in the area in the early hours. For the time being, Horgan's grenade attack was forgotten, although the seconded counter-terrorism officers continued their work. Catching the killer of a police officer took priority.

'It's no good, guv. The bastards have gone to ground.' A hollow-eyed Jack stood in the doorway to Emma's office, late in the evening, radiating total defeat. Other officers and support staff sat at their desks, exhausted and dejected.

'So, what have we got? Anything?'

'We tracked the van as far as the Eastside, with CCTV. At some point, they must have changed the plates, because the van we were watching had a different number from the one the DCI phoned in. But we're pretty sure it's the same one, even though the plates were obscured by dirt. Once it got into that rabbit warren, we lost it. We knocked on doors, opened garages and combed every alley and dead end. One of the shittier residents put up a poster in their window saying Eastside 1: Pigs 0. I'd half a mind to torch their fucking flat myself.'

'Glad you didn't,' replied a weary Emma. 'So, what you're saying is that the van somehow changed its appearance. New plates, possibly a respray, then sneaked out of the Eastside this morning, under our noses.'

'Looks like it, I'm afraid. And we can't stop every medium-sized coloured van on the streets of Mexton, on the off chance that it used to be white.'

'What about visible damage? Was anything broken when it ran over her, or a bumper twisted?'

'Not as far as we can see from the cameras. A headlight could have been broken but the bulb was working, so we can't be sure. There was no debris in the road. All we know is that it was medium-sized, white, most likely a Nissan and driven by two people, probably males. We'll keep talking to people and appealing for witnesses, of course. We'll never let it go. But, as of now, we've got fuck all.'

'All right, everyone,' said Emma, despair colouring her voice as she addressed the detectives in the incident room. 'We've been on this for fourteen hours. Time to go home. Thanks for all your efforts. Pick things up in the morning.'

She knew that they wouldn't rest until DCI Gale's killer was caught, but exhausted officers miss things and make mistakes. With no leads, witnesses or forensics, the chances of getting justice for their colleague looked slim. But that wouldn't stop them trying, with everything at their disposal.

Chapter Seventy-Four

Day 43, Thursday

THE *MEXTON MESSENGER*'s front page carried the stark headline 'Police Officer Murdered' and included an appeal for witnesses. For once, the paper's tone was wholly in support of the police. It even offered a reward for information leading to the arrest and conviction of the killer, or killers.

For the group of exhausted detectives, assembled in the incident room at seven a.m., this was small consolation. Everything else had come to a halt. Nobody puts the death of a police officer on the back burner. But for all their efforts, there was no progress. No-one interviewed admitted they had seen anything – not that there were many people about at the time and place of the killing. All the local informers had been contacted, with nothing forthcoming. Detectives would contact them again with news of the paper's reward offer. They had visited every garage within five miles of the town centre but all the proprietors had denied respraying a van in the past two days. As Emma feared, the murder scene yielded nothing in the way of forensics, despite the efforts of a team of SOCOs, apart from a few fragments of headlamp glass that might not have come from the vehicle at all. Water from the fire engines had washed away anything else.

So the team carried on, re-examining CCTV images, setting up roadblocks and talking to individuals, their rage building as they realised that their colleague's killer might never be caught.

———

'I'm really looking forward to meeting your brother, darling, but why on earth is he visiting that dreadful mosque full of Arabs?' Jeannie asked.

Arden shrugged.

'He feels he needs to. He wants to try to promote racial harmony and smooth over the effects of our campaign, including the failed burning. Not that he's got much chance of that. But he has to be seen to be doing something. Always the politician.'

'But we're not going there, are we?'

'No. I must, but you needn't. Gavin will come to the hotel for lunch and we should be able to have a private chat with him then. Oh, do remember that you're my PA and Mrs Arden was indisposed, so you've taken her place.'

'Lovely,' replied Jeannie, who wanted nothing more than a private chat with the Home Secretary.

'Right,' said Arden, briskly. 'I've got some tedious constituency business to look after and you'd better change into something a bit more formal. I'll meet you in the dining room at one. We've got a reserved table at the back, away from the hoi polloi.'

'Don't worry. I've got everything I need in my case and I'm sure I can make myself look presentable. I think I'll go blonde for the occasion.'

She kissed him on the cheek and went back to her room to make her preparations.

In a blouse, skirt and smart navy jacket, with a convincing wig and make-up, skilfully applied, Jeannie McLeod looked just like any other respectable woman, used to dining with government ministers. She walked past the armed officers at the entrance to the restaurant and approached the corner table where two men were sitting, her heart pounding and a trickle of sweat running down her back. A third man stood watchfully to the side. Gavin Arden, smart in a well-pressed two piece and crisp white shirt, stood up to greet her as she approached the table.

'Delighted to meet you my dear. Shona, isn't it? Max, here, has been telling me how hard you work for him.'

He extended his hand for Jeannie to shake and she mirrored his gesture, then snapped her forearm downwards. A thin, sharp-pointed knife slid down her sleeve, the hilt settling into her palm. Before anyone realised what was happening, she rammed the knife between his ribs and into his heart, twisting it to maximise the damage. A small scarlet flower bloomed on the front of Gavin Arden's shirt as he gazed at Jeannie with incredulity.

'I'm Iona McLeod's sister. And this is payback.'

She elbowed Maxwell Arden in the face and dodged between the tables as the Home Secretary's minder bent over him, groping for his weapon and simultaneously shouting into his radio.

'Ambulance to the Hawthorn Hotel. Minister wounded. All units to look out for a blonde woman in navy jacket and skirt. Suspected attacker. Armed with a knife.'

By the time he had finished his message, Jeannie was clear of the restaurant and heading for the hotel's service entrance. She knocked a delivery driver out of her way and leapt on the small motorcycle that she had parked there earlier that day. Discarding her wig and jacket, she jammed a helmet on her head, turned the ignition key and sped off.

Ten minutes later she was well clear of the hotel and the clamour of sirens that surrounded it. She dumped the bike in a side alley and ran towards a row of rubbish bins, which served the kitchens belonging to a couple of restaurants. She pulled a black plastic bag from behind them and exchanged her skirt for a pair of jeans. She was glad of the warm hoodie she pulled over her head. Riding a motorbike in February, with just a thin bra and blouse above the waist, was a chilly experience. A woolly hat completed her change of appearance and she sauntered out of the alley, unrecognisable as the woman who had assassinated the Home Secretary.

On the way to the car park, where she had left her hatchback, she stopped off at one of the few remaining public phone boxes in the town and made a couple of calls. Smiling broadly, she reached her car and drove sedately away to a safe flat she had prepared, on the outskirts of Portsmouth. And didn't she feel great!

'You know who I think that is?' said Emma to Jack, as they pored over CCTV stills from the hotel.

'Enlighten me.'

'It's Jeannie McLeod. The missing IT woman from Maybrick and Cream.'

'How can you tell?'

'Look. Ignore the hair – it's probably a wig. The shape of her chin is distinctive and she's about the right height and build.'

'Why on earth would she want to kill the Home Secretary?'

'That, lad, is a three pint problem,' replied Emma. 'She seemed perfectly normal when we interviewed her. Calm, competent and just a little bit boring.'

'She escaped through the back of the hotel and rode off on a motorbike that she'd left there,' said Jack. 'We're talking to all the hotel staff who were on duty during the morning. There's no CCTV there. It's just a back alley. We put an appeal out on social media for any sightings of a woman riding a motorbike around that time and somebody tweeted that he'd seen, quote, "This bird on a bike in a blouse that showed her nips" crossing Tavistock Street. This was a few minutes after the attack. Where she went after that is anyone's guess.'

Emma was about to comment on the tweeter when Martin came over to the group.

'We've found the bike, in an alley behind Gloucester Street. She left her skirt there so she must have changed clothes. She's vanished. Again.'

'Fuck,' said Jack and Emma, simultaneously.

'I'd better go and talk to our beloved MP,' said Emma. 'I gather he got a black eye when McLeod pushed past him. Also, a bag of cocaine fell out of his pocket when he pulled out his handkerchief, but he swears it wasn't his. He's not been arrested but he's waiting at the hotel. In the bar, no doubt. Get someone round to McLeod's address and see if there's any clue as to where she might go, would you? Split the team. I want half of you continuing to work on DCI Gale's murder. I'll take Martin with me.

'Yes, guv.'

Chapter Seventy-Five

As EMMA PREDICTED, Arden was sitting in the empty bar of the hotel, his solicitor by his side and a large Scotch in front of him. Apart from a developing bruise beside his eye, his complexion was pallid and he looked nervous.

'Mr Arden, I'm very sorry for your loss,' began Emma, 'but I'm sure you appreciate that we need to talk to you. I assume you would prefer to speak here rather than at the station. This is not a formal interview but we do need to establish what happened.'

'Yes. All right. We've met before, haven't we?'

'That's right, in a different context. I'm DI Emma Thorpe and this is DC Martin Rowse.'

'Before you start, Inspector,' interrupted the solicitor, a dapper man with the expression of a hungry ferret and a suit that cost more than three months of Emma's salary, 'my client denies any knowledge of the white powder that was in his pocket. It is his assertion that it was planted there, probably by the offender you are seeking.'

'I'm not dealing with that, sir,' Emma replied. 'My

colleagues will examine it for fingerprints and DNA. If there are no links with Mr Arden, then, obviously, we will not pursue the matter.'

She turned to address the MP.

'How long have you known Jeannie McLeod, Mr Arden?'

'Who?'

'Jeannie McLeod. The woman who stabbed your brother.'

'I think there must be some mistake. Her name is Shona McKay; at least, that's what she told me.'

'I'm afraid she was using an alias, sir.

'Oh. Yes. She did say she used a different name at work. Well, I've known her for about six months. We met socially and became friends.'

'The Home Secretary's bodyguard heard you referring to her as your PA. But I thought your PA was Mrs Celia Davenport. Can you clarify this for me?'

Some colour returned to Arden's face.

'That's correct. Shona was very keen to meet my brother. She said she admired his hard-line stance on drugs.'

Emma suppressed a snort.

'In addition to your brother's murder, we want to speak to her in connection with a number of other matters, including the importation of controlled drugs that were found on the premises where she worked. She disappeared immediately after our raid, which concerns us.'

Arden looked stunned.

'That is all news to me, Inspector. I'm shocked. Obviously, I will help you with your enquiries in any way that I can. I'm afraid I don't know much about her private life. When we met, she told me she worked in IT and could maybe help me with the constituency computer system.'

'Is there anything else you haven't told us, sir?'

Arden thought for a moment then spoke, tentatively.

'There's something that may help. When she stabbed Gavin, she mentioned an Iona McLeod. Her real name is Jeannie McLeod, you say. That can't be a coincidence.

'Thank you, sir. That could be useful. We'll certainly look into it. When did you last see her, apart from lunchtime, that is?'

Arden looked embarrassed.

'We spent the night in the hotel. We'd booked separate rooms. My wife was away, taking part in a Scrabble tournament, but I would never have brought Shona back to the house.'

'You bloody hypocrite,' thought Emma. 'Happy enough to screw her but not to bring her into your home.'

'And how did you meet?'

'At a party fundraising dinner. She sat on my table and we got talking. We seemed to click and she came to the office the following evening.'

Emma nodded.

'So, you had no idea she harboured any animosity to your brother?'

'No. None at all. As I said, she seemed to admire him.'

'Finally, sir, do you have any idea where she might have gone? Her registered address has been empty for some time and her car hasn't been used.'

'Well, she did talk about a cottage in Scotland. Near Dumfries, I think. But I don't have the address, I'm afraid.'

'OK. Thank you. I'll get Police Scotland to keep an eye out for her. We will need to take a formal statement from you in due course. Again, I'm sorry for your loss. We'll be in touch.'

Arden appeared to relax as the officers made their farewells. As soon as they left the hotel Emma swore.

'He's bloody lying. I'm sure of it. But I don't know what about.'

'He's a politician. It's part of the job description, isn't it?' Martin replied. 'But I agree. He's hiding something. He's clearly not happy talking to the police. Do you buy that stuff about how she got involved with him?'

Emma chuckled.

'It doesn't ring true. I've asked Mel to do some discreet digging on Mr Arden. Time to find out if she's come up with anything. We'll do an interview under caution with him when we've got a bit more ammunition. Oh, and can you find out who Iona McLeod is?'

Chapter Seventy-Six

'So, what have you found out about our esteemed MP, then?'

Mel sat uncomfortably in Emma's office and hesitated before answering.

'The official biog is that he went to a minor public school. He scraped into Cambridge, after travelling around with his brother for a while, doing nothing particularly useful and spending his parents' money. He got a 2.2 in PPE and briefly held down a job in the City, until he turned his hand to politics. He's been Mexton's MP since 2017 and is likely to be there for life. It's a safe seat, despite the social problems in places like the Eastside. He has a number of business interests, including Carter's, and is a college governor. He sits on the board of the local health trust and was instrumental in getting two of the hospital wards reserved for use by private patients.

'He married the daughter of one of the local gentry. She's a regional Scrabble champion but seems to do little else. Gossip columnists put his politics considerably to the right of Margaret Thatcher. He has no offences on record, apart from a few speeding fixed penalties and a very recent parking ticket. The warden reported that he was abusive, but we haven't taken it further.'

'OK. That's the official line. So, what are you not telling me?'

Mel fidgeted.

'Well. Information has come into our possession, information that we cannot use, which suggests that Arden has been accessing child pornography sites. He was also in contact with Charles Horgan's former commanding officer, Colonel Horrocks, shortly before the grenade attack.'

'Shit. Shit. Shit. I knew he was hiding something. He was distinctly uncomfortable when Martin and I were talking to him after his brother's murder. And it wasn't just grief. So how do we get a warrant to look at his phone and computer, given that your information is unusable?'

'You said he had some cocaine on him, boss. Can we arrest him and get warrants on that basis?'

'Not a chance. He denied all knowledge and there were no fingerprints on the bag.'

'He would, wouldn't he?'

'The drugs were almost certainly planted by Jeannie McLeod. She must have a grudge against him, too. Even if they weren't, there wasn't enough to consider intent to supply. We'll never get warrants on the basis of a small amount for personal use, especially as he's an MP and grieving for his brother. If it ever went to court, he'd only get a fine. We have to find another way.'

She looked at her watch.

'Get a few people together and we'll toss a few ideas around in the pub. A couple of pints might lubricate some brain cells. Six o'clock in the Cat and Cushion. There's a snug we can take over and talk without being overheard.'

Chapter Seventy-Seven

'DIDN'T this used to be the Crown and Cushion?' asked Martin, as the barman passed him a tray of drinks.

'Yep. But the new landlord's a republican and prefers cats to royalty. The beer's just as good, though. He even stocks Royal Oak on occasions.'

Martin grinned and took the drinks over to their table, where the group of detectives thanked Emma for getting them in.

'OK folks. Get your thinking caps on. How can we, legally, get a warrant to look at a dodgy MP's tech?'

The silence was broken only by the sounds of sipping and supping.

'Come on,' continued Emma. 'Work for your beer. We need to do it discreetly or the press will be all over it.'

'How about talking to the wife?' suggested Mel. 'Find out if she had any suspicions about his interests.'

'Possibly,' replied Emma. 'But wives often stick with their husbands, even when they're guilty. They can't stand the shame of exposure. Worth thinking about, though.'

'Could we set a trap, like Mel's new best friend did? Get him to log on to a fake paedophile website?' Karen asked.

'Come off it,' replied Mel. 'We're not that close. He's a good guy and Tom and I are just protecting him for a while. I think he fancies Tom, though.'

The others laughed.

'Anyway,' said Emma, 'that's entrapment and any evidence we found would be thrown out.'

'Are any of these sites monitored to see who's using them?' asked Addy.

'I'll talk to Tom about that when I get home.' Mel looked thoughtful. 'If the sites require payment there would probably be credit card details, unless he's using bitcoins or some other cryptocurrency.'

'Sounds promising,' said Emma. 'He strikes me as rather old school. Bitcoins are too modern for him, like as not.'

'What about the terrorism angle?' Addy, again.

'MI5 and SO15 have no suspicions about Arden,' said Angela. 'They know he's very right-wing and has made some inflammatory speeches in the past. But he's stopped short of suggesting violence or telling people to march on the mosque. I've made some enquiries about Colonel Horrocks. He has a distinguished military record, earned a DSO for bravery and retired a few months ago. He served in Afghanistan on several occasions. He's unmarried and there's no scandal surrounding him. The address the MoD has for him is the same as the one you searched.'

'How about social media?' asked Karen.

'He doesn't use it much but he is a member of a couple of private Facebook groups,' replied Mel. 'One of them is political and the other's name doesn't indicate what it's about. It would be very interesting to know who else is in the group with him.'

'Pity we can't join it,' Martin said.

'No, we can't. But I know someone who might be able to. And he's not subject to RIPA.'

'Careful, Mel,' warned Emma. 'I don't want you doing anything illegal or putting someone at risk.'

'Course not boss. I wouldn't do that, would I?'

Jack frowned but refrained from saying anything. The session broke up shortly afterwards and people drifted home, thoughts of how to nail Arden competing with the urge to catch DCI Gale's killer.

They chose the Eastside because people there minded their own business. The battered, crudely resprayed Nissan van, with its patchy paintwork and broken headlight, blended in amongst the other semi-derelict, and probably untaxed, vehicles scattered around the estate. And half the kids were semi-feral. Another plus. Good money for easy work.

It only took them half an hour to find a target. A boy of about nine, on his own, going to the mini-mart that provided the estate with much of its nicotine and alcohol when smuggled supplies from booze cruises ran out. He had probably been sent out to buy fags or cider while his parent or carer, a term used in its loosest sense, watched sport or soaps on the TV. Illegally, of course, but Istvan Malik, who ran the store, couldn't afford to turn away business or deal with the violence should he refuse to provide the necessary intoxicants.

Tony Evans, the less intimidating of the two men, stood close to the shop doorway while Johnny Wallace, shaven headed and extensively tattooed, remained in the driver's seat. The van was waiting at the kerb, its engine idling and the sliding door at the side open. As the boy came out, a large bottle of White Lightning under his arm, Tony called to him.

'Fancy earning a few quid, son?'

The boy turned around and looked interested, although wary.

'Doin' what? I ain't on the game.'

'No. Nothin' like that. Here, fancy selling these round the estate?'

He gestured to a cardboard box, just visible in the depths of the van.

As the boy approached the vehicle and peered at the box, Tony grabbed him by the back of his hoodie and his legs, hurling him into the van. He slid the door shut, jumped in the passenger seat and the van roared off.

Davey North had never been so scared in all his life. Not even when one of his 'uncles' had come back hammered from the pub and started hitting his mother. If he'd had anything to drink that afternoon, he would have pissed himself.

'Where are you takin' me, you dirty fuckers?' he yelled, banging on the partition that separated the back of the van from the driver's compartment.

'You'll find out soon enough, so shut it,' Tony sneered. 'And stop banging or I'll get in the back with you. And you won't like that.'

Davey shut up and tried not to cry. He attempted to hold on to something as the van bounced around and cornered erratically. The cardboard box was empty and provided no anchorage, so all he could do was wedge himself between the wheel arches, making his arms and legs ache viciously. Eventually, the painful journey ended and the van door opened. He caught a glimpse of a large building with boards over its windows as he was pulled roughly through a doorway, then down some steps. Another door was opened and he was half-dragged across a floor and dumped on a bed. A handcuff snapped around his wrist and the two men left without saying a word. A door slammed and he was alone.

He pulled at the handcuff, which was connected to a chain fixed to the leg of the bed. There was no way he could get his hand out of it. He felt sick with terror. A dim bulb above the doorway cast enough light for him to make out a small table, on which there were two sausage rolls and a bottle of water. A bucket stood nearby with a toilet roll next to it. The chain was just long enough for him to reach these items but no further. He couldn't see far into the darkness but he thought he could make out some sort of table with chairs around it. The room was cold and smelt of mould, whisky, tobacco and something else he couldn't place. Something unpleasant. Curling up under the thin blanket on the bed, and for the first time since he was six, Davey North cried.

It was purely by chance that Istvan Malik looked out of his shop window as Davey North was thrown into the van. He hauled his bulk from behind the counter and opened the door just as the van drove off. Despite the black diesel smoke pouring from the vehicle's exhaust, he could just make out the number plate in the pallid light from his shop window, which he memorised.

He'd always been good with number plates. It was useful to keep track of unmarked police cars and trading standards vehicles, which might interfere with his business. The problem, now, was what to do with the information. He wasn't a grass and he knew that if anyone found out he'd talked to the police, he would be targeted. At the very least he could expect a beating and might even find his shop on fire one night. But he liked Davey North. He had a cheeky sense of humour and didn't steal from him that much. So, reluctantly, he picked up a burner phone from under the counter and dialled 999.

'A kid's been snatched from the Eastside,' he told police control, trying to disguise his voice. 'His name's Davey North. Someone threw him in a van five minutes ago.'

He gave the van's description and registration number then rang off before the operator asked him any questions. Then he removed the SIM card from the phone. His civic duty done, he returned to his seat behind the counter and resumed sorting ecstasy tablets into small plastic bags.

Within five minutes of Malik's call, two police cars arrived at the Eastside estate and all mobile units had been told to look out for the kidnappers. The van's number had been checked against the PNC and was found to be registered to a high court judge in London, who drove a Daimler. The plates, obviously cloned, were later found dropped by the roadside a few hundred yards from the estate. Whoever had been driving the van had taken great care to avoid public CCTV, although there was always the possibility that a private camera, in a car park or petrol station, had picked up a van answering the suspect vehicle's description. That would be something for detectives to explore in the morning, when likely premises would be open again.

Uniformed officers visited Davey's mother, who insisted that she had only asked him to get some milk from the shop. Although she was slightly drunk, it was clear she was worried. Istvan Malik confirmed that Davey had been in his shop, couldn't remember what he had bought and denied seeing any van. Door-to-door enquiries at the flats near Davey's had resulted in nothing apart from the ritual abuse of police officers. No-one admitted to having seen Davey since the afternoon. Police cars continued to patrol the Eastside and its surroundings throughout the night, stopping and interviewing anyone seen on the streets, but found no sign of Davey or the van. Areas of waste land, and a few derelict buildings, were searched by torchlight, with a more thorough examination planned for daylight. The duty inspector, thirty years in the job and more familiar with the workings of the Eastside than he would have liked, leant back in his chair and addressed his sergeant.

'This is bloody nasty, Jim. If a rich kid is snatched it's usually for ransom or some sort of child custody thing. But a kid from the Eastside? Fuck knows what's going to happen to him.'

Chapter Seventy-Eight

MEL RETURNED to the flat bearing a carrier bag full of Chinese food. It was her turn to cook but she had other things on her mind. When they had eaten, she broached the subject of investigating the private Facebook group with Tom and Robbie.

'I can't do anything,' said Tom, but Robbie was only too eager.

'Just give me the details and I'll find a way in. What do you want to know?'

'Who's in the group for a start,' replied Mel. 'Also, info on what the group is for. It may be perfectly innocuous. Overgrown schoolboys liking secret societies and that sort of nonsense. But it may be something more sinister. And please, Robbie, don't put yourself at risk again. Someone's tried to kill you before and we don't want a repeat.'

As she spoke, a thought chilled her spine. Robbie had been targeted because of his paedophile hunting and somebody IT savvy had tracked him down. And a hitman carried out both the chemical attack in the flat and the shooting of Michael

Harris. The terrorist group and at least some of the paedophiles were clearly connected in some way. Which also meant that Robbie was still in danger. Mel kept these thoughts to herself, intending to discuss them with Tom later. For the moment, she asked Tom about tracing credit cards used on the child pornography sites.

'Yes, it can be done. You might remember a singer was cautioned a few years ago when he used a credit card on a nasty site. That sort of thing had no attraction for him. He was just trying to lay some childhood ghosts. The problem is, there could have been thousands of people paying to visit these sites.'

'Is there any way of whittling the numbers down?'

'Well, I suppose if we generated a list of users accessing all four sites within the past year, we might get a manageable number. Someone in CEOP owes me a favour. I'll see what I can do.'

'Thanks love,' she whispered. 'I'd kiss you but it might make Robbie jealous,' she giggled.

Robbie, who was busy with his laptop in the corner, didn't seem to hear.

Tom looked puzzled for a moment then flushed. He led Mel out to the kitchen.

'You're a rotten tease, Mel Cotton. I'll clearly have to prove myself later tonight.'

'I'll look forward to it.'

Chapter Seventy-Nine

Day 44, Friday

'LOOK AT THIS, guv. The *Messenger*'s outdone itself this time.'

Mel thrust the morning edition of the paper in front of Emma as she entered the office. Splashed across the front page was 'MP's alleged mistress slays Home Secretary' and, as a subheading, 'Cocaine found'. The hunt for DCI Gale's murderer had all but disappeared from the paper.

'It's so much rubbish. Half made up and with more innuendoes than a box of Spanish suppositories. Where did they get all this stuff? Has somebody leaked?'

'It's all right, Mel. Take it easy. I've already seen it and I spoke to the editor. He swore blind that nothing came from the police. He maintained that, shortly after the killing, a woman phoned the paper and said that she had committed the crime. She said she was Maxwell Arden's mistress and gave sufficient detail about the attack to establish her credibility. The paper's lawyers crawled all over it before it was published and there is nothing actionable there. It doesn't even say where the coke was found, apart from at the scene. And, just to reassure you, our friend Jenny Pike has been nowhere near the story.'

Mel looked slightly mollified.

'Not helpful, though, is it?'

'On the contrary, it might be useful. Arden's wife now knows about the affair, if she didn't already. She might be more inclined to give us something. I suspect Helen Causton-Taylor will be using her maiden name from now on. I'll see if she's free for an informal chat over lunch. Did you get anywhere with the things we spoke about yesterday?'

'Yes. Tom's getting me details of credit cards used on the four paedophile porn sites we're interested in. And someone else is looking at the Facebook group. Discreetly.'

'Good. Well, I won't keep you. I need to brief the Super on what's been happening. Thanks, Mel.'

Before her meeting with DSup Gorman, Emma spoke to Jack.

'A nine-year-old boy, Davey North, was abducted on the Eastside last night. Uniform are doing the usual door-to-door and poster campaigns but they would like some help scanning CCTV for a suspect vehicle. Could you organise a couple of people?'

'But we're rushed off our feet looking for the DCI's killer and McLeod.' Jack looked pissed off. 'I suppose I could spare Addy for an hour or so. He's pretty good at camera work.'

'Thanks, Jack. Just do what you can.'

He nodded reluctantly and went in search of the DC.

––––––––––––

Mel spent the morning working through e-mails and other admin tasks. Just before lunch, an email arrived from Tom with a spreadsheet attached. Three hundred rows displayed the computer user names of people who had visited all four of the sites since August and their credit card numbers. A separate column linked the credit cards to named individuals. She printed the document out and took it to the canteen, where she studied it while eating a sandwich. Arden's name was nowhere to be found, and just as she was on the verge of abandoning the idea, something rang a bell. She looked back over the spreadsheet and found what had niggled her. She grabbed her phone and dialled Emma.

'Guv. It's Mel. What did you say Mrs Arden's maiden name was?'

'Causton-Taylor. I'm just about to meet her. Why?'

'Well, a Roger Causton-Taylor has accessed all four sites several times over the past six months.'

'Bloody hell, Mel. Great stuff. I'll make some discreet enquires about Mr Roger. I'm glad you caught me.'

Mel rang off, almost glowing with excitement. Could they be a whole family of paedophiles? Surely that was too much to credit. But it wouldn't be without precedent in the evil world of child abusers. She finished her sandwich and dashed back to the office to let the others know what she'd found.

Chapter Eighty

'THANK you for agreeing to meet me here, Mrs Arden,' said Emma, as they sat down in one of Mexton's posher tea rooms. Emma felt slightly out of place in her working clothes, but her companion's smart, yet restrained, London fashions fitted in perfectly.

'Actually, it's Causton-Taylor now, Mrs, if you don't mind. I'm sure you have your reasons for talking to me but I am rather busy and I am certainly not going into a police station.'

Her disdain for such vulgar locations was evident.

As the two women ordered, Emma first offered her condolences for the loss of her brother-in-law, then tried to make small talk, asking about Scrabble tournaments and other matters unconnected with the purpose of the meeting. Her Yorkshire accent contrasted with Mrs Causton-Taylor's cut-glass tones and it was clear that the latter regarded Emma as her social inferior.

'Firstly,' Emma began, 'I must ask you whether you knew Jeannie McLeod, also known as Shona McKay. Your husband described her to Gavin Arden as his PA but I gather that this wasn't the case.'

'No, it wasn't. He was fucking her, though I'm damned if I know what she saw in him.'

Emma was slightly taken aback by Mrs Causton-Taylor's bluntness, but continued.

'So, you knew about the affair?'

'Yes of course. Maxwell couldn't hide a daisy in a meadow. He left credit card bills around listing stays in local hotels when he was supposed to be in Westminster. I found receipts for lingerie that I certainly wouldn't wear. I could smell her perfume on his clothes. And his demeanour suggested he was getting his sexual urges dealt with somewhere. Certainly not by me.'

'Pardon me, Mrs Causton-Taylor, but I take it that your relationship with him was rather distant. May I ask why?'

'I suppose you may. And I'll answer provided you don't quote me publicly. You promised me this talk would be off the record. Can I trust you?'

'You're not a suspect, you've not been cautioned and I'm not recording our conversation. Anything you give me I may use in our enquiries, but I can't use it in evidence unless I interview you formally. Will that do?'

Helen Causton-Taylor thought for a few seconds, then spoke.

'Our marriage was not exactly one of convenience, but it was certainly useful for both of us. Maxwell seemed to be the right sort. He wasn't unattractive when I first met him. My family fortunes, such as they were, had declined and I needed a husband. I wasn't a dazzling deb but I looked all right. Maxwell, with his ambitions towards politics, needed a wife from the right sort of background.

'We met at a Young Conservatives dance and sort of ended up together. His performance in the bedroom was less than adequate and I became aware, not long after we married, that he had certain...proclivities. I found photographs in his desk when I was looking for a stapler one afternoon. I confronted him about them and he admitted he was, frankly, a disgusting pervert. From that night on we slept apart and I just thank God we never had any children.'

'Why didn't you contact the police?'

She looked at Emma pityingly.

'Don't be silly. We don't do that sort of thing.'

'You've been very frank, Mrs Causton-Taylor, and I'm grateful. Can you tell me anything about his political views and his associates?'

'One thing Maxwell and I did agree on was politics. We're both sick of the way the country's going. Thank God we'll be free of Brussels at last. As to his friends, I don't know many of them, but I think they're all decent people. English to the core.'

'I see. One more thing. Can you tell me about Mr Roger Causton-Taylor?'

'He's my father.' She prickled. 'What do you want to know about him?'

'Are you in touch with him? Do you know if he uses the internet at all?'

'That's hardly likely. He has Alzheimer's and has been in a care home for the past nine months. And damned expensive it is. Maxwell has been managing his affairs and keeping the fees paid, but I don't know how much longer the funds will last. Why do you ask?'

'I'm sorry, I can't discuss that. But it's nothing for him to worry about.'

'I should think not. He's barely capable of doing anything

for himself. Now, if you'll excuse me, I must get on. Does this establishment have a bathroom?'

Emma couldn't help herself.

'No, Mrs Causton-Taylor, but there's a ladies' toilet over there, behind the potted palm.'

Her companion stalked away with a frosty glare, leaving Emma feeling that the class system was well and truly still alive.

Chapter Eighty-One

MEL HAD HARDLY SAT down at her desk when her phone rang.

'It's me, Robbie. I've got the names of the group members.'

'Brilliant, mate.' She jotted them down as Robbie read them out.

'Was there anything else?'

'Err...no,' Robbie replied, but Mel had a feeling he wasn't being entirely truthful.

'That's great. Thanks so much. I'll find out who these people are. I recognise a couple of names already. And Robbie.'

'Yes?'

'Please don't go hacking them. It is illegal. Promise?'

'Scout's honour.'

As Robbie rang off Mel realised that he had never said anything about being in the Scouts. And he wasn't the outdoor type. She would have to reinforce the message when she saw him later.

Looking through the list of group members, as well as Arden she identified Colonel Horrocks. Another man, Paul

Black, seemed familiar. She Googled him and realised where she had come across him. His nightclubs had a reputation for glamour, but were also suspected of being conduits for cocaine, although nothing had been proved. Then she recognised the fourth name, Councillor Gordon Lewis, one of the directors of Carter's Commercial Vehicle Hire. PNC checks showed that none of the group had a criminal record.

Half an hour's background checking found nothing compromising and Mel wondered what the four men had in common, apart from, possibly, political views. Lewis was a member of Arden's party, Horrocks had briefly been a local spokesman for the Brexit party and Black had urged his customers to vote for Brexit in the referendum. But why would they bother to form a private Facebook group when they were doing nothing illegal? The more she thought about it, the more she believed that something seriously nasty was going on. But it was still not enough for a warrant. She resolved to talk to Tom and Robbie about it that evening.

The flat was strangely quiet when Mel returned home. Usually, Robbie's laptop would be clattering, complemented by a tinny sound of techno music escaping from his headphones. Tom was working late, so Mel made herself a coffee and put her feet up. Robbie's absence began to worry her. He wasn't supposed to leave the flat, except in emergencies, and certainly not without letting her or Tom know. A phone call to Tom confirmed that he must have slipped out on his own.

Now seriously worried, Mel turned to Robbie's laptop. He had left it switched on and open, and he had shared his password with his hosts in case of emergencies. Mel's stomach turned over when she saw what he had last done. A message on Facebook had invited him to join the secret group in person. A car would pick him up in the railway station car park to take him to his first meeting. Mel phoned Tom.

'The bloody idiot's playing detective. He's gone to meet the Facebook group on his own. He must have created a credible persona and they've invited him.'

'Do you think it's a trap?'

'Probably, but even if it isn't he'll never maintain the pretence in front of these bastards.'

'Has he got Find my Phone on his laptop?'

'Yes. I'm opening it. His phone's moving.'

'Right. I'll leave now. Tell me where he's going and I'll get there as quick as I can. I'll borrow a blue light.'

'OK. He's moving down Denny Street at the moment. Turning into Thompson Street.'

Mel kept up the commentary as Tom dashed to his car and screeched out of the police station car park.

'Now on Matthews Road. Crossing Conway Avenue. Turning into Swarbrick Street. Stopped.'

A few minutes later Mel cursed.

'Shit. It's switched off. They must have found it. Get over there as quick as you can.'

Ten minutes later, Tom called back.

'There's nothing here. Most of the buildings are boarded up, as if for redevelopment. You might remember one of them. The Maldon Club.'

Mel shivered. She and Martin had almost been killed there, by a maniac with a knife, the previous autumn.

'Any sign of life?'

'Not that I can see. Hang on. Something's happening. I'll call you back.'

'Thanks. But be bloody careful. I'll call the DI and ask her to send backup. Love you.'

———

Davey North was hungry, cold and scared. He'd eaten the sausage rolls and drunk the water many hours ago. He'd peed in the bucket and the smell reminded him of the uncleaned toilet at home. His brothers had often frightened him with tales of what can happen to kidnapped small boys, just to wind him up. Now their horror stories looked like becoming real. He hated them. A tall man with a hard voice had taken most of his clothes off him and looked him up and down as if he was inspecting something on sale in a shop. The man terrified him. The blanket offered little protection against the chill in the room, and however hard things were at his mum's flat, he wished with all his heart he was back there.

Chapter Eighty-Two

ROBBIE FELT as though his heart was going to leap out of his chest as he stood in the station car park, waiting for his contact. It had felt like a good idea, in the comfort of the flat. The Facebook group seemed to comprise old blokes who didn't look very threatening, unless you were a child, that is. Now, standing in sleety rain under the harsh lights of the station, he began to regret it. Detection by computer was his forte. Doing it in the real world was uncomfortable and possibly dangerous. Perhaps he should have left it to the police.

He'd left his laptop open so Mel and Tom would know what he was doing. He realised that if he had told them in advance about what he was planning, they would have vetoed it. But this was his chance to infiltrate a vile group and he wasn't going to miss it. He could do it when the police couldn't. He was thinking of getting a T-shirt printed with the slogan 'If you can't get a warrant get a hacker' but realised that Tom wouldn't approve. And he really wanted Tom's approval.

He pulled out his phone and, under the pretence of playing a game, filmed the car park, streaming the images to the cloud. The meeting was supposed to be at seven o'clock and he had arrived a few minutes early. At seven precisely, a smartly dressed man, with a scarf over his face and a trilby pulled down over his eyes, approached him from the side, unseen by the station's CCTV cameras.

'Are you Gary?'

'Yes, I am,' said Robbie, his stomach lurching. He put his phone away, leaving it switched on, and turned to face the man, who introduced himself as Howard. That's odd, he thought, there isn't a Howard in the group. The man held out his hand to shake but grasped Robbie's wrist instead.

'Get him in the van,' he hissed. Two men, who had crept up behind Robbie while his attention was focused on Howard, seized him and dragged him to a dark blue van parked a few metres away, its engine running. They threw him in the back, slamming the door, and all three attackers piled in. The van hurtled off and Howard yelled at Robbie as he bounced around in the back.

'I don't know who you are, you little oik, but you're in serious trouble. You've got some questions to answer and you'd better co-operate.'

Robbie started to sob.

Ten minutes later the van pulled up with a jerk. Robbie was hustled out of the back and a hood was rammed over his head. Before his vision was obscured, he caught a glimpse of a boarded-up building, but he had no idea where he was. Someone rifled through his pockets, pulling out his phone and wallet. He heard the sound of his phone breaking as someone stamped on it. He was dragged, stumbling, across the pavement and through a doorway.

'Steps down,' a voice shouted.

Robbie cautiously descended a flight of stairs. He heard another door opening and he was pulled into a room that smelt of stale drinks and cigar smoke. Someone shoved a chair into the back of his legs and he sat down. A rope of some kind was wound round his body, securing him to the chair. Nobody spoke to him for a while, but he could hear the murmur of conversation some distance away and what sounded like a child sniffling.

Then someone struck him in the face, nearly knocking him and the chair over.

'Who the bloody hell are you?' a voice shouted.

'Gary. Gary Morris. Why are you doing this to me? I thought we were friends.'

'Don't be funny. Your bank card is in the name of Robert Woods. So, answer again.'

Another blow.

'All right. I am Robbie Woods. I use an alias online. Everybody does, don't they? Particularly on...special sites.' Robbie just managed to get the words out without throwing up.

'Who is Maurice?'

'I don't know anyone called Maurice,' replied Robbie, his voice quavering. 'Oh, wait a minute. He has a site. But there's nothing much on it.'

'How did you find us?'

'Umm. Just looking around, really. I like getting into secret sites. It's a hobby.'

'A dangerous one. How did you hack us?'

'I learnt with some mates at college. But they chucked me off the course 'cos they said I was accessing inappropriate content. But you could improve your security settings. I can show you how.'

Robbie heard his interrogator step away and confer with other men in the room. There seemed to be some kind of argument going on, and after a few minutes the speakers appeared to have come to a decision.

'OK, you pair can go,' a voice said. Robbie heard footsteps as two people climbed the stairs, closing the door behind them. The hood was pulled off his head. The light in the room dazzled him for a few moments, then he saw three men, all wearing masks, sitting around a table several metres away. A fourth masked man, who he recognised by his stance as Howard, stood beside him, holding the hood. To Robbie's horror, he saw a young boy, wearing nothing but underwear, chained to a bed in the corner. The child had obviously been crying and he looked terrified. A video camera on a tripod was pointed at the bed.

'Right then, Robbie Woods. You're a bit younger than the rest of us, but I see no reason why you shouldn't be admitted to the group. But first you have to prove that you really share our interests and aren't just a nosy parker. I should mention that, if you fail the test, you will never be seen again. So, there's your challenge.'

He untied Robbie and pointed to the child.

'Get undressed and get on with it.'

Robbie screamed inside. He would rather die than harm a child. He knew what it meant. But he was holding on to the faint hope that Mel and Tom would realise where he was and would rescue him.

'I...I'm a bit nervous. It's kind of public. Could I have drink or something?'

The man closest to him walked to the table and poured him

a large whisky. He drank it slowly, wondering how long he could draw it out. After ten minutes of sipping, the others were clearly impatient.

'Get on with it,' someone shouted.

'Prove yourself,' another called.

Robbie considered smashing the glass and using it as a weapon, but he knew he had no hope of taking on four grown men. He'd never won a fight in his life, although he'd been bullied many times. So, tears in his eyes, he stood up. He was just about to tell them he couldn't do it when he heard a bell ring and a light flashed above the door. A rescuer or just another pervert come to join the vile gathering?

Howard stepped briskly to the door and jerked it open. And yanked DC Tom Ferris through the opening and threw him to the floor.

Chapter Eighty-Three

Tom Ferris had parked his car a hundred metres up the road from the boarded-up Maldon club. He'd made good time with the aid of the blue flasher clamped to his roof but had turned it off several blocks away. A wise precaution because, as soon as he switched off the engine, he saw two men leaving an alley that ran down the side of the club. He waited for them to get into a dark blue van and noted the registration number. As soon as they drove away, he climbed out of his car and approached the building. Something glinted on the pavement where the van had been parked and he stooped to examine it. Robbie's phone. Speaking as quietly as he could, he called Mel.

'I think I've found Robbie. At the Maldon Club. It looks deserted but I've just seen a couple of heavies come from what looks like a side entrance. I'll take a look.'

'For fuck's sake, Tom, be careful. IT have come through with the location of Horrocks' phone. Swarbrick Street. He must be in the club. An ARV is on its way so don't do anything until it arrives. Last year you were telling me to be cautious and you were right. We nearly got killed. Now I'm telling you.'

'OK, OK, I'm not going to kick down the door like Arnie. I'll just check out the entrance and get back to you.'

Tom gave Mel the van's number and ended the call.

Rubbish had piled up in the alley, the usual collection of discarded fast food wrappers, beer cans and plastic cider bottles, but there was a clear path through the debris. Half way along, Tom found a door and eased it open. It made no noise. The hinges had been well oiled. He tiptoed down the stairs, his phone light illuminating the way. A door at the bottom of the stairs appeared to be firmly shut and he pressed his ear against it. He could hear the murmur of speech from inside, followed by a couple of shouts that he couldn't make out. Then he heard the faint ringing of a bell.

Fuck, he thought. An alarm.

The door was jerked open and a hand pulled him through the entrance. He tripped and crashed to the ground, pain flaring through his elbow where it hit the concrete floor. Three things caught his immediate attention. Robbie, in obvious distress, standing next to a chair. A half-naked child, apparently chained to a bed. And the muzzle of a Browning semi-automatic pistol aimed steadily at the space between his eyes.

'Another visitor. We are popular tonight,' mocked the man with the pistol, casually kicking Tom in the gut. 'You have five seconds to tell me who you are or I'll shoot you.'

'Detective Constable Ferris. Mexton CID. And I'm not alone.'

'Oh, but I think you are. If you were with other officers, you wouldn't be sneaking around. You'd be knocking on the door en masse. Give me your phone. And sit on the floor by the bed.'

Tom complied, his eyes focused on the muzzle of the gun. He looked around the room, at three men in masks sitting round a table, at Robbie looking petrified and at the cringing child on the bed. He nearly threw up.

'So, this is what you filthy bastards are up to. That's Davey North, isn't it? You kidnapped him from the Eastside for your perverted pleasures.'

The man with the pistol removed his mask and Tom recognised him, from an MoD photo, as Colonel Horrocks.

'DC Ferris,' he said, in a chillingly matter-of-fact tone. 'You are in no position to pass judgement on what we do. I am armed and you are not. You are quite alone. Woods, here, will not help you. And you must realise that you aren't going to leave here alive. Your choice is to die quickly and cleanly, or be tortured to death.'

'No, Peter, you can't,' one of the men at the table shouted. 'This was supposed to be fun, not murder.'

Horrocks turned towards him.

'Do you think this officer will keep what he's seen to himself? Don't be so bloody naive. If he lives, everything comes crashing down.'

He turned back to Tom, who spat at him. A streak of saliva ran down Horrocks' immaculately polished brogues.

'We know who you are, Horrocks,' called Tom. 'Not only are you a fucking paedophile, you're a terrorist. A traitor to the oath you swore when you joined the army.'

Horrocks seemed annoyed, then smiled.

'Yes, I served my Queen and country. But look at the way the country's gone. Infested with immigrants, dole scroungers, homos, druggies and Muslims. I'm working to make Britain great again and grubby little policemen like you aren't going to stop me.

'But I've had enough of this. I need to know exactly what the police know about my activities and you will tell me. Quickly. If you don't, I will shoot you in the foot, then the other foot, then one hand, then the other. Have you heard of the Belfast six-pack? You get the picture. So, what do you know?'

'I know that we have enough evidence to put you away for a very long time. I know that you were involved in the hand grenade attack. And I know that your campaign is financed by the proceeds of the drug trade, which brings untold misery to the country you profess to care about.' Tom's last point seemed to confuse Horrocks. 'As to the rest of it, you can go fuck your-self with your pistol. Sideways.'

'Suit yourself.'

Horrocks stamped on Tom's ankle, holding it firm against the floor, and aimed his weapon. Before he could pull the trigger, a screaming Robbie crashed into him, knocking him off balance. A shot echoed round the room and Robbie yelled, clutching his leg. Horrocks recovered his stance and cursed.

'You first, then, you little bastard. I knew you were a fake.'

He raised the pistol towards Robbie's head but, before he could take aim, the sound of boots on the stairs, and the crash of the door being smashed off its hinges, made him hesitate. A spasm of alarm crossed his face.

'Armed police. Drop your weapon. Get on the floor. Now.'

The shouted commands of the Armed Response Unit frightened even Tom, for whom they signalled deliverance. The three men seated around the table ducked for cover but Horrocks switched the aim of his weapon from Robbie and turned towards the AFOs, who continued to shout.

'Throw down your weapon. Throw it down. Now.'

'I am Colonel Peter Horrocks, formerly of the British

BRIAN PRICE

Army,' he said, drawing himself up into a military posture, his back straight and his voice unwavering. 'I do not surrender.'

He aimed at the nearest firearms officer and fired, hitting him in the chest. The AFO staggered backwards but Horrocks never saw it. Two 9mm rounds from Heckler and Koch G36s hit him in the forehead and blew the back of his skull out, splashing blood and brain matter over the wall behind him.

'Don't shoot. Don't shoot,' screamed Paul Black, emerging from under the table with his hands held high. 'I'm unarmed. Please.'

Gordon Lewis followed suit but the third man remained out of sight. Before the ringing in his ears from the previous shots had faded, Tom heard the muffled crack of a pistol fired close to human flesh. Maxwell Arden stumbled into sight, with a gunshot wound to his chest, a Walther PP pistol falling from his hand and the light rapidly fading from his eyes.

Mel rushed over to Tom but he waved her away.

'See to Robbie. He's been shot.'

Robbie sat on the floor clutching his leg, which was bleeding copiously from a hole in the back of the calf. Mel tore a strip off Robbie's T-shirt and formed it into a pad, holding it against the wound. She used his belt to secure it then turned her attention to the child on the bed, who was staring wide-eyed at the scene.

'I bet it's the first time you've been glad to see the coppers,' she said gently. 'It's Davey, isn't it?'

The child nodded.

'Did they do anything to you?'

He shook his head.

'Can...can you call my mum?' His voice quavered as he spoke.

'Yes, of course. But first you need to see a doctor. You don't

366

look very well. Then you can go home.'

Mel found the key for the boy's handcuff on the floor, freed him and passed him his clothes. When he was dressed, she asked a couple of uniformed PCs to drive him to the hospital.

By the time Emma arrived, the two surviving members of the paedophile group had been arrested and placed in separate police cars. The AFOs had made the weapons safe and boxed them up. The forensic physician had examined the two corpses and also the shot AFO, whose body armour had stopped the bullet. He was uninjured but the impact had left him with a painful bruise. The dark blue van had been stopped by a traffic patrol and the two men inside had been arrested on suspicion of kidnapping. Robbie had been taken to hospital, white as a snowdrift, and Tom had promised to visit him as soon as he was allowed to.

'He's a good kid is Robbie,' said Tom, shivering in the Tyvek suit he'd been given to replace his clothes, taken for forensic examination. 'He saved me from a nasty injury at least. Probably saved my life.'

'Well, you were bloody lucky. Why the hell didn't you wait until we got here?' reproved Mel.

'I was listening at the door but I must have set off an alarm on the stairs.'

'Didn't you see a sensor or something? You're supposed to be the technological whizz kid, you idiot. Are you sure I can trust you with the toaster in future?'

Tom grinned.

'Toast would be great but I'm freezing and need to get somewhere warm.'

'I'll find a way to warm you up later. But, right now, we need to get back to the station and write our reports. It looks like the Grateful Dead T-shirt for you again.'

Chapter Eighty-Four

Day 45, Saturday

'So, what it boils down to,' began Emma, as the team sat, subdued, in the Cat and Cushion the following evening, 'is that Horrocks was behind the racist campaign and didn't know it was funded by drug money. Arden was involved in the campaign but, as far as we can tell, his brother wasn't. He provided the money from his drugs operation, which Jeannie McLeod laundered through Carter's. But we still don't know why Jeannie killed the Home Secretary. And what did she see in Maxwell Arden anyway? She's an attractive woman and he's far from being a chick magnet.'

'Henry Kissinger once said that power is the best aphrodisiac,' offered Martin.

'Yes, but Maxwell Arden was hardly powerful. A backbench MP, who was an unspectacular minister for tourism for a few months, is hardly turning the wheels of destiny.'

The others managed a smile.

'We have no idea where Jeannie McLeod is and we don't know if she's planning anything else,' Emma continued.

'I rather think,' said Jack, slowly, 'that killing Gavin Arden was her end game. Suppose she was cultivating Maxwell Arden in order to get close to his brother. She's nothing else to strive for. She's presumably got plenty of money from the drugs racket and may well just ride off into the sunset. We'll probably never hear from her again.'

'You may be right, Jack,' said Emma, grimly. 'But we'll not stop looking for her. I'll not be having her running rings around us, not on my patch.'

The others raised their glasses in agreement.

'Something that might be relevant,' said Karen. 'I looked into Iona McLeod. She was an undergraduate at Cambridge who committed suicide in 2010. She left no note but had very recently become pregnant. The interesting thing is that both the Arden brothers were there at the same time, as mature students. Also, she had a sister, Jeannie.'

'So, you're thinking Gavin Arden was the father, Jeannie blamed him for her sister's suicide and vowed revenge. She got at him via his brother, giving Maxwell a false name in case he recognised McLeod?'

'Yes, I am. Pure speculation, I know. But it's possible.'

The others nodded.

Emma's phone rang. She turned away to answer and listened in silence.

'Thank you, sir. That's good. I'll share it with the others.' She switched off and turned back to her colleagues. 'That was the DSup. The blue van that they used to kidnap Davey had been resprayed and cleaned thoroughly, but SOCOs found blood and tissue inside one wheel arch. There was some flaking white paint, too, which may match traces of paint on DCI

Gale's body. So, we believe it was the same one used to kill her. We're waiting for DNA to prove it, but when the interviewing officers put what we'd found to the two suspects, Tony Evans caved in and shopped his mate, Johnny Wallace. They'll both be charged with murder. So, Fiona will get some justice.'

An air of bittersweet satisfaction settled over the detectives as they finished their drinks and, one by one, left for home, each one thinking there but for the grace...

Chapter Eighty-Five

Day 47, Monday

JEANNIE MCLEOD SAT in her Portsmouth flat feeling like shit. She had been coughing for several days now, and breathing was becoming increasingly difficult. She supposed she must have picked up a chest infection. She'd managed to get some paracetamol from a late-night corner shop, after venturing out with a scarf, glasses and a hat concealing her features. Her face was all over social media, a heroine to some of the more deranged anti-authoritarians but a villain to the vast majority of the population. The drug helped with her fever but didn't make her feel much better.

She didn't want to risk going to a doctor but she knew she would have to, soon. She was running low on vital immunosuppressants, and, without them, her sister's kidney would be rejected. She still liked to feel that a little bit of Iona lived on inside her and without it she would die.

She cast her mind back over the past few years. Evolving from victim to predator, creating a false identity and working her way to her target. What a blast it had been! It hadn't all been fun, of course. Sleeping with the vile Maxwell Arden in order to get close to his brother had been unpleasant, to say the least. But every time he flopped, grunting and sweating, on top of her, she thought of what he and his brother had done to Iona and she overcame her revulsion. The revelations in the news about the paedophile ring had come as shock to her, although he did once ask her to dress up as a schoolgirl, a request she firmly rejected.

It was a pity that the planted cocaine hadn't worked, although she derived much satisfaction from Arden's suicide and subsequent disgrace. But any disappointments and unpleasantness were far outweighed by the exultation she had felt when she plunged her knife into Gavin Arden's heart.

She resolved to set it all out in a draft email. When she had recovered, and was far away, where she wouldn't be troubled by extradition, she would send it to the police and the media, explaining her actions. For now, this illness was worrying her. Suppose she couldn't get the immunosuppressants? She was too weak to leave the flat and every hour she seemed to be worse. She set the email to send in five days' time. If she felt better, she would delay it but, if she didn't recover, it would go and tell her story. But, as she sat down to another ready meal, which smelled and tasted of nothing, a puzzle still niggled her. Who the hell was Emeraldchalice2019?

Chapter Eighty-Six

Day 52, Saturday

Email received at Mexton police headquarters

From: Jeannie McLeod
To: CID@mexton.police.uk

If you receive this email it means that something has happened to me.

I want to explain why Gavin Arden had to die.

I loved my sister, Iona, more than anyone else in the world. When our parents were killed in a car crash I was badly injured and she willingly donated the kidney that saved my life. We protected and supported each other as, apart from an aunt, we had no-one else.

In 2010, Iona was at Cambridge University. Gavin Arden seduced her. He and his brother, Maxwell, insisted that she had an abortion, left Cambridge and never contacted them again. They backed this up with deadly threats against her and also me. Devastated, she committed suicide, primarily, I think, to protect me. I hold these two despicable men wholly responsible for Iona's death.

She did not identify these men but I had a blurred photo of them. When I moved to Mexton I recognised Maxwell Arden from his picture in the paper and realised that his brother was Home Secretary. I resolved to get sufficiently close to Gavin Arden to destroy him and I used Maxwell Arden as a means. I slept with him, a revolting experience, and eventually he took me to meet his brother. You know what happened.

I must put it on record that I do not espouse Maxwell Arden's vile racist beliefs. I pretended to support him to get close and this was extremely hard. I found out many unpleasant things about him but his paedophilia was a complete surprise to me, although I did suspect there was something odd going on. I helped him launder money from his drug business but that money has been redistributed elsewhere, most of it to rehabilitation centres and charities. I'm glad he's dead but I would have liked to have seen him stand trial and suffer in prison.

I am attaching a list of all the individuals involved in Maxwell Arden's illegal activities, together with their roles. I hope you catch them and they go to prison for a long time. I also attach details of various bank accounts that you should find interesting.

I do not regret, for one moment, killing Gavin Arden. For too long, people like him have got away with things at the expense of people like Iona and me. It's an old song but it's true:

'It's the same the whole world over
It's the poor what gets the blame
It's the rich what gets the pleasure
Ain't it all a cryin' shame?'

Jeannie McLeod

Epilogue

JEANNIE MCLEOD's body was found by Portsmouth police after Mexton CID received the email, which gave her address. A briefer email went to news outlets and posts appeared on various social media channels. Police Scotland traced her aunt and Jeannie was buried in Scotland, next to her sister, with few mourners in attendance.

Paul Black and Gordon Lewis received long prison sentences for their part in the paedophile ring and for the possession of indecent images of children, found on their computers. Lewis was fatally stabbed in prison three months after sentencing and Black was wounded in a similar attack a day later. DNA from two other kidnapped children was discovered in the Maldon club, but their bodies were never found.

Michael Harris recovered and his prison sentence was reduced significantly because of the help he gave to Mexton CID in dismantling the terrorist group. He never walked properly again. Derek Farren was sent down for life. Darren Lorde and Mark Dickens received twenty-year sentences for kidnapping, drug importation and conspiracy to commit an act of terrorism. Dickens received an additional, concurrent, sentence for attempting to murder Addy.

Tony Evans and Johnny Wallace received life sentences for the murder of DCI Gale, in Wallace's case with a 35 year minimum term. Twelve year sentences, for kidnapping Davey North and arson, were also imposed, to run concurrently.

The names on the criminals' phones, and in Jeannie's email, were passed on to SO15, MI5 and the drugs squad, who carried out their own investigations. A few middle-ranking drug dealers were picked up, following the raid on the warehouse, and supplies were disrupted for several weeks. Other dealers quickly filled the vacuum. Maybrick and Cream continued in business under another name.

Duncan Bennett was cremated following a simple, non-denominational service. There were few mourners, just three of his former colleagues, a couple of cousins and Mel, representing the police. DI Steve Morton sent a simple wreath, anonymously, bearing the message 'Thank you for your service'. There was no wake.

DCI Gale was buried with full police honours, following a packed ceremony at which the Chief Constable read a eulogy. Her name was added to the growing list of officers killed in the line of duty.

Mel received the Queen's Gallantry Medal for her bravery in defusing the bomb and, after the ceremony, announced her engagement to Tom.

Robbie eventually recovered from his gunshot wound, although he limped for the best part of a year. Following Lyndon Johnson's dictum, the National Crime Agency reckoned it was better to have him inside their tent and offered him a job in cybercrime. For him, a dream come true.

Postscript

The new head of MI5, the UK's domestic security service, has warned that nearly 30% of the major terror plots it has disrupted at a late stage since 2017 have been from far right extremists.

CNN Online 15 October 2020

Acknowledgments

I would first like to thank my wife, Jen, for enduring my early drafts and making so many helpful comments. Without her support, I would not be a crime writer.

Thanks are also due to Rebecca and Adrian at Hobeck Books, for their constant encouragement, to Jayne Mapp for another excellent cover and to Sue Davison for her invaluable editing. It is really great to be part of the Hobeck family.

I would also like to thank Graham Bartlett (https://policeadvisor.co.uk) for advice on police procedures, Kate Bendelow, for help with forensics, and my son, Corin, for information about gyms and fitness. Any mistakes are, of course, my own.

Thanks are also due to Christopher, most excellent chocolatier of Weston-super-Mare (www.facebook.com/christopherhouseofchocolates), for supporting the competition and to my daughter, Cait, for painting the chocolate box lid.

Finally, I would like to thank all the readers and reviewers who said nice things about my first novel, *Fatal Trade*. I hope you will find this one just as enjoyable. Please feel free to leave reviews on amazon, Goodreads and social media and to subscribe to my newsletter via my website.

Brian Price
www.brianpriceauthor.co.uk

Glossary of Police Terms

AFO: Authorised Firearms Officer

ANPR: Automatic Number Plate Recognition (camera)

ARU: Armed Response Unit

ARV: Armed Response Vehicle

CEOP: Child Exploitation and Online Protection Centre

CHIS: Covert Human Intelligence Source

CPS: Crown Prosecution Service

directed surveillance: planned, covert observation of somebody (*see* RIPA)

DSO: Distinguished Service Order, a medal awarded to officers

DVLA: Driver and Vehicle Licensing Agency

DWP: Department for Work and Pensions

ESDA: Electrostatic Detection Apparatus

hang fire: when a cartridge fails to fire immediately when the trigger is pulled but goes off later

HMRC: Her Majesty's Revenue and Customs

MET (the): Metropolitan Police Service

NABIS: National Ballistics Intelligence Service

NCA: National Crime Agency
PNC: Police National Computer
RIPA: Regulation of Investigatory Powers Act
RTC: road traffic collision
SOCO: Scene Of Crime Officer (aka CSI)
SO15: Counter-Terrorism Command

Hobeck Books - the home of great stories

We hope you've enjoyed reading this novel by Brian Price. To keep up to date on Brian's fiction writing please subscribe to his website: **www.brianpriceauthor.co.uk**.

Hobeck Books offers a number of short stories and novellas, including *Fatal Beginnings* by Brian Price, free for subscribers in the compilation *Crime Bites*.

- *Echo Rock* by Robert Daws
- *Old Dogs, Old Tricks* by AB Morgan
- *The Silence of the Rabbit* by Wendy Turbin
- *Never Mind the Baubles: An Anthology of Twisted Winter Tales* by the Hobeck Team (including many of the Hobeck authors and Hobeck's two publishers)
- *The Clarice Cliff Vase* by Linda Huber
- *Here She Lies* by Kerena Swan
- *The Macnab Principle* by R.D. Nixon
- *Fatal Beginnings* by Brian Price
- *A Defining Moment* by Lin Le Versha
- *Saviour* by Jennie Ensor

Also please visit the Hobeck Books website for details of our other superb authors and their books, and if you would like to get in touch, we would love to hear from you.

Hobeck Books also presents a weekly podcast, the Hobcast, where founders Adrian Hobart and Rebecca Collins discuss all things book related, key issues from each week, including the ups and downs of running a creative business. Each episode includes an interview with one of the people who make Hobeck possible: the editors, the authors, the cover designers. These are the people who help Hobeck bring great stories to life. Without them, Hobeck wouldn't exist. The Hobcast can be listened to from all the usual platforms but it can also be found on the Hobeck website: **www.hobeck.net/hobcast**.

The Mel Cotton Crime Series

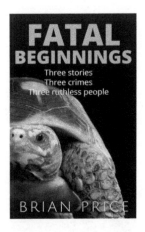

Fatal Beginnings

Martina Baranska only has one desire – to escape. She might not be able to erase the memories of her past but that doesn't stop her going out with a bang.

When investigating an accidental drug overdose, PC Melanie Cotton finds herself with an unexpected new house guest. Mel is unconvinced by the circumstances surrounding the death. Keen to prove her worth to her superiors, she is determined to seek the truth, but to what cost?

It was supposed to be the perfect robbery yet sometimes even the best laid plans can go wrong. Just as Jimmy thought he had successfully buried the truth, it makes its presence known in a most unexpected way.

Fatal Beginnings is free to subscribers of Hobeck Books: go to www.hobeck.net.

Fatal Trade

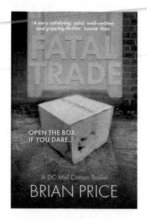

Glasgow, 1999

Reaching the point of no return, Martina is ready to make her move. After years of being the victim, it's now time to turn the tables.

Mexton, 2019
The small grey-haired woman grimaced as she entered the police station, dragging a tartan shopping trolley containing her husband's head.
'What are you useless buggers going to do about this?'

DC Melanie Cotton's fledgling career is about to take an interesting turn. Freshly promoted to CID, Mel is excited by this disturbing and mysterious case – her first murder investigation as a detective.

She's determined to make her mark.

But as she discovers, there's far more to this case than a gruesome killing, and Mel's skills and courage are about to tested to the limit.

Praise for Fatal Trade

'A very satisfying, solid, well-written and gripping thriller.' Louise Voss, best-selling thriller author

'A fast-paced edge-of-your-seat thriller from a major new talent. Gripping stuff!' David Mark, best-selling author of *Dark Winter*

'One of the best books I have read this year so far!' Kaz W.

'This is one o the best police procedurals I have read this year... a clear five star from me.' Lynda Checkley

'Some really nasty villains in this remarkable debut novel.'
Marie

'This had me gripped instantly and my intrigue initiated and I
knew I was in for quality read.' Ann-Marie